Home Repair

**Center Point
Large Print**

**This Large Print Book carries the
Seal of Approval of N.A.V.H.**

Home Repair

Liz Rosenberg

CENTER POINT PUBLISHING
THORNDIKE, MAINE

This Center Point Large Print edition
is published in the year 2009 by
arrangement with Avon Inspire,
an imprint of HarperCollins Publishers.

The text of this Large Print edition is unabridged.
In other aspects, this book may vary
from the original edition.
Printed in the United States of America.
Set in 16-point Times New Roman type.

ISBN: 978-1-60285-541-0

Library of Congress Cataloging-in-Publication Data

Rosenberg, Liz.
  Home repair / Liz Rosenberg.
    p. cm.
  ISBN 978-1-60285-541-0 (library binding : alk. paper)
  1. Married women—Fiction. 2. Marital conflict—Fiction. 3. Domestic fiction.
    4. Large type books. I. Title.
  PS3568.O7874H66 2009b
  813'.54—dc22
2009011770

This book is lovingly dedicated to my family, first. And to all our friends and neighbors in Binghamton who have made this a sweet place to live for the past twenty-five years.
Thanks to Larry Rakow, for his amazing, perspicacious eye.
And to Jenny Bent and Carrie Feron, as close to fairy godmothers as it gets.

Chapter 1
The Garage Sale

As garage sales go, this was a disaster from the start. First it hammered rain all night, then morning brought the typical gray Binghamton gloom, with dreaded Early Bird bargain-hunters ringing the doorbell at dawn.

Eve answered the door. Chuck was still sleeping, clutching at the covers like a drowning man. Eve wasn't sure what time he'd finally come to bed. "Our ad said nine o'clock," she told the two figures standing on her porch.

They were an older couple, thin and angular, shadowy in the morning half-light, in their early seventies, she would have guessed. Both wore the sort of cheap flimsy blue rain ponchos that looked like pool covers. They stared sharply around the porch, and, leaning past her, peered into her living room, as if everything in sight was up for grabs.

"Do you have any git-ars?" the man asked in a piercing voice. It was a country voice; he must have driven a long way to get to town. "Any musical instruments a-tall?" He craned his neck to look further into her house.

"No, I'm sorry," Eve said. "Nothing like that."

She moved in front of the door, blocking his view, self-conscious about standing there in her robe and slippers. "Maybe you could come back later. The sale starts at nine. The ad said no Early Birds." It was still so dark that she could not read her watch till she pressed the little button that made her Timex glow green-blue.

It was not yet 6:00 a.m. "Good God," she said.

"Any flo blue chiner?" the man's wife chimed in. "Or English? Any tea sets? I'm always in the market for chiner."

"I don't think so," Eve said, "but please come back later." She swung the door shut gently and locked it. She stood another few seconds staring at the door, half expecting the bell to ring again.

When she climbed back into bed, Chuck murmured "What was it?" but was asleep before she could answer.

Soon the bell rang again, three sharp rings in a row. This time it was a young Asian man, shabby, with a determined air. Eve had been working at the state university for fifteen years; she knew the look of all the students. This one appeared to be a Korean graduate student; his English was not very good. "How you doong!" he sang out in a cheery voice. "You have any Cokes?"

She was startled. "You want Coca-Cola?"

"Coke like you wear. Inna winna."

"Oh, you want a winter coat," she said, too loudly.

"Yeah, that's right." He smiled and nodded. "Winna coke."

"A coat," she echoed stupidly. She tried to picture everything they had stuffed into boxes, or hung on poles in the garage, she and Marcus, and even nine-year-old Noni, who mostly just liked playing with the price gun. Chuck refused to have anything to do with this garage sale. "Just give the stuff away," he said. "Toss it."

"But that's like throwing money away." Noni had turned her dark, serious gaze on her father's face. Nearly everything she said or did sounded like it came from a worried little old lady.

"Can I see the cokes?" the young man asked.

"Not now," Eve said. "I'm not sure we have any. Come back later, please. It's very early—all the signs and ads say nine o'clock. Can you come back?" She felt like she was pleading.

"Nine o'clock?" He looked unhappy. "That's so long. Maybe . . . seven?"

"No," Eve said. "I'm sorry. We're still asleep. Come back at nine."

"Mom?" She heard Marcus's gentle, sleepy, deep voice from the top of the stairs. At seventeen, Marcus sounded more mature than her husband. But she kept expecting his old childish treble. "Mama? 'oo doing?"

"Go back to bed," she told her son.

"Is everything okay?" he insisted. He came down the stairs a few steps, steel-rimmed spectacles perched on his nose, crouching down to see better, barefoot and gangly in sweatpants and a T-shirt that said CAT: THE OTHER WHITE MEAT. Noni was a fanatical animal lover and a vegetarian. Chuck had bought him the T-shirt at the Jersey shore earlier that summer. Both he and Marcus thought it was hilarious.

"Everything's fine," Eve said firmly.

"Eight o'clock?" the Korean student wheedled, looking from mother to son, as if he thought Marcus, at least, might relent. Marcus would have, too, if Eve had given him the chance.

"Nine," she said sternly, and for the second time in her life closed the door right in someone's face. She felt bad immediately, but there was no point opening the door and calling apologies after the young man. Through the sheer white curtains she watched him trot slowly down the walk, then stop and turn to look at the house reproachfully.

"Back to bed," she told Marcus. "—It's Saturday, remember? You can sleep in."

This time Chuck did not even stir when she came back. He was clinging to the covers, his long strong fingers curled around the quilt's edge. A sweet and peppery smell always clung to his T-shirts and skin. But now she was too tense to go to sleep; as soon she began to drift off, she heard a doorbell ringing or imagined she did. She lay there stiff as a board, staring at

10

the bedroom clock, its frantic buzzing set to go off at eight. She tried turning her back on it, but that was worse; it felt like the alarm might sneak up on her from behind. She climbed out of bed, shut off the alarm—no point annoying Chuck, he hadn't wanted the sale in the first place—showered, dressed, and began hauling boxes out of the garage and onto the driveway. The lawn was still shaggy with last night's summer rain.

Her first customer was the shabby-looking graduate student who returned to the house exactly at eight. He seemed delighted to see her. "How you doong!" he called, waving, hurrying up the driveway.

The air felt autumnal, though here it was the end of July, still really the height of summer. Only the sumac leaves had started to turn, in brilliant quadrangles of red. Soon would come the overheated days of August and September, art students wilting in the sunlit studio classrooms. Nonetheless she brought out the blue down jacket she had given Chuck last Christmas. It was brand new, all the store tags dangling from the sleeve, stirring in the air like paper wind chimes.

The young man—a graduate student in the School of Management, originally from Seoul, it turned out—bargained her down on the price of the jacket. The coat had cost a hundred and fifty, but Chuck said it was too damn puffy, and

Marcus said he wouldn't be caught dead in it, and she had been too lazy or busy, or both, to get it back to the store on time to return it—one of those hiking and camping places filled with hyperactive young men. Typically American, she consumed and discarded. Here she was, getting rid of junk she never should have owned in the first place. People elsewhere were starving; the planet was filling up with refuse; meanwhile her closets were bulging with useless stuff, stuff she didn't even want.

Reselling the jacket was a form of recycling, she told herself. The young man wore her down quickly. "You sell for ten?"

"Twenty," she offered.

"Ten?" he said again, smiling piteously. "Ten, you sell it for ten?"

"Fine."

It turned out all he had was a twenty dollar bill, so she went inside the house to get his change, and came back with a cup of coffee. "Coffee?" she offered, holding out the mug.

"How much?" he asked.

"No," she said, giving him his change and proffering the coffee. "The coffee is free."

He looked at her blankly, not extending his hand.

"My treat," she said. "No charge."

"No—thank you," he said. "Do you have tea? I love drink tea." He accepted the ten dollar bill, folded it up and tucked it carefully into his pants pocket. He took the coat, still on its hanger, and held it up to admire it in the watery blue morning light.

Eve asked the young man to keep an eye on the driveway while she went inside to boil the water for his tea. Of course she didn't know him from Adam. That was her way—trust everyone, believe everything. Once she'd heard a man on National Public Radio interviewing a coho salmon, and was so excited she called her first husband, Ivan Fidelman, at work to tell him about it. "It can talk—even sing!" she exclaimed. "He was singing 'Tiptoe Through the Tulips.'"

In retrospect, it was a peculiar song choice for an underwater creature. Ivan had been silent a moment. "Eve," he said gently. "Do you know what day it is?"

"Tuesday?"

"Yes it is. Tuesday, April first. April's Fool's Day."

Years later, she was still a fool. She half expected to find all her things stolen, which would have served her right, but the young man was standing in the driveway, holding the coat on its hanger, a sentinel, his arm upraised. "Some woman come by," he told her. "I told her come back at nine. You have more cokes?"

"She wanted to buy a coat, too?" Eve asked. Maybe she should have gone through their closets more carefully.

"No." He smiled again, brightly. "I need light spring coke."

By eight-thirty she had both kids roused and out of bed and ready for the sale. Chuck mumbled something about getting a few things together, and off he went a little too fast in his bright blue Ford Focus, like a blue jay, leaving a streak of color behind.

People began drifting down the sidewalk toward the sale, and she set Noni up behind a folding table, with a cardboard box for change and a large printing calculator. Noni had hand-drawn all the signs for the sale, in colored markers. The little girl was as happy as a clam. She had a cool head and was good at math. She kept her pet parakeet, Tweetie Bird, in a cage beside her and turned down countless offers to sell him—most of them kidding, of course. Nine-year-old Noni was literal-minded. No one could bargain with her. She never cut a price by a dime. More than once Eve heard her daughter say, gravely, "No, the ticket says one dollar and fifty cents. No, look, this says four dollars."

The sky had cleared and was now a rare, pale, rain-washed blue. Binghamton got perhaps five or six days a year this pleasant. The city was famous for its impossibly grim gray winters—a season that seemed to drag its feet from late October through April. Their luck had turned. All of last night's puddles had dried. It was cool enough that people were out and about, walking their dogs, strolling their children. Business was brisk. Maybe they'd make enough to splurge on one last weekend vacation before school began.

Marcus moseyed around, rearranging items, claiming several for himself, and charming the customers; then lost interest and drifted inside. By nine-thirty Eve's mother had come out to help. Chuck called and left a message with Marcus; he was running late.

"He'd better not be *too* late," Mrs. Dunrea—her mother—said sharply. "He's got to drive me to the airport."

"Your plane doesn't leave till four this afternoon," Eve said.

"Yes, but I like to get there early," her mother answered. She sat in a lawn chair that had a tag hanging from it marked eight dollars. "This chair isn't very comfortable," she announced.

The woman who had bent over to examine it walked away. Eve rolled her eyes.

"What?" Mrs. Dunrea said. "I didn't say she shouldn't buy it. You want me to run after her and tell her to buy it?"

"Maybe you could make Noni some breakfast," Eve said.

"I'm going to be late for my plane," her mother said. "Wait and see."

"I'm not hungry," Noni called over the boxes

15

and poles between them. "We're raking it in here!"

"You need nourishment," Eve said, watching a woman lift a necklace from a spice rack draped with costume jewelry. The woman was young and fair-skinned, in her mid-twenties. The way she was holding the necklace, the glass beads glittered deliciously in the sunlight and cast rainbows over the driveway.

"You're saying I'm in the way," Mrs. Dunrea grumbled. She too was watching the young woman and the necklace.

"How much?" the young woman asked. Even her fingers were long and beautifully tapered. Her face seemed to glow above the necklace and her white summer T-shirt.

"Thirty dollars," Eve lied. She had decided not to sell it.

"Let me see that," Noni said.

"Noni, go inside with Grandma Dunrea," Eve ordered. "I'll watch the cash box till you get back."

"No way that necklace costs thirty dollars," Noni insisted. The only jewelry Noni ever wore was an elastic hair band around her wrist for soccer.

"Breakfast time!" Charlotte Dunrea clapped her hands and stood. She was small but extraordinarily upright, her hair so white it looked electrified. Her voice, after all these years, still held the hint of a Tennessee accent.

Mrs. Dunrea's parents had owned a furniture store, and her grandparents were peddlers lost in the flood of Jewish immigration at the turn of the century, lost to history. Eve would never understand what made a few of her ancestors turn left instead of right into the Lower East Side, ending up in strange southern places like Alabama and Tennessee. Maybe a fear of crowds?

"I'll make you some grits. How's that sound?"

To Eve, under her breath, she muttered, "What do you need that bead necklace for? It's a piece of junk."

By noon Eve was inwardly fuming at Chuck for having run out on the sale to do who-knows-what: buy a piece of plumbing to fix the leaky upstairs faucet, maybe. Theirs was an old house, things were starting to break down. He'd put off the repair for months, but today of all days he decided it had to be done. Or he'd found a softball game going on at Rec Park. Chuck never could resist a game of any kind—touch football, shooting hoops, softball in summer. He played in the local league; most of the players on his team worked at one of the car dealerships in the Triple Cities. Granted, he hadn't wanted the sale, but he could have done something, almost anything, to help out.

Marcus always came forward to help when a pretty woman stopped by. But otherwise he objected strenuously to Eve actually parting with anything. She'd had a sense, lately, that she was drowning in unwanted things, the wrong things, things she had bought by mistake and never found the courage to throw away. Wherever she walked, she stepped over or around something, picking her way through a cluttered mess.

"I love this soap dish," Marcus announced, cupping it to his chest. "I grew up with this cookie jar!" He kept reclaiming items and bringing them back inside the house. He'd try to do something useful, wrap up half a set of bowls, but he was easily bored and distracted. It was a miracle he was awake so early. Noni was a far greater help than her brother. Or her father. Eve sighed, caught herself—and then sighed again.

As the sun rose higher and stronger in an enamel blue sky, Eve kept busy, rearranging tables, wrapping items in newspaper for the customers. Her mother had gone from petulant to worried to fretful, as she so often did nowadays. Every few minutes she muttered about Chuck's absence and her flight back to Tennessee.

"If I miss that plane, I'll kill Chuck," she grumbled. "Murder him with my own two hands."

Neighbors had emerged from their houses, women with baby strollers, couples holding hands, whole families on bicycles, all amazed that they actually had a pleasant summer's day.

Eve could feel her own movements growing

more tense and staccato. At one o'clock she sent the kids inside for lunch, partly so they wouldn't see her looking so grim, mostly because her mother was starting to drive her crazy.

"I just don't understand it," Charlotte said. "Chuck's not a baby. Doesn't he remember that he has to drive me to the plane?"

"Yes, Mother, he does," Eve said, annoyed that she had to defend him.

"This is what you get for marrying a younger man," Mrs. Dunrea said in an automatic-sounding voice, she'd said it so many times before.

"Six years—it's not like I robbed the cradle." Still, Eve knew what her mother meant. Chuck acted young for his age—he acted young for any age except maybe that of Marcus, his teenage stepson. Chuck liked to stay up late, sleep late, drink hard, play video games, and eat junk food. He watched too much TV. He would have been a perfect teenager, but it was much too late for that.

Too late. A sudden panic gripped the center of Eve's chest; a feeling of hollow-bodiedness, as if she were about to levitate up off the ground. She reached out for something, anything, to grab hold of. She repeated the words that had floated into her brain: too late. She gripped the back of the plastic lawn chair in which her mother, Charlotte Dunrea, was sitting, craning her neck around with a sharp, eagle-eyed look. "What is it?" her mother said. "What's wrong?"

19

"Nothing," Eve said quickly.

"Dad is so weird," Noni said, as if she'd been reading Eve's mind. "He just, like, vanishes."

Marcus overheard. He had come out to hover around them, one by one. He looked unusually pale. His feet were bare, which somehow made him look even more vulnerable. "Chuck'll be back soon—right?" he asked.

"Does this mean he won't be able to drive me to the airport?" her mother said.

"I can drive you, Mom."

"But I need help with the bags!"

"He'll be back." The words rang hollow in Eve's ears, but the kids, even her mother, seemed to accept them and relax a little.

Eve fought back her own terror, wrestled against the thought that had floated into her head unbidden, but it returned like a household ghost. Where was her second husband? Actually, where was he? When she tried to picture him, she drew a blank, as if Chuck had been gone for months or years, instead of a few hours.

An elderly Indian couple picked their way slowly down the driveway, examining each object with infinite slowness and care. They studied a floral rug, examining it front and reverse, talking animatedly in another language, then together walked away down the street holding hands, the wife swaying in her bright pink silk sari, the husband in a short-sleeve polo shirt and jeans. It made Eve's chest ache to see them go. They came back twenty minutes later and she sold them the rug for next to nothing. She felt limp, wilting under the July sun, set out like something in the garage sale. There was no fight left in her.

When things finally slowed down, mid-afternoon, she sat in the lawn chair alone and let the sun beat on her head. No way around it, she thought. She did not pass Go, she didn't collect two hundred dollars. She felt amazed, defeated. It seemed to come along with the tuna sandwich her mother set down in front of her, centered on its little flowered plate, cut on the diagonal. This terrible, almost comical thing.

Her husband had walked out on them in the middle of a garage sale, in the middle of a rare blue Binghamton summer's day. She knew as surely as if he had bent over her, lanky as he was, and whispered it into her ear, his blond hair brushing her skin. He was simply—gone. She pushed the plate away with one hand—not far, she was sitting at the little square card table with the money box.

"You have to eat," her mother said.

Eve shook her head. It felt like she had dropped ten pounds that morning; her summer dress hung lankly on her bones.

Chuck had called the house again, around one in the afternoon, but no one heard the phone ring. His voice on the answering machine sounded strained, like he was hoping to get off before anyone would pick up. "Don't worry. I'm fine, and I'll call again later."

Eve stood by the phone, listened to the message twice, three times, then pressed the delete button. The phone emitted some kind of mechanical sound—to Eve it sounded more like a squawk than a beep—and then he was truly gone.

Chapter 2

Cleaning Up

Her mother cancelled her flight back to Tennessee. Mrs. Dunrea's stubbornness was solid and spiny, like the Tennessee mountains. "I am not about to abandon my own daughter," she said. The words hung heavy in the air.

Marcus and Noni looked at each other. Their faces carried the code of siblings, even if half siblings: danger. Keep quiet.

"I don't see any point in going just now," Mrs. Dunrea corrected herself. "Chuck's running around somewhere. The man never sits still. He simply cannot sit still."

Marcus and Noni were staring at their grandmother, their lips parted in fascination. "I mean, I'm sure he'll be back very soon," Charlotte plowed on.

"We all know what you mean, Mother," Eve said.

It was getting toward evening. Eve could almost feel the blue sky sinking into navy, closing around them. Soon it would be violet, and then pitch-black. By now it would have occurred to most wives that something terrible had occurred, for instance, a car accident. Exactly this had happened, in fact, to Ivan Fidelman—Marcus's father. He'd gone out to run an errand late at night and was killed in a car crash, thirty-seven years old. That had been thirteen years ago. It's not as if one could erase an event like that, or just let it go. Eve carried it around with her, like a stone tucked in a coat pocket.

But she never even considered that Chuck had been hurt or killed. It wasn't that she could not believe that lightning might strike her twice. God had a bizarre sense of humor, she was convinced. But she had known immediately, in some deep-down, secret way, when Ivan didn't come right back from the supermarket, that hideous night. He was as reliable as rain and hated to be away a moment longer than he had to. Ivan never dawdled. He never forgot to call. He was the quintessential good Jewish husband —dedicated, calm, kind, brilliant, and reliable. When his ten minute errand took one hour, then two hours, while she was waiting with the phone shaking in her hand, pacing—long before the doorbell rang—she knew. It was as if one of the planets had been sucked out of the sky. She remembered the emptiness that night, staring at a frozen sunflower nodding like a ghostly giant beside her front door. She would walk outside, look at it, come back in again, the beige phone slick in her hand, like an orthopedic appliance. It had happened in November, a month she could never love again.

Chuck was not gone with that kind of finality. But Eve didn't believe he was coming back, either.

By nine that night she and the children had dragged everything back up the driveway and into the garage. It was pitch-dark, they kept bumping into things—the extra lawn mower that hadn't sold, the garden tools someone had said they were coming back to buy. Eve wouldn't have thought they could manage everything, but Noni was surprisingly strong for her age, and Marcus seemed to be everywhere at once, lifting things, muscling them up the driveway with his newly broad shoulders and back. He looked like a man. It amazed her. She could not reconcile this handsome young adult with the round-cheeked baby in the photo album, chewing on the telephone cord, his hands folded into fat fists.

Danny Schwartz, Marcus's best friend, stopped by around suppertime and he helped, too, which was even stranger. He and Marcus moved the two heavy tables she had rented from Taylor's and placed them out of the way. Danny was skinny, dark-haired, pale-skinned, wavery as a reed. He was always telling Eve that he was lifting weights at school, flexing his terribly skinny arms with one hard little lump popping up in the bicep, but she never believed him. She could not imagine Danny Schwartz involved in any athletic activity. His father was their family doctor, a tiny heavy-lidded man who always wore gray and looked gray. Even his skin and hair were a sandy gray. Dr. Schwartz was kind, intelligent, steady, everything one would ask for in a physician, but there was a touch of gloom about him. Danny never did anything physical. He didn't even play video games with Marcus—just stood behind him, waving his arms around, flapping them like some land-bound bird attempting flight.

Eve ordered pizza, and Danny called home to get permission to stay. Noni and Marcus huddled close to him, as if Danny now represented sanity and safety. Eve's mother seemed to have shrunk, and was simply curled in the flowered living room chair, not saying anything.

"My mom wants to talk to you," Danny said, holding out the phone with his arm straight as a stick. His voice was deadpan. Everything about him was deadpan. He had a straight, deadpan nose. Straight deadpan hair. "The pizza has to be vegetarian. She, uh, she wants to tell you something about Chuck."

"Chuck?" Eve reached for the phone. She and Maxine were friendly the way parents of best friends were—inexplicably joined at the hip. Maxine was a modern Orthodox Jew, and loudly conservative in her opinions and politics, while Eve was half Reform Jew (her mother) and half Presbyterian (her father, whose grandfather had been a lay minister in Tennessee). Maxine's attitude toward her was irritable and motherly. Maxine behaved as if Eve had no idea what she was talking about, ever.

"I saw Chuck on his way out of town," Maxine announced without preamble. Her speech was rapid-fire, a downturn on each note. Even questions snapped out like orders. "The car was all loaded up, like he was moving out. Where's he going?"

"You tell me," Eve said. Talking to Maxine, her own intonation changed; she *felt* more Jewish.

"Joel and I were wondering," Maxine pushed on. "Is Chuck on drugs—He was acting very strange." Maxine assumed that everyone was a drug addict—her own children, friends, neighbors. Maxine must have wondered about her, too.

"Strange how?" Eve tried to keep the fear out of her voice. Both of her children were looking at her. Danny was studying the ceiling, squinting, his arms rising from his sides.

"Is that a spider up there?" he said. "I think I see something moving on the ceiling. Let's kill it."

"Shh," Marcus told him. He was sticking close to his mother.

"Chuck was getting his oil changed, I stopped for gas," Maxine said. "I can't believe the prices, all because of your liberal Democrats. Get them out of Congress, we could bomb the Arabs and the price of gas would drop like a rock."

"Chuck," Eve reminded her.

"Right, so Chuck jumped when I said hello. He looked like he was high. Joel says men keep drugs in their sock drawers. Chuck said he was on his way out of town and would I please keep an eye on the kids. Did he get a new job or what?"

Eve was conscious of the children listening to every word. She spoke cautiously. "I'm sure everything will be fine. I'll let you know as soon as he comes in."

"No. I told you," said Maxine. "Chuck said he was leaving. For quite a while, I had the impression. Did he join the reserves—wasn't he in the Marines."

"Okay, great," Eve said. "That's good. Danny's behaving like a perfect gentleman. Don't worry, I'll send him home before dark."

"Listen," Maxine said. "In your shoes I wouldn't be talking sense, either. Do you need anything? Can Joel—"

"Fine, fine," Eve said.

"Whatever you're doing, it's not good," Maxine said. "Make sure Danny comes home before dark. Walk with him. This town is full of human garbage, it's not safe."

"Mm-hmm," Eve said. "I should get off, in case Chuck's trying to call."

"Call me later," Maxine said. "Don't let Danny wander home by himself. If you turn your back, he'll do something stupid. What good is a Jewish education if the child is dead?"

"Right," Eve said.

She hung up and stood for a moment with her back to her children and to Mrs. Dunrea. The phone, she noticed as if for the first time, was beige. Probably the same one she'd been holding the night her first husband was killed. She could not remember buying a new one. Why did people have beige phones? Like cars, or houses. Everything in dull, flat colors. Why? What was wrong with beauty?

She knew she was being cowardly. She was afraid to turn around, to start her new life alone.

"Somebody give me a shoe," Danny said. "I'm going to flatten that spider."

Eve swung around to face them. "Nobody's killing anything under this roof," she said.

Chapter 3

Sorry

"I'm sorry," Chuck said again, his voice breaking up over the cell phone.

He was calling from Ohio, where he'd bought a used motorcycle from a farmer. At least that was what Eve thought he'd said.

She couldn't be sure. He might have said he bought it from a Father. That didn't seem likely, a priest selling a motorcycle. Chuck said something about the blue Ford. She strained to hear the words. Maybe, on top of everything else, she was going deaf.

"I'm really sorry," Chuck said. "I know it's crazy. You always said motorcycles are for kids."

She shifted the phone back to her right ear. The side of her head was sweating, her hair was matted to her temple. She was still wearing what she'd slept in the night before. The receiver had been pressed to her ear for nearly an hour, and they were getting nowhere. She didn't want to miss this next part. She needed to hear him clearly. "Are you alone there?" she asked.

"Of course," he said. "What do you take me for?"

She didn't answer.

"I love you and the kids, you know that, Evie. This is breaking my heart."

"You don't get to say that," Eve said. "You're out there in the middle of Iowa, breaking ours."

"Ohio," he corrected her. "I didn't *want* to leave. I had to." The words sounded canned, rehearsed. Probably he had discussed these things with his buddies at Diute Ford. With Marty, his assistant manager, or Sal, the top used car salesman at Diute. "You weren't happy either —Eve, this is going to be the best thing for all of us."

"Best for the kids?—No discussion, no warning." She meant it as a question but it came out as declaration.

"I know what I did was wrong." He sounded like a child forced to apologize for throwing spitballs. "I'm going to make it up to you all, some way." The silence lay heavily between them. Through the phone receiver came the familiar but magnified sound of his breathing. "If we had sat down and talked about it, you would have talked me out of it."

"People don't just walk out on their lives," Eve said. "Even your dad was an alcoholic for years before he took off. He was a terrible father. You had some warning."

"You think that would have been better?" Chuck said. "Listen to what you're saying."

She heard male voices talking in the background, laughing. Chuck came back on. "Some guys I met at the motorcycle shop. They invited me out for steak dinner."

Eve wanted to warn him about befriending strangers—bikers, no less, with long hair and spiked leather bracelets. Chuck was worse than a kid; he was a big dumb guy "with no inner resources," as her mother always said.

She wanted to yell at him for being so happy about going out to eat steak when she could not push a bite of food past her own lips. But what was the point? The phone receiver felt heavy in her hand. She just wanted to hang up and crawl back to bed.

"I'll keep in touch," Chuck said. "But I—Selling car parts. Sitting in an office. It was never for me."

"Try to call here around nine." She was amazed at how calm she sounded. "The kids are done with their homework by then, but they're still awake."

"You're a great mother," he said. "I'm sorry—" His voice broke. "This was never about you."

"That's for sure," she said.

She could go on being brave as long as he was at the other end, while she still had his voice there in her ear, keeping her afloat. That was why, long after he had hung up the phone, after she'd pressed the talk button herself, she kept on holding the dead phone in her hand. Then she cradled it to her chest. The phone cord was like an umbilical cord, binding her to the life she had known.

That night, three days after the garage sale, it rained again. The wind came at midnight, blowing her white bedroom curtains into billowing ghosts. Eve managed to get the window shut before the worst of the storm broke. The rain rattled against the roof as loud as marbles. She listened to water drum against the heavy air conditioner—who would drag it inside, come winter? What if the roof leaked, what if the house flooded, what if they all washed away? Between one stroke of lightning and the boom of thunder, the empty side of the bed lit white. It seemed Chuck would reappear in one of these thunderclaps, his long, familiar body against her side, hanging onto her hand the way he often did in his sleep, the safe, known world restored. But the storm raged, and at last died down, and when dawn came she still slept alone.

It was raining when Eve awoke. It was so green outside, the trees full of leaves, and the streets running with rain—through the window it looked like the world was streaming green past the glass. Their driveway had become an unfordable river. Everything left over from the yard sale was soaked and ruined—the cardboard boxes appeared to be melting. She had wanted to unburden herself, to rid the household of unwanted things. She had lost more than she'd bargained for.

Refrigerator, the elder and larger of their two shih tzu dogs, came slowly up the stairs and jumped onto the bed. His fur was damp from having gone out in the rain, and he smelled pungently of wet dog—dirty socks mingled with singed hair and bathwater. Still, she was so grateful for his company she could have wept.

Directions for Heartbreak Diet, Week One

Supplies required: toaster, bread.

Take slice of bread out of the fridge. Place in toaster oven.

Wait five minutes. Try to read news-paper while waiting. Burst into tears at the wedding announcements.

Check cold bread. Plug in the toaster. Wander upstairs. Make the bed with cotton sheets bought on last anniver-sary. Sit on made bed, staring blankly. Rush downstairs when smoke alarm goes off in the kitchen.

Blackened toast is probably done. Throw away. Repeat each day for a week.

Chapter 4

Alone

It was strange to be alone in the middle of her life, when she'd least expected it. Of course she should have been prepared—this happened to women all over TV and in magazines, to women in her own neighborhood. How embarrassing to be a fool in the face of the world. Her clothing hung on her, meant to be worn by someone else— someone married and plump. She had said she needed to drop those extra ten or fifteen pounds. Now they were gone, too.

Joel Schwartz prescribed something to help her sleep; "just for the time being," he said. She usually forgot to take it anyway. She had grown forgetful. She walked bent over, hunched like an old person. She felt old. She dressed straight out of the hamper, pulling out whatever came to hand—wrinkled pants and a stretched-out college T-shirt; a blouse in need of ironing, and a pair of old gray stretch pants, the elastic frayed and showing at the waist. One day she'd put on a pair of mismatched socks. Noni pointed it out reprovingly. She drew cartoony pictures to show Eve just how bad she looked. Mrs. Dunrea compressed her lips but said nothing.

34

Eve put the familiar things in front of her: the kids' sneakers, lined by the front door in neat rows like protecting soldiers. Their favorite brands of cereal almost hid her husband's box of Frosted Flakes. She piled their hooded sweatshirts and windbreakers over Chuck's jackets, but his were longer, bigger, brighter; they revealed themselves, hanging from hooks.

Noni refused to speak about this. She posted an elaborate homemade sign on her door: NO TALKING ZONE. Marcus treated it like a big joke. Eve knew her kids too well to think that any of this was a good sign.

In most ways, of course, the whole situation was awful, humiliating, sickening—and yet day by day her bed felt lighter and wider, her day more open. It was as if someone had punched her straight in the face, handed her twenty years and said, "Start over again."

She hid photos of Chuck in the back of her drawers, face down. One of them cracked down the middle, and she looked at the fractured glass with as much horror as if she'd broken the man himself. She threw away old country CDs that he listened to in the car, because the soppy, clever lyrics made her feel she too was swimming in tears. She could not afford to drown.

The first week passed as slowly as an ice age, then a whole month slipped by. She dropped another ten pounds. She watched a moon wax and wane till it was the same sliver it had been when Chuck first left. There was something irrevocable about the way it came around full circle.

She increased her summer hours at the university, working to bring order into the Art Department, an endless, hopeless task. Sometimes Noni came along and sat at one of the flat wooden desks in the drawing studio, doodling. She created a comic book superhero girl, Speed Demon; a teenage boy superhero named the Sleeper; and an avenging female character she called the Amazing Shrinking Mom. Mostly, though, Noni stayed home and played cards with her Grandmother Dunrea, who had stayed on in the house, like an image stuck on the TV screen.

Eve wore sweats to the office and tried to convince herself she looked sporty and athletic. What she really looked like, she knew, was Carol Burnett in her old cleaning lady routine. "Aren't you *hot*?" Noni demanded. "It's summer!"

But Eve felt exposed even with the heavy clothes. It was all she could do to undress long enough to take a shower. Naked, she could see her own ribs under the streaming water. When she got out, she wrapped herself in layers, creating a cocoon out of clothes: a sleeveless tank under an old T-shirt under a baggy cotton sweater. She could not bring herself to wear anything colorful, anything pretty. It didn't matter; no one was around to care.

She hadn't weighed this little in years; she felt insubstantial, wrapped in fog and vanishing, the way her superhero alter ego did in Noni's comic strips. The gray hood of the sweatshirt flopped behind her neck. If she needed to, she could just pull it up over her head and disappear. In the air-conditioned office, she was always cold. There was one fuzzy gray sweatshirt she wore a lot, with thin black stripes. Noni told her, "You look like a giant caterpillar."

Eve filed memos, answered phones, arranged for lights to be repaired and studios to be repainted. She barely left the office. The support staff at the university was halved in summer—everyone off on vacation, taking family leave time. The days poured toward the end of summer—the university was mostly deserted, but would soon be boiling over with students petitioning to get into art classes, faculty members hunting for lost office keys, oceans of paperwork.

Chuck's voice over the phone no longer made her heart clench with hope. It was slowly, steadily being replaced by something else. Time was slipping away, and all that happened was she kept getting smaller inside her thick clothing. Despair made her look older, and at forty-six, she already felt middle-age.

She'd been wearing size 14 for years; now even the tight size 10s bagged around her waist. Sometimes, just for a moment, she'd stand inside her crammed closet, place herself in front of Chuck's clothing and breathe in. There it was again, the sweet, sweaty, sexy smell of him, so close she could touch it. She was tempted to sleep in his shirts but knew better.

Heartbreak Diet Dinner and a Movie

Rent one of the following movies:

1. *The Heartbreak Kid*
2. *First Wives' Club*
3. *An Unmarried Woman*

Take out a pint of favorite ice cream. Spoon half into the dogs' dish. Fall asleep halfway through the movie. Wake when ice cream is well melted.

Eve had not laid eyes on the department chair, Frederick Cummings, all month. That was not unusual. He traveled summers and hid out as long as he could. The chairmanship had fallen to him ten years earlier and stuck. No one else would take it on, not even Helen Gollow, who preferred to run things with secret department alliances and cabals.

Eve and Olivia Zarembo, the Permanent Collections curator, made up an Arts Events calendar earlier than ever before. They booked the rooms, double-checked the dates, everything. At Olivia's insistence, they went out to lunch to celebrate. Eve ordered a martini, extra dry, with olives. The olives were her lunch. They might as well have written the events calendar on wastepaper, Olivia pointed out. It would all have to be revised once the faculty came back in the fall. Helen Gollow alone would change her mind six or seven times.

Eve was grateful that at least she didn't have to feign good cheer at work. She saw almost no one but Lev Schooner, the administrative assistant in Music, who also ran the box office. "What are you—cold?" he asked her.

Noni snorted. Lev was small, an inch or two shorter than Eve, with black curly hair and dark eyes, and an angry edge if you did or said something that rubbed him the wrong way. His voice rang out like the rapping of knuckles on a hard surface, even when saying the most ordinary things, like, "Don't forget the file folders." He kept hundreds of CDs, tapes, and long playing records stacked on every wall of his office, lined up on both sides of the door. "If anything happened to my music," he once told Eve, "I would be lost."

His nose looked like it had been broken and

bent several times over by some insane plastic surgeon. It was a truly terrible nose, a beaked, crooked nose. If not for his nose and unpredictable black moods, he might have been handsome. His slender build made him look smaller and younger than he was. He was a rare creature around campus, an unattached male. The female staff debated endlessly whether he was gay or straight.

Lev and his wife Hannah-Lore had once lived in Eve's neighborhood, the West Side of Binghamton, known as the university ghetto, with its flat streets, gardens, boxy old 1920s houses, and square front porches. Now he lived alone in a farmhouse on a lake twenty minutes from campus. Eve heard it was beautiful out there, if remote. Hannah-Lore moved to Ithaca three years earlier to be with a woman, but Lev had no interest in filing for divorce. If anyone broached the subject, he bristled like a fire cat.

When Eve told him about Chuck leaving, he said, "Gee, that's too bad," in a voice surprisingly vehement and husky. His black eyes peered into hers. Two years after the separation, Lev and Hannah-Lore were still best friends. He sat for her cats when she went away, took her to doctors' appointments. Maybe he was a saint.

"I'm not a saint," he told Eve. "Forget that." He laughed, but his laughter was an angry bark.

"The world is a terrible place," Lev would say.

"People aren't what they seem . . . But the end is coming," he would almost sing. "It's coming one of these days." Clearly he thought the end of the world was a good idea.

The administrative staff was an anomaly, midway between janitor and provost. Half the faculty treated them like servants, others behaved as if they were angelic, or just dumb. She'd had a few students snap their fingers at her as if she were a slow waitress. Money poured into the sciences, business, athletics. The arts withered away unattended.

"It's getting worse." Lev shook his head, his black eyes ferocious and gloomy. "The end is coming." He read two newspapers a day, combing through for word of the apocalypse.

If not for Noni and Marcus, Eve wasn't sure she'd care if the world did end. She wanted it to go on for their sake. Then she'd start thinking about her mother, who had still not flown back to her little condo in Tennessee, though she missed her friends and bridge games. And there were the dogs, Refrigerator and Toaster, who had moved into her bedroom now that Chuck was gone; and the neighborhood children; the art students; her neighbors. Even Chuck. You didn't stop loving someone because they'd broken your heart. She couldn't even wish for the end of the world without getting tangled up about the exceptions.

Charlotte Dunrea cooked what in Tennessee was called "home food"—corn pudding and grits, fried chicken and greens. Noni and Marcus loved it. Eve toyed with her food. It was hard to swallow. She had already been widowed once— shockingly, without warning. One day she had a husband, a normal life. The next, she was alone. It was remarkable how many of life's great events happened that fast. She could not go through it a second time. Yet here she was, going through it a second time.

It was strange to lock the door at night and feel frightened.

To look at herself in the mirror like a teenager, fretting. She worried about windows jamming, peeling paint, appliances breaking down. Why hadn't she learned to be more capable? Noises out on the street sounded dangerous—the screech of car brakes, a door slamming, voices outside behind their backyard.

Heartbreak Diet Midnight Snack

One glass of tap water, one Ambien.

There were still four seated at the square maple table in the kitchen. But Mrs. Dunrea was old and frail—more like a third child than another adult. It was hard for Charlotte to reach things on the top shelves, so she left them out on the counters. She drove warily and, it seemed to Eve, more slowly each day.

After Eve got home from work, Mrs. Dunrea went out and shopped, bringing back an odd assortment of things from the local dollar store —bags of stale licorice, dollar store decorations, a large plastic American flag to hang on the porch.

"I'm not hanging that," Eve said, looking inside the bag.

"Why not? You're an American. Aren't you proud of your country?" Her mother's voice was truculent.

"But we all have to live on the same planet."

"That makes you a Communist," Charlotte Dunrea said. "I've been listening to talk radio and they're right. The country is falling to pieces."

"Who's saying that?"

"Rush Limbaugh," her mother said. "Don't laugh—I like him."

"Rush Limbaugh is a drug addict," Eve said.

"He's got brains," her mother snapped. "People are out to get him."

"Stop fighting!" Marcus piped up. "You're ruining my birthday party!" He was grinning, but he crashed the dishes into the sink, and Eve winced, wondering what he had broken now. Between Marcus and her mother, she had lost three drinking glasses just that week.

"You ruin everything," Marcus said, his voice near tears.

"Don't blame me," Mrs. Dunrea said. "I only came for a few days. Blame your mother."

"I was just kidding," Marcus said, his voice shaky. "Chuck is a craphead."

"Who taught him to talk like that?" Mrs. Dunrea said.

"Don't call your stepfather a craphead," Eve said.

"He's not here," Marcus said. "I can call him anything I want."

"Not—that word," Mrs. Dunrea insisted.

"Okay," Eve said. "Call him a fathead."

"Shut up!" Noni hollered from the living room. She was watching her favorite sit-com. She planned her day around it, and if for any reason she had to miss an episode, she made Eve tape it. Eve had watched a few times, trying to understand her daughter's fascination. The only sign of life on the show was the laugh track, and that was canned. She tried to explain that to Noni, but Noni said, "No, people are laughing because it's funny." Maybe she liked the program *because* it was boring.

"You're losing weight too fast," Charlotte scolded. "At your age it shows in your face. It doesn't look good."

"Thanks," Eve said.

"I mean it," Mrs. Dunrea insisted. "I'm your

mother, I'm telling you for your own sake."

"I'm on the Heartbreak Diet," Eve said.

"Really?" called Noni from the living room. "There's such a diet? We studied diets in health class. I don't remember that one." She muted the TV, a sure sign of her fascination.

"I was kidding!" Eve called back.

"You don't want to look old, you'll never get another man." Mrs. Dunrea stood by their kitchen window, hands behind her back, watching the birds in the backyard. She was crazy about birds. Eve believed she preferred them to people. "Look at that pair of cardinals," she said.

"What do you mean, another man?" Marcus asked. A muscle jumped at the side of his jaw and he reached up to rub it. The kids still believed that Chuck was returning any day now, that he was on a strange and extended vacation.

"I'm still married, remember?" Eve held up her left hand with the diamond wedding and engagement rings on it. Chuck had long ago tucked the two rings inside a box of Cracker Jacks, at the movies, as a surprise. It should have been an omen.

"Hold up the other finger," Marcus said. "The middle finger, Mom."

"Look what you teach them," said Mrs. Dunrea, offended.

Eve took a breath and handed the newspaper to her mother, feeling she was sealing her own

45

fate. "Here are the apartment ads. You wanted to look at places."

"I certainly do not *want* to move to Binghamton," Mrs. Dunrea said. "But I feel it is my duty."

"It is not," Eve said. "It might even be a burden, looking after you, along with the kids."

"I am your mother," Mrs. Dunrea said.

Was this said as a reminder of her mother's love? As a reproach? Eve had the panicky feeling of someone sliding down an icy hill, her whole life heading in a direction over which she had no control. "Whatever you want is fine with me," she said.

"Good," said Marcus. "Then I should tell you something."

Both women turned toward him.

Marcus smiled shyly and proudly. He was making an announcement. "I'm homosexual," he said.

"You are not!" cried Noni from the other room. "You like Alicia Adams."

"But I might be," Marcus said. "It could happen."

"What is he saying?" asked Mrs. Dunrea, tottering to a chair and sitting down. "I don't understand."

"Okay, let's say I'm not," Marcus said cleverly. At such moments he resembled his late father, Ivan Fidelman. "Can I start smoking cigarettes?"

"No!" both women exclaimed at the same time.

"Can I drink, then? Just on the weekends?"

"Gross! No," Noni called.

"Okay, then," Marcus said, sounding reasonable. "How about if I run for state senator? It pays $65,000 a year."

"What is wrong with you?" asked Mrs. Dunrea. "Your mother is skin and bones and you sit tormenting her."

"He's just being funny," Eve said, though she too was confused.

"What's funny about it? It's sad, really." Mrs. Dunrea looked affronted.

"Can I learn how to drive? Teach me how to drive," Marcus begged. "I promise I'll leave you alone about everything else."

"I will teach you how to drive," said Mrs. Dunrea. "If I get killed in an automobile accident, it won't matter. I may be old, but I'm not infirm or stupid."

"Deal," Marcus said happily.

"Deal," said his grandmother.

They shook on it.

Chapter 5

On the Diet

The flood of students swept in at the end of August. You could no longer find a parking space on campus. There weren't enough art classes to go around, sometimes not even enough chairs in a room. Even the painting teachers who used to stroll in at the last minute like visiting gods ran around the halls looking panicked. Blue petition slips piled up in faculty inboxes as students argued, wept, threatened, and begged to be added to overflowing studio classes. Eve's work began before eight and she usually left after five. There was no catching up. Her desk was piled high; in her pocketbook she carried long lists of tasks left unchecked at the end of the day.

Heartbreak Diet Breakfast on the Go

Perfect for the busy woman: paper cup of coffee, and the half-eaten granola bar your daughter left on the car seat.

Professor Gollow, the printing teacher, threatened to resign. Helen Gollow was an imperious

48

woman with a limp from childhood polio. She volunteered for dull committee work, labored nights, and worked her printing students to the bone. Her son, an only child, was gaunt and pale like Helen, moody and unpleasantly sly—Eve had caught him stealing from the departmental supply closet—and like his mother, he wore black. Gollow listed to the right when she walked, a ship keeling in wind. People ducked back into their offices when they saw her coming.

Once Helen had stalked off to a new position in Comparative Literature. The Art Department heaved a collective deep sigh of relief—but that alliance fell through. Alliances with Helen Gollow always did. There was something heavy and uncompromising about her, like the musk perfume she wore. She was sweet to Eve, but Eve had seen too many students, and a few young faculty members, fleeing Gollow's office in tears. Helen Gollow pursued her friends as relentlessly as enemies, keeping them talking in the hall for hours. One drawing teacher retired early because Helen would not stop calling and dropping by. First he changed his office phone number, then he disconnected the phone, and the following year he was gone.

Gone, too, was summer, which sank toward its end in a series of muggy hot days that rolled miserably from the Susquehanna River to the Chenango. Chuck seemed to have snuck away with the season under one athletic arm, leaving them the dregs. Now there was only the Labor Day weekend, that last drop of freedom before her kids were back in school.

Mrs. Dunrea sat in the air-conditioning and watched old black and white movies with Marcus and Noni. There was no Chuck to make them watch action movies and what Eve secretly thought of as dumb-guy comedies. No Chuck to leave behind empty bags of chips and a trail of cookie crumbs. And sometimes there was something even stranger than her sense of relief. One day she said to her mother, without thinking, "I really miss Ivan."

"Ivan?"

"I mean *Chuck*—I mean I really miss Chuck. That's who I miss."

"Hmm." There was a longish silence. Then Charlotte asked, "How long has Ivan been gone?"

"Nine years and ten months."

Charlotte shook her head. "I should have said something when you married that man."

"Ivan?"

"Of course not. We all loved Ivan. I mean that other man."

"His name is *Chuck*."

"He had sex appeal—well, he did. But he was like Silly Putty. He took on whatever shape you wanted him to be. He always seemed half-baked to me. He wasn't for you."

The truth was, the longer Chuck was gone, the more unreal he seemed, as if he'd never been there at all. And in his absence, Eve thought of her first husband, Ivan, more than she had in years. She remembered the deep timbre of his voice. It was his photograph, not Chuck's, she wept in front of. Once, coming into the living room very late at night, she thought for an instant she saw Ivan sitting there, his long legs extended in front of him in well-worn corduroys. She nearly mentioned it to Charlotte but she knew her mother was superstitious; it would only make her anxious.

Everything made Mrs. Dunrea nervous—Noni's bike-riding, Marcus' habit of wandering off to find his friends. Her mother's driving lessons went as far as letting Marcus drive circles in the church lot next door. He threatened to convert to Catholicism; he said he was spending all his time at church anyway.

"I can't in good conscience take you on a highway," Mrs. Dunrea said. "Not till you prove you can steer and brake."

"I can steer, and I can brake," Marcus said.

"At the same time," Mrs. Dunrea said.

The dogwood leaves shone a furious red. Maples began to turn at the ends of branches. The hills around Binghamton were slowly dipping themselves, like strands of tapestry wool, in darkening shades of russet and orange and bronzy green. The heat wave broke in a thunderstorm one night that lashed branches, tumbled across Riverside Drive and tore down telephone wires in Endicott. September brought the first white frost to the front lawns, sugaring the grass. Chuck called less and less often, promising nothing; the sheets no longer smelled like his aftershave. Eve had to give in and wash the pillowcases she'd been preserving for the last faint trace of his shampoo.

She tried to face a few hard facts. She had married two men she'd barely known. The first time, she was lucky. Ivan turned out to be kind, brilliant, gentle, wise, talkative. But it was pure dumb luck. She'd known him less than six months when they married. She'd jumped in the same heedless way with Chuck, but with entirely different results. Chuck remained a charming, good-natured, good-looking stranger. She didn't share his hobbies or his politics. She didn't get his jokes. To be fair—if he was not the right man for her, she probably wasn't the one for him, either. But that was cold comfort most days, and almost all nights.

Heartbreak Diet Sunday Morning Brunch

Pizza crusts left over from Saturday night pizza. Do not serve to guests.

Summer stepped out of its pale yellow dress into its brightest attire. Light shimmered and shone on the commonest things—red stop signs, plastic lawn chairs, the last roses, making them leap painfully, jabbing at her in unfamiliar colors; sulfur yellows and vivid reds. This beauty only lasted a few weeks, under lapis blue skies, but sometimes she'd find her face wet with tears without realizing it—standing on line at the grocery store, driving to work, staring out the window. Better not to look, not to feel too much of anything. Joy led to sorrow, in a straight line. She'd sit on their king-size bed and sob, muffling the sound with her pillow held up to her face, till Marcus and Noni knocked on the bedroom door.

"Mom, it's scarier when you do that. It sounds like someone's trying to strangle you." Marcus spoke for both of them.

They stepped gingerly into her room, looking around.

"It's okay to cry," Noni said.

"Right," Marcus said, but looked worried that Eve might take them up on it. Her eyes were red, her cheeks tear-streaked, but she forced herself to smile.

"I'm done now." Eve opened her arms. Maybe she had been a failure as a wife, but she could still be a good mother.

After that she did her crying in the locked

ladies' room down the hall from the art office, but students kept knocking on the door, and finally she realized she simply didn't have any time or space to weep in. She'd have to give it up and move on.

One night, Marcus lit a fire in the fireplace, but forgot to open the flue. They were driven out onto the damp lawn in their nightclothes and slippers, while the house slowly emptied itself of smoke. Marcus had to shut off the alarm with the stick end of a broom, breaking it in the process. It was moments like these that made Eve feel how vulnerable they were. Chuck deposited money directly into their joint account—so either he'd picked up jobs or had sold a few of the bonds his father left him in his will. But that could all change. Chuck seemed to be riding all over the country, calling first from his stepmother's in Nebraska, then the apartments of old boyhood friends in Indiana. Her conversations with him ran about the same:

"How are the kids holding up?"

"They're doing okay," evenly.

Or, "Fine."

Or, "What do you want, Chuck?"

The kids didn't stay on the phone long; their conversations were full of murmurs and grunts of agreement, and long silences, then, "It's okay, Dad," or, "Love you." Afterward they'd come into her bedroom and lie on Eve's bed.

Mrs. Dunrea would already be asleep in the guest room—the old lady tired easily these days. She needed peace and quiet. They kept their voices low. Marcus hated a quiet house; as a child, he'd been so afraid of the dark that Eve left his radio and the overhead light on. She'd read that the latter was bad for children's eyes, but too late—by age thirteen Marcus already wore owlish metal-rimmed spectacles, and now he could barely see across a room without them —or go to sleep without background noise.

Strangely, Marcus persisted in the idea of running for senator, though he didn't have a snowball's chance in hell of even a nomination. She'd had a similar sinking feeling the year he went out for wrestling and she watched him get creamed at every match. "I'm proving a point," he said. Their local Republican state senator, Byron Filliman, was running unopposed for a third term. The Filliman family had been in Binghamton for a hundred years; there were streets named after them, and a park. The senator was well-connected and popular—a former high school basketball hero—the local boy who'd made good.

Eve had let Filliman put his last election sign on her front lawn, and it happened that the *Binghamton Press* took a photo of the senator hammering it into the grass, with Eve looking on and smiling from the porch. The way the photographer took the picture, the tanned, silver-haired senator looked very large, and Eve looked tiny. Chuck had the picture laminated; it was lying around in her closet somewhere under the kids' report cards, their art projects and essays and homework with little blue and silver stars on top. The garage sale barely made a dent in all the accumulated junk. She had to step on squishy black plastic bags filled with who knows what just to reach her own closet shelves.

Maybe she should hold another sale, she thought. She imagined Chuck showing up at the end of it, like a man gone in an enormous circle around the block.

Marcus's twelfth grade Social Studies teacher, Ms. McLain, had sent out a summer letter offering extra credit to anyone involved in a civic project that year. Marcus adored Ms. McLain— he'd had her before, in ninth grade. She was enthusiastic, young, blond, and pretty, with ultra-bright aqua-blue eyes that always looked surprised. Now, in his senior year, Eve knew they'd be hearing about the wonderful Ms. McLain all over again.

"Why don't you work for Project Paw?" Noni suggested. "I'd rather save animals than people." This was certainly true. Noni, as a toddler, had refused to walk, crawling and barking like a dog instead.

"Or practice your driving," Eve suggested. Marcus had never been coordinated, even as a child. He kept falling, skidding into bushes, slamming into parked cars. The night he gave up riding a bicycle, he told her to give his bike away or sell it. His light gold hair, nearly white in summertime, was covered with a slick-looking black helmet that Chuck had bought him. The boy loved his helmet more than the bike. Sometimes he'd tried to go to sleep wearing the thing.

"You already take me wherever I want," Marcus had said. "When I'm older, I'll learn how to drive a car." He'd come out of the garage holding the black helmet in front of him, like John the Baptist's head. "I guess I have to give this back," he said.

"No way," Chuck told him. "You never know when you'll need protection. Hang onto it, man."

Eve had never loved Chuck more than at that moment. So Marcus had worn his helmet around the house, playing his insane make-believe games. The black helmet made him look like Darth Vader. He and his friends argued over whose turn it was to wear it.

"In a true democracy you need more than one candidate," Marcus lectured them now. "No one is willing to debate this guy."

"You're only seventeen," Eve said.

"I'll be eighteen in two months."

"You have to be twenty-one to run for office."
She'd looked it up.

She had even called Albany, to double-check.

"I'm old enough to join the army, but I'm not old enough to run for office. I can get a license for a gun. I'm old enough to vote in an election, but not old enough to take part! That's wicked stupid, don't you think?"

Marcus had the capacity to wear her down faster than anyone else on earth.

"And anyway, I'm taking my driving test soon. Thanks to Gramma." He still pronounced it as he had as a child: *Gramma.*

"He's coming along," Charlotte Dunrea said. But she gave her head a hard little shake, which meant she was lying.

Noni said, "I would vote for you, Marcus."

Marcus was sitting at the kitchen table looking so eager it broke Eve's heart. Marcus, her firstborn, would be away at college this time next year. She could not imagine the house without him in it. How had her mother borne it?

She herself was an only child. At least when Marcus left, she'd have Noni around to nag her.

"I'm going to SUNY Albany," Marcus said. "Where the state senators have their offices, and it isn't too far away in case you need me for anything."

"Can I walk there?" Noni asked.

"It's a little far for that," Marcus said.

"Can I ride my bike?"

"Probably not," he said. He looked to Eve for help.

"It's still a year away," Eve said.

When she thought about her son actually leaving to go to college, she felt dizzy and a little sick to her stomach, as if she'd heard about a fatal disease. Next year at this time he would be gone.

The Empty Nest Heartache Diet

Take out various high-calorie items from refrigerator and freezer: a quart of ice cream, coconut cake, fancy cookies reserved for guests.

Stare at your child's sneakers lying cockeyed on the floor, one big sneaker fallen on its side, the other standing upright, both with filthy white socks crumpled inside. Imagine them gone. Imagine his room empty.

Put plate down on table.

Repeat as needed.

Worrying, it seemed, had become her true full-time job. She put in hours every night, staying up till one, one-thirty, two, two forty-five, turning on her side to gaze long and solemnly at the glowing clock, as if into a lover's face.

She worried about global warming. She worried about deadly rays coming from the microwave and cell phones. What if the furnace broke down? What if the roof went? What if her children grew up alone and unloved?

She saw new lines around her mouth and her eyes, on her forehead, even delicately scribed on her cheeks. She would be forty-seven next month. She looked into the mirror with morbid fascination. Having her mother so close only added to her feeling of being old and doomed. Three decades separated the two women. Once it had appeared a vast chasm. Now it seemed a mere step.

In thirty years, she would think she'd have a hard time climbing up and down the three front stairs. She'd have to sell the house, move into a ranch or condo. Her hands would shake, her throat would wobble, her blood pressure would drop, her hair would thin. If she ran out of ideas, she had only to glance over at her mother.

"What?" her mother would say sharply. "Is there a stain on my blouse?"

Often, in fact, there was.

Charlotte Dunrea, the meticulous, the upright, was beginning to drip gravy down her front, to spill coffee in her lap. The seat of her slacks sagged. She complained that it was harder to do everything—to get in and out of the car with Marcus. You could see what an effort it was, getting up out of the kitchen chair after dinner, clinging to the table for support. She might need a walker soon. She was slowing down. It seemed to Eve as if her stubborn little mother was now a permanent fixture in their lives, and the only way she'd ever leave was for her to be carried out, feet first.

Instead, three weeks after school began for the children, as matter-of-factly as Charlotte had decided to stay on, she flew back home to Tennessee.

Chapter 6
The Floating World

Eve could not decide if she felt injured or relieved by her mother's desertion. Now there was no cushion for them to break the fall of bad moods or bad news.

Marcus had failed his September driver's test by forgetting to put on his seat belt. The man administering the test wouldn't even let him drive away from the curb after that. When they sat at the table after supper, Marcus stared into his ice cream bowl as if watching a movie in there. Maybe this was how adolescence prepared you for a child's departure from home, Eve thought. They were gone before they actually left.

Noni lived at the opposite end of the spectrum;

absolutely nothing escaped her eagle eye. "Okay," she lectured Eve. "Your wardrobe is getting a tiny bit better, but it's all huge on you. How about some color once in a while?" She scribbled with her colored pencils, blue, green, purple squiggles, and held them up. "You remember—color? It looks like this."

Noni threw herself into soccer practice, schoolwork, and the intricate web of female friendships that defined fourth grade. Some of her friends already wore makeup and high heels to school. Children seemed to hit adolescence earlier and then stayed there longer. Noni walked home with her soccer teammates—they practiced on the field right behind the park—then she spent most of the night literally sitting in Eve's lap, planted there like some exotic orchid, her lanky, hard muscular arms and legs wrapped around her mother.

Noni's hair smelled sweet and edible. She and her friends traded shampoos and conditioners, and each experiment brought a different tropical scent—pineapple, mangos, coconut. "Mmm." Eve would pretend to nibble on the end of a light brown braid. "Delicious."

Noni twisted around to look at her sternly. "If you ate my hair at least you'd eat something." She looked and sounded like a miniature Mrs. Dunrea. "Tell me about the Heartbreak Diet," she said.

"I made it up," Eve said. "There's no such thing."

"Yes there is." And Noni put one small, delicate hand flat on her mother's heart. "Tell me . . . Once upon a time there was a Heartbreak Diet," Noni prompted her.

"Okay," Eve said. "She was so skinny that when she turned sideways, she disappeared. This was handy when she wanted to travel, because instead of paying for a ticket, she could turn sideways and no one would know she was there.

"She traveled all around the world, growing skinnier and skinnier . . ."

Eve's voice trailed off. Dimly she heard Noni saying, "Mom? Mom! What's the end of the story?"

I'm getting as bad as Marcus, Eve thought. She tried to remember where she'd left off.

"Then one day she met a sandwich, and she liked it so much she ate it all up. And that was the end of the diet. The End."

"Mom!" Marcus howled. "If Noni ends up bulemic or morbidly obese, it'll be your fault."

"Grandma says always eat breakfast," Noni said. "She says it's the most important meal of the day."

"It is," Eve said gravely. "That's why I keep it simple. Coffee. Coffee with coffee. No additives, no artificial ingredients."

"Coffee stunts your growth," Noni said.

"Though maybe that's not your problem anymore."

"Quit worrying about me." Eve gathered both children into her arms and held them, their big bones jabbing into her.

"Hey, Mom," Marcus said. "I know the Ultimate Heartbreak Diet."

"What?" Both mother and sister turned to look at him.

"One cyanide pill."

"That's cold, Marcus," Noni said, and Eve agreed, "Very dark." Marcus laughed maniacally.

But mornings after the kids had gone to school, the house seemed to swallow her whole. The upstairs was cramped and dark. She had to turn on lights just to make her way down the narrow hall. The house had been built by people who wanted to save money and space. Ceilings were low, rooms were small, every corner utilized. The upstairs was deserted and dim as she wandered from room to room, picking up the kids' socks, and closing dresser drawers. Neither child ever closed a single door or drawer.

She still looked in the bedroom mirror sometimes thinking she'd see Chuck's lean smiling face above her shoulder. She could almost feel his sharp jaw against the side of her neck. Noni was right, she thought. Her clothing did look ridiculous. It provided great fodder for Noni's comic strips. Eve had dropped another seven pounds. Everything was too long, too wide, too big, too baggy. Sweaters stretched down past her knees. She rolled her sleeves up two and three times, and still they fell over the tops of her hands. She looked like she was wearing webs and tents. But she couldn't bring herself to do better.

Once, she'd had someone to hold and be held by. Now she had the dogs. Every woman she knew who lived alone got a dog, sooner or later. You saw single women out every morning, walking their dogs. The only men out walking dogs were old. They had a widowered look. Probably the wife had died, leaving the dog.

Single men always had cats. Basically, cats lived like guys. It was no wonder that men and women couldn't get along. When men went on vacation for two weeks, they'd call someone to come feed the cats. If a woman went away for a day, she had to arrange for her dog to be walked, fed, played with, petted, let outside and given treats.

Eve took to walking her dogs the five blocks to Rec Park. As soon as they heard the jingle of leashes in her hand, the shih tzus were ecstatic— they leapt joyfully, throwing themselves against the front door—though, walking, one or another of the little dogs would tucker out and want to be carried home. Still, it gave her a sense of purpose in those first drowning moments of the day.

She strolled in wordless dog company past the bulky Binghamton houses with their sagging square front porches, not thinking, not carrying her cell phone, not even worrying, for once. Walking the dogs was like riding on a train. The landscape passed by; no one could call you or fax you or ask you to do anything—you were unattached, gliding along. It reminded her of the Ukiyoe Japanese prints called *Pictures of the Floating World.* Plus, she could talk to herself without looking crazy. "Hang in there . . . It'll get better." People just assumed she was talking to her dogs.

Rec Park was quiet and still in the early morning. She saw a few dawdlers on their way to school. She headed almost hungrily for the depths of the park. One Down syndrome boy dragged what looked like a dead animal on a red leash, which turned out to be a stuffed dog. The boy wore a big green varsity jacket with saints embroidered in gold on the back.

She spotted couples holding hands, sometimes a mother pushing a stroller—one energetic young woman jogged by with a three-wheeled stroller designed for speed. Eve pitied the poor baby, whose eyes were wide, it seemed to her, with terror. She had to resist an impulse to jump in the young woman's way and lecture her.

"Slow down!" she wanted to yell. "Let the kid

see something. He'll be grown up and gone soon enough."

There were the senior citizens who played tennis in the park before the high school tennis team took over the courts. The old men yelled at each other as if they were furious over some ancient grudge, while the women played like peaceful children.

The only hard part was her two tiny dogs barking hysterically at every passing animal: big calm dogs, other small dogs, even old and blind dogs. Eve hurried across the street each time one headed in their direction. Toaster, the younger dog, practically strangled himself on his leash. She would try to look friendly, overcompensating. She'd smile or wave and say something stupid like, "Their bark is worse than their bite!"

At home she had a fenced backyard, but was afraid that one day they'd escape and run into the street. She considered taking them back to obedience school but she barely had time to get the essential things done in a day, much less going to night school for dogs. She decided to train them at the park. The safest place was inside the handball court, which was both fenced in and, in mid-autumn, always empty.

One morning, she heard a large black man in an orange jacket shouting across the park. She assumed he must be hollering at truant school kids hiding out under the trees. There were always a few hanging around. But he was waving his arms and heading straight toward her. He was still half a football field's distance away when she understood the words.

"Get out of the handball court!" His voice was so loud it sounded like he was blasting through a megaphone. "I said, get the dogs out of the court!" Before he could come any closer, she called the dogs—for a change they actually obeyed—and ran home, breathless by the time she reached her front door. She supposed he was an overzealous parks worker, there to rake the leaves that fell from the oaks in huge, soft mounds, dizzying piles, like waves in a coppery-brown sea. She decided to wait it out, see if he was there the next time she walked the dogs. He always was.

She was afraid to go back into the handball court, though it seemed ridiculous—the place was deserted. Apparently the bellicose worker in his puffy orange jacket was a permanent fixture in Rec Park. She'd see him talking genially to other parkgoers, helping an old neighbor ease his walker over the curb, waving and calling to the school kids. He seemed to know everyone except her. Most of the time, he wore headphones, listening to rap music that floated faintly from the headset. She felt slightly outraged. No one else was using the court. She considered calling Mayor Nick Garguillo, whose son she'd known since he was in kindergarten, a square-headed boy playing blocks with Marcus.

All the same, she dreaded being yelled at again. Anything these days could wound her. All day, she'd put her hand to her chest, resting her fingers there, pressing down to contain it, and detect the dull little constant ache in her chest bone. Here's what no one ever told you about heartbreak, she thought: it actually, physically, hurt.

She shied away from anyone who had a mean streak, which gave her new perspective about people she'd known for years. One day Lev Schooner said something snappish and she felt a lump form in her throat. They didn't speak again for days, because she couldn't risk his saying something worse. The dean, a curt black-haired woman with a pointy nose, was to be avoided at all costs, but her assistant, Eugene Trueblood, was as soft-spoken as Mister Rogers. He wore zippered cardigans, like Mister Rogers, and stayed inside his small gray office. Probably, Eve thought, he was hiding out from the dean, too.

Mrs. Dunrea phoned from Tennessee, but she kept the phone calls brisk and matter-of-fact. "Bloom where you're planted" was her motto. It was stitched on a rectangular pillow propped up on her white sofa in her Tennessee condo. She was not a coddler. "Buck up," she'd say, and Eve would wince. She prayed she'd never say anything so stupid to her own children.

One evening just as she and the kids were finishing supper, the doorbell rang. The shadowy figure standing behind the locked screen door looked familiar, but she could not put her finger on where she'd seen him before.

"How you doo-ing?" he asked cheerfully. He was holding a familiar-looking winter jacket over his arm.

Eve pushed the door open a crack without actually inviting the young man inside. She was conscious of her children behind her in the house. The dogs circled around her feet but had already stopped barking, a good sign. "May I help you?"

"This coke, it cannot fit me," he said apologetically. "I wonder don't you have other coke?"

"It doesn't fit?" she echoed stupidly. Now at last she remembered him from the garage sale.

"Sadly, no," he said. "What I do with it?"

She reached out to take it from him. "How much did you pay for it?"

"Ten dollar," he said. "I sell it back to you—for five dollar."

"I'll give you ten," she said. She called back into the kitchen, "Noni, will you bring my purse, please?"

"I cannot take ten. Only five." The young man tilted his head at her like a friendly bird. His smile was broad and white. It was hard to believe she was still bargaining with him.

"Who is it, Mom?" Noni said. She came running with the purse in her arms, then stopped short at the sight of the young man standing on the porch. "What's he selling?" she asked.

"Coke," he said, hoisting it up in his arms. "Maybe fit you in another few year."

"Maybe," Noni said doubtfully. The little girl stood next to her mother with her arms folded. "My dad's not here anymore and my brother's too tall for it."

"Nice," he said, smiling. "Nice girl. Very polite."

As if on cue, Noni said, "Would you like to come in?" She pushed open the screen door, and the young man came inside, immediately stepping out of his shabby-looking loafers. When Eve saw his worn-out socks, her heart gave an unwanted lurch of sympathy.

"Would you like a cup of tea?" she asked, handing him the five dollar bill.

"Thank you, no." He gestured vaguely. "My wife is waiting."

Eve peered through the screen door. A young Korean woman was standing out on the sidewalk. Her hands were folded in front of her.

"Come inside!" Eve called.

The woman was very pretty, and very thin, wearing a pair of overalls and a bright red ski jacket. Her hair was cut short, the bangs straight across her forehead. She was dressed like someone Noni's age, except she wore neat red pumps and had a matching red plastic purse. She waved both hands emphatically. "No, no sank!" the young woman called. Her voice was low and musical. She said something in Korean to her husband. There was an urgent tone in whatever she said, and she was looking straight at Eve.

The young man was still standing in the foyer in his stocking feet. He had tucked the five dollar bill into his worn leather billfold and put the billfold away. Yet he appeared to be waiting for something.

"I don't have any more jackets to sell," Eve said. "I'm sorry." She wondered if she should go upstairs and give him whatever was still hanging on Chuck's side of the closet. She wondered if the young man would be insulted.

"My wife want me to ask," he said. "She say you look like very nice person. You teach at university?"

"No," she said. "I work there." She made a typing motion with her fingers. "In the Art Department. Secretary." She did not feel up to explaining the difference between an administrative assistant and a secretary.

He looked disappointed. His wife, still standing on the sidewalk, asked a question. He answered briefly.

"You could teach English?" he said, turning back to her.

"I—uh—" Eve was flabbergasted. Noni was looking at her.

"She definitely could," Noni said. "My mother is a very good teacher. She taught me how to knit."

"Please," the young woman said. She came forward a few steps up the walk. She said something to her husband in Korean.

"She work very hard," he said. "I pay you. See?" He reached into his pocket and displayed the folded five dollar bill she had just handed him.

"I couldn't take your money," Eve said.

"Not enough?" the man said.

"No," Eve said. "I'm not charging anything."

"Free!" Noni said cheerfully.

"Okay," the man said, grinning widely. "We come back tomorrow. Eight o'clock p.m. Eight o'clock?"

"Sank you," his beautiful wife said. She was nodding and smiling. The man slipped his feet back into the loafers and bowed slightly.

Noni bowed back. "Tomorrow night at eight!" she said.

Eve closed the door weakly. "Noni," she said. "For heaven's sakes."

"You can do it," Noni said. "Buck up! You need some new interests. New friends!"

"You'll be great," Marcus said.

"Right," said Eve. "Thank you very much, both of you."

"You're welcome," they said together.

Chapter 7

Jonah

It was a cold, clear morning in November. The tennis players were gone, the nets down. Eve supposed the angry park worker's job was finally done. There were fewer glove-brown leaves heaped below the oak trees, whose branches hung as empty as coat hangers. Soon there would be an utter end to blue skies. Binghamton was settling in toward winter. Snow would gather and drop from endlessly gray clouds, and no one would see a sidewalk for months.

Binghamton's population was aging, like many upstate New York towns; its dismal climate was only a piece of the problem. Half the downtown buildings stood empty with vacant or soaped-up windows, the younger people were fleeing, and more welfare cases were moving in from metropolitan New York. This brought a new set of problems: drugs, gangs, smash-and-grab robberies—things nobody wanted to talk about. Not even the mayor, who enthused about the influx of new people. But now there were always two police cars parked by the basketball hoop, which had been moved to the edge of the park. Twice, there were drive-by shootings late at night.

Eve hunkered down in the cold empty handball court, smoothing her skirt over her knees—and held up her hand. The dogs sat and looked at her expectantly. They stayed. She called and they trotted across the court for their treats. "Good boys!" She petted and praised them and they squirmed under her touch, like teenage boys embarrassed and pleased by the attention.

"How many times I got to tell *you* to stay *out* of the *court!*" a voice boomed in her ear. She practically fell backward, then scrambled to her feet to face the big parks worker. He had snuck up on her this time. Close up, he seemed even tougher and bigger, more muscular and less fat. He looked menacing and mean, not the trace of a smile on his face.

"I'm sorry," she said.

"No dogs, allowed on the handball court," he chanted, jabbing his hand toward a sign hanging on the gate.

"Sorry," she said. "I won't do it again."

"I got better things than chasing you around this park!"

"I'm really sorry," she said again, meekly.

"How many times I got to be telling you the same thing over again?"

"Okay, *okay*—brother! I apologized. Now I'm leaving." She was struggling to attach the leashes to the dogs' collars as she spoke, but her hands were shaking.

"*What* you just call me?" He jerked the words out furiously. "You call me a brother?" He looked enormous now, puffed up with angry indignation.

"What? No," she said. She had never in her life called anyone "brother"—least of all a black man.

"My name is *Jonah!*" he said belligerently.

A few snowflakes dropped from the pulpy-looking gray sky, wearily, with no intention of sticking around. She got the dogs' leashes attached and put out one gloved hand. Her glove, she just now noticed, had a rip along one seam. She was determined to be polite to the end. "Nice to meet you, Jonah."

He stared at her hand a moment, then shook it. "I got better things to do," he said. "Got to shovel out this whole park every time it snow. 'Course," he suddenly smiled, "if it happen late enough, I get overtime."

More flakes fell, dissolving as soon as they touched her coat sleeve and her hair. "I'm sorry I took up your time," she said. The cold was seeping up into her thin shoes, old brown leather pumps with buckles. Eve thought they must have been her mother's, handed down. They looked unfamiliar. He was keeping her inside the court and she was afraid the dogs might choose that inopportune moment to break another rule.

Jonah wore orange gloves as big as a fighter's boxing gloves. He stretched them out to the dogs, who sniffed at them. His skin was so dark it looked blue-black. "They smelling my lunch," he said. "Made myself a turkey sandwich on white, a little bit mayo. Some carrot sticks, and an orange, and a piece of pie." He patted his jacket pocket. "Got it wrapped up in here. Got a whole quart of milk in my office, too." He nodded toward the closed pool pavilion. Now that he was so close, she noticed his strong scent of cologne, spicy and lemony.

"Keep my equipment back behind the pool area. Got me a little desk, a couple chairs and a heater. Uh-huh. It's nice. Not as nice as my apartment, but still nice."

"That's—nice," she said.

"I am also superintendent at the Chestnut Arms apartments," he said. "Over on Chestnut Street, you know where that is at?" He pointed across the park.

"I think so," she said. "Well, I'd better be going."

"That's after I'm done here at the park as

head maintainer. I am responsible for twenty-one tenants, make sure no druggies come around, no dealers, no trouble. I make all the needed repairs. I got to get a part for the furnace soon as I'm finished here in the park. See, I'm trying to fix it myself, save them some money. They appreciate that. They give me a big beautiful apartment for free. Nice-sized bedroom and a very large living room. I got one of them big-screen TV sets last year, 'cause my nephew likes to come watch the games. Oh, the ladies like it, too, I'll tell you. I got it done ni-iice." He drew out the words. "Got a third job also. Guess what."

"Cook?" She was thinking of the lunch he'd brought to work.

"That's a good guess! I'm a better cook than most ladies. I make chicken, lamb chops, grill them with a little rosemary and olive oil, or a chicken breast marinated first, with mashed potatoes—real mashed potatoes, none of that boxed stuff—and beans and greens. My mother raised me right. You know what I mean by greens?"

She nodded. She wouldn't have believed this large sullen man could be so voluble. It was as if she had pushed some button that got him going. He put long-winded Marcus to shame.

"Most white people don't have the first idea what is meant by greens."

"My mother is from Tennessee," she said.

"Oh yeah? That explains it. Where she at now?"

"Now?" Eve repeated stupidly. "She's in Tennessee."

He laughed as if she had made a joke. "I work at the Sports Authority on the weekends," he said. "That's the gym over in Johnson City. Nice place, very nice." He nodded. "I train every morning. I can lift two hundred, two twenty, without breaking a sweat. I don't brag but that's what I do. With great strength comes great responsibility. Some of the other guys at the gym, they look at me like, oh no, man, what is he doing next? I'm tougher than I look."

She wanted to say he looked plenty tough. "I'd better go," she said. "Work." The snowflakes were gathering in white patches on the dogs, and she was worried about the new construction jamming things up around the Johnson City traffic circle. She moved to go around him, the dogs trotting obediently in a half circle, their leashes jingling pleasantly, like sleigh bells. He followed her out of the court and shut the gate behind, rattling it to be sure it latched.

"I observe the older gentlemen, give them a hand. I run the kids' basketball program every first Sunday I'm not in church. My mother raised me to go to church. I don't always get there, but always mean to go."

She walked quickly toward the edge of the park, but Jonah kept up without breaking stride.

"Don't make me be chasing you no more," he said with a smile. Close up, he had a broad, handsome face, with a closely shaved mustache and beard. She wasn't sure if she was imagining it or if he was flirting. The way he was looking at her made her feel almost pretty, for the first time in months. "You and these cute little dogs of yours." He bent down again to ruffle them behind the ears. "What kind of dogs?"

"Shih tzu," she said.

"Uh-huh," he said. "They very nice." He put his orange work glove out, and Toaster, the smaller dog, leaped up shamelessly to be petted. He'd gotten his name from the high leaps he made straight in the air, like bread popping out of a toaster. "Another young lady, she comes through the park with a dog like this one, little bit bigger. She got only one. You got the pair. They brother and sister?"

"Actually, they're cousins," she said.

"I got fifteen cousins," Jonah said. "No wait— sixteen! Got a new one this summer. One of them live at the Chestnut Arms. Actually, she my mother's cousin but I call her cousin. The Chestnut management trust me to keep the drugs out of the apartments and off the sidewalk. Black people, white, yellow, purple, don't matter to me. The only color I care about is the green." He rubbed his gloved thumb and fingers together.

"Well, I can't be late," she said, but he put one hand on her arm. She was wearing Ivan's old Irish tweed overcoat. It was thin but warm.

"I enjoyed conversating with you," he said. "I didn't mean to skeer you, but this park is my responsibility. Good people are my people. Not everybody who come through is like you. We got some head cases trying to ruin it, strung-out whack jobs, knuckleheads, we got third generation welfare don't got no place else on earth to be. I call them the dollar store mamas with the dollar store marriage and the dollar store baby carriage."

Jonah strode in front of her and held up his orange-gloved hand, stopping traffic on Beethoven Street to let her cross. The locals pronounced it *Beeth*-oven.

"You have yourself a very nice day," he said in a formal voice, nodding at her and at the dogs. It must be his official farewell to all the visitors to his park. She now thought of the park as belonging to this large, talkative man.

He waited till she was at the other side of the street, then fitted his earphones over his head, squared his broad shoulders, and walked off. She watched him go, and was embarrassed when he suddenly spun around, catching her looking. He lifted one earphone slightly away from one ear.

"I never did catch your name!" he called.

"Oh!" she said. "Eve."

"Okay, then. *Eve.*" He said the name as if it were an object he was tucking away, alongside his lunch. "You have yourself a *very* nice day."

Chapter 8
Bad News

Frederick Cummings was literally pulling his hair when she came into the office—twenty minutes late, thanks to her encounter with Jonah in the park, the snow, and traffic snarls at the bridge. Frederick's long curly hair had been bright red but had faded to an orangey brown and was now mostly gray. When he saw her, he sank back in his chair, visibly relieved.

"Thank God!" he said. "We meet with the dean today. You've got the budget proposal?"

She slid the file out of the filing cabinet.

He refused to take it from her hands. "No—keep it! " He held up his red-knuckled hands, which were spattered with paint. "If I touch it I'll lose it."

The staff from the Music and Theater departments were already sitting in the anteroom outside the dean's office, glumly clumped around a low table covered with out-of-date magazines and on-campus publications, but the dean, as usual, kept them cooling their heels, while her secretary, a small untidy woman, fluttered at them from behind her gray desk.

"The dean will be out in a moment," she said every minute or two. She kept offering them coffee or tea, till finally Lev took a Styrofoam cup. He was in his plaid flannel shirts again; winter had officially begun.

Routinely, the chairs of the art, music, and theater programs came to the dean for adjunct money, line items, increases to the graduate students, and new faculty lines. Just as routinely, the dean turned them down. People joked that SUNY Binghamton had gone from being state funded, to state supported, to state located. Budgets got tighter with every new governor.

Eve could remember when the dean seemed distressed by her inability to fund the arts. Now she called it "learning to make do." She groused at the faculty, as if the lack of money were somehow all their fault. She warned about cuts and advised them to write more grants. "Think outside the box, people!" she'd bark.

The chair of the Music Department, Walter Blair, was a passionate little man given to fits of temper. His department had fallen on hard times. Instruments were now entirely taught by adjunct faculty, and the dean talked about removing the old Steinways from the practice rooms instead of refurbishing them.

"What are the students supposed to practice on?" Blair fumed. "Pieces of wood? Paper with the keys drawn on? Are we going to burn the Steinways for fuel, for Chrissakes?"

The Theater chair, Jack Veneer, was tall, laconic. He was surrounded by the usual assortment of lunatics, outcasts, and geniuses that comprised the Theater Department, but was himself more at ease talking about real estate and classic cars. He was neither dramatist nor actor, director, dancer, or theorist. She thought he'd had something to do with stagecraft—lighting. He still worked the boards in a pinch.

He had been chair for the past twenty-five years uninterruptedly. His name, Jack Veneer, suited him; all anyone saw was a calm, smooth surface. His wife had run the box office, but for the past ten years, at least, she'd been battling brain cancer. The vibrant, vivacious Tiffany was now frail, ghostly white, and seldom appeared in public. Jack spent his time taking her to doctors and clinics all over the country. Friends attributed her having survived this long to his constant, tender care. Yet if you asked him about Tiffany, he'd just smile blandly and say, "Doing all right, doing her best."

The dean finally opened the door of her office. "Come in," she said. She dashed one hand down toward the conference table and chairs. "Have a seat." Her office was dominated by a large, old grandfather clock, which ticked through their meetings.

"Ohmygod," said Valerie, the Theater Department assistant. "I totally left my stuff downstairs."

"Go get it," Jack told her calmly. Everyone knew Valerie needed an excuse to step outside and smoke. She smelled of tobacco. Her fingernails were bitten to the quick, her hands inflamed-looking. She smoked three packs a day, easy, and as a result her voice was rough, her face gaunt and yellow. She looked much older than her age. She was skeleton-thin and dressed in what could only be called costumes. Valerie was costume designer for the student productions, dressing the kids straight out of her own closets. Her eyes looked wild now as she stared around the dean's wood-paneled office. She exited mumbling under her breath. She wouldn't return, Eve knew, till a few minutes before the meeting ended.

"Things look very bad," the dean said, smiling grimly, as soon as Valerie closed the door. "We may be cutting whole programs." She glared around at all of them. The big clock ticked loudly. "Probably no extra funds for any of you," she said after a pause.

"For God's sakes!" Walter Blair exploded. "Why don't we all just lie down and die, then. What is the point of these damned meetings?"

The dean and Jack Veneer turned sideways to look at him. Frederick Cummings fidgeted. He reached for the Art Department folder. Eve slid it into his waiting hands.

"I guess I'll start," he said.

An hour later they emerged from the dean's office with no idea which, if any, of their requests would be granted. Eve had noticed that the angrier the dean seemed, the more virulently she opposed them, the more likely they were to get what they had asked for. If the dean spoke sympathetically, they would not get a dime.

"I think we're in good shape," Eve said. The dean had been especially nasty toward the Art Department, which might mean they'd finally get a junior hire in painting.

"What meeting did *you* go to?" Lev grumbled. The dean had disputed every figure he'd presented—the number of music majors, even the head count at last year's concerts.

"Wait," Eve said. "You'll get that cellist, and she'll increase the concert budget, too."

Lev looked at her suspiciously. "What makes you so cheery, all of a sudden?"

"Nothing," she said. "I just have a naturally sunny disposition."

He frowned. "You've lost weight," he said. "You look like hell."

Frederick Cummings emerged engrossed in conversation with the other two chairs. He patted

Eve absently on the shoulder as he walked by. "Well, we did our best," he said. "If she shuts us down, I can finally move to Brazil." Cummings's wife was Brazilian; they spent all their vacations on the coast. "And don't worry about Helen Gollow," he said. "We've got her covered."

"Helen Gollow?" Eve echoed.

She felt rather than saw Lev stiffen at her side. He took a step forward as if to shield her. He seized her hand tightly in his. His touch was so unexpected, she flinched. Lev's hand was small but surprisingly warm and square and hard. He squeezed hers once, convulsively, then let it drop. That touch frightened her more than anything. He had never so much as brushed her shoulder before. The surge of contact was like an electric charge. I must be in big trouble, she thought.

Frederick Cummings's face turned bright red.

"What about Helen Gollow?" Eve said, looking at Lev.

"She's all talk," said Frederick. "She goes after every woman in the department, you know that. She hates her own kind."

Lev turned toward Eve. "She's trying to get you fired. She went to the dean, offering to trade you for a new hire in Graphics."

"When?" Eve said blankly.

"It'll never happen," Frederick said. "Nothing to worry about."

"Fired?" Eve said. "Me?"

"I called the union rep," Lev said. "She can't touch you."

"You see?" Frederick waggled his hands. "The dogs bark, but the caravan moves on."

"I don't understand," Eve said.

"It's nothing personal." Lev frowned at Frederick. "Now Eve's upset—understandably," he added. He nearly patted her arm but this time jerked his hand back before making contact. "I'll buy you a cup of coffee." He turned to Frederick. "Can you spare her?"

"Absolutely. But not for long." Frederick's smile wavered. He reminded Eve of a clumsy golden retriever. His office was perpetually tumbled, as if a large dog had been there knocking things over—empty food packages, spilled papers, gin bottles, paintbrushes left out to dry like quills. He ran his fingers through his red hair till it stood straight up, then pushed it down again. "Forgive me. I was just afraid you might hear about it from someone else."

Lev walked so fast she had to trot to keep up with him. "You want a bagel?" he asked. "You should eat."

The Fine Arts lounge smelled of toast and melted butter and coffee. Eve ordered hot tea, and Lev insisted on paying. This worried her, too. He was notoriously tight.

The students were bundled up in winter coats

and down jackets, even indoors. A few sported handmade-looking knitted hats, brightly colored, with long silly tassels. Outside the tall windows, snow slanted down, batted this way and that by the November wind. "Don't take it personally. Everyone knows Gollow is completely off her rocker."

"I guess," Eve said, blowing on her tea with milk. Today it seemed too rich to swallow. *The Bad News Diet: It is safe to order anything on the menu in this diet.* "She must believe she's doing the right thing for the department."

"Well she's not," Lev said flatly. "Is *she* going to do all the work? Schedule meetings, fix everything that goes wrong or breaks? Get the files and transcripts to the registrar? Counsel the students the way you do? You're worth three graduate advisors. Everyone knows it."

Eve was unused to praise from Lev; it was unsettling. "How are your cats?" she asked, to change the subject.

"Okay," he said. "You know—" he added, "I'm — not just living with cats anymore."

Eve's stomach gave a hard jump. Some woman had moved in with Lev, out at his isolated farmhouse. At times she'd pictured the place, and even imagined he'd invite her out to hear the CD collection he bragged about. It was a pathetic friendship that never extended beyond the walls of the university. Now she would be the only member of the administrative staff on her own. Everyone else was either married or partnered. She set the cup of tea down on the table. And there was something else. She couldn't put her finger on it, but Lev rushed on. She fixed a bright, artificial smile to her lips.

"I've been meaning to tell you about it," he said. "I got a dog. Last month."

"A dog?" she asked.

"They were going to put her to sleep. No one wants a middle-age dog, I guess."

"No one wants a middle-age anything," Eve said.

He looked at her. "I wouldn't be too sure about that. Cummings was wound up about this. He wouldn't let anyone touch a hair on your head. Those were his words—Of course, he may have been drunk when he said it."

"What's the dog's name?" she asked.

"Ginger." Lev had already polished off one toasted bagel and started on a second. "You sure you won't eat?" he asked. "You should eat something."

She shook her head. "Ginger as in the spice?" she said.

"Rogers," he answered, crunching into the bagel. "I've got a cat named Fred. Fred Astaire was a terrific singer, you know. I'll lend you his CDs sometime, you'll be surprised."

"Maybe I could meet him." She spoke into her tea.

"Fred Astaire's dead," Lev said.

"I meant your dog."

"Oh!—Ginger. Maybe I'll bring her into school sometime." Lev stood abruptly, his cup clutched in his hand, the tea bag dangling over the side. Lev liked his tea strong and bitter. "I've got to get back to work. You're okay, right?"

"Fine."

He was standing, she was sitting, her tea untouched. Still, something made her plow on ahead. "Would you like to have dinner together sometime?"

"Gee." Lev rubbed one hand through his curly black hair. He tilted the unfinished bagel into a nearby garbage can. "I don't think so. Thanks anyway, Eve, that's nice of you. I sort of like to —once I leave this place, I'm done for the night. And now I've got Ginger—"

"Sure," she said. This was turning out to be a completely humiliating morning. "I understand. I get tired early myself."

"No offense," Lev said, and hurried out the door.

Chapter 9
Seven at One Blow

When Eve got home, she found Marcus on the phone with his grandmother, practically in tears. "What's wrong?" she said.

He waved her away and pushed his bedroom door closed with his foot.

She hurried to find Noni. "What's wrong with Marcus?"

"He flunked his driving test again." Noni said. "How many times can he try?"

"I don't know if there's a limit," Eve said.

His friend Dev had driven him in for the test. "For moral support," Dev had said.

She went back upstairs and knocked lightly on Marcus's door. "Marcus—are you all right?"

He came to the door holding the phone. "I'll never learn to parallel park! It's so dumb. Why can't I just avoid those parking spaces, what does it matter?" He listened over the phone for a minute, nodding but not saying anything. "Gramma wants to talk," he said, holding out the phone.

"Well my goodness," Charotte said. "He's so emotional. Life is full of ups and downs. Marcus needs to learn that." She said it as if it was something Eve had neglected to mention.

"He can take the test again," Eve said. Marcus shook his head. "I'll bet he passes next time." His head drooped lower.

"And what about you?" Charlotte asked crisply. "How was your day?"

Without intending to, Eve told her mother about Helen Gollow.

"Why would anyone try to get you fired? You're such a nice person. Everyone loves you. Everyone has *always* loved you."

Eve was stunned. Her mother had never said such a sweet thing to her in all her life. Not even in this matter-of-fact voice, as if she were quoting something she'd read in a newspaper.

"Trust me, you are a very lovable person."

"I don't know about that," Eve said, hoping to hear more.

"I do," her mother said. "This Gollow woman must be a lunatic. Stay away from her. A woman like that could be carrying a firearm."

"I doubt it."

"Look at all those school shootings. One day a teacher will be toting the gun, mark my words."

"I'll wear a bulletproof vest to work."

"I'm glad you think this is funny," Charlotte said stiffly. "What about Marcus? That boy doesn't stand a chance in Alabama of getting his license. He's not cut out for it."

"You're wrong," Eve said. "There's nothing he can't do if he puts his mind to it."

"We'll see," Charlotte Dunrea said. "It sounds like you've got your hands full."

Marcus wanted to know where Helen Gollow lived, what kind of car she drove. "I've got friends, Ma," he said. "I'll tell Dev and the team. They'll put sugar in her gas tank—or sand, I forget, but it wrecks your engine."

"I'm old enough to fight my own battles." She and Helen Gollow had always been cordial even though they were completely unalike. Once or twice they'd had a cup of tea, while Helen went into great and alarming detail about all her medical problems. Helen kept her students and herself to a rigid work schedule. Her gourmet cooking was legendary. She wore operatic black capes in winter. This would be quite a year, Eve thought, if she lost her husband *and* her job. What was that fairy tale about the man who killed the flies? Seven at one blow.

She went downstairs to make supper. First she forgot to turn on the oven under the meat loaf. Then she forgot to put the meat loaf into the hot oven. She also forgot to use her pot holders, and not to use bad language in front of Noni.

They ended up eating cold cereal and milk.

"You should put this into the Heartbreak Diet Cookbook," Noni said.

"How about playing Boggle?" Eve suggested.

That might bring Marcus downstairs.

"Mia is coming over," Noni reminded her. She came now for English lessons every Tuesday night. Her name wasn't really Mia, but must have sounded vaguely like it in Korean—all her friends took on American-sounding names: Mary Ann, Joo-Lee, Lucy, and so on. It seemed to Eve shameful, young men and women giving up their names because Americans were too lazy to learn to pronounce them. Mia didn't mind; she loved everything American. She often dressed in red, white, and blue. Her husband was eager to return to Korea once he earned his doctorate, but Mia wanted to stay in Binghamton.

"Here better for my chir-en," she said. "Good for boys in Korea, not good for gir-uls."

Eve knew she was supposed to be correcting Mia's pronunciation—that was why the young woman came to her house every Tuesday night without fail. Her eagerness to improve her English was touching. But Eve thought that English words sounded better the way Mia said them—more interesting and musical. Tonight, Mia looked upset, shrugging off a short black jacket—she always dressed as if she were going to a party, her handbag matching her outfit, a pretty coordinating necklace.

Noni offered Mia a cup of green tea, and Mia accepted unsmiling. Eve kept sweets in the house for Mia—just one reason the young woman was so popular with Eve's children. Marcus was bowled over by Mia's beauty. Noni seemed fascinated by Mia's endless series of matching handbags and shoes.

"She's like an Asian Barbie," Noni once remarked.

"That's not a nice thing to say," Eve said.

"I don't see why. Everybody wants to look like Barbie," Noni replied, ever practical.

"You want to have pointy boobs with no nipples?" Marcus chimed in.

That ended that conversation.

Noni poured hot water into Mia's cup. Noni and Marcus each grabbed a few of the cookies Eve had set out and vanished into the den, leaving the two women facing each other.

"How are your children?" Eve asked. This was how they began their sessions, like two women easing into a swimming pool.

Mia's face brightened. "John made the straight A for his first marking period."

"Wonderful!" Eve said.

"But . . ." Mia looked down.

"Have a cookie," Eve said, sensing trouble.

Mia accepted it and placed it on her plate but made no move to take a bite. "I went shopping at the Gap," she said. "For my chir-en."

"Chil-dren," Eve reluctantly corrected her. "They like the Gap?"

"Chil-jen," Mia said. "Yes, they like. I don't so

much. Not now. I bought a pair of girl's pants. Made from—" She fumbled for the small translator she carried with her. It was the size of a calculator. She typed rapidly and waited, scanning the machine. "Cor-dur-oy," she said. "Pupple."

"Purple," Eve said. "Go on."

"They fall apart after one wash. So I bring them back. I ask please give my money back." Mia took a sip of her tea. "He say, you all alike. You want everything for free. He say it not nice."

"This was a young man?" Eve said.

"Teenager, maybe your son age. But your son very nice boy. This woman not nice. So to say —only assistant manager."

"I see," said Eve. "She, then."

"She. You think I did wrong thing? Whole seam open down leg."

"No," Eve said. "It was the saleswoman who behaved badly."

"Behaved . . . ?" Mia reached for the translator again.

"Very badly," Eve said.

"I don't want go back," Mia said. "I think she does not like Koreans. Maybe not any foreigners. She threw pants at me. "

They composed a letter to the store manager. Mia wrote each phrase slowly and seriously, frequently stopping to look up a word. At the end of the hour, she nibbled at her cookie. "You very good cook," she said. "I don't understand you not married."

"I am married."

"Oh—" Mia looked embarrassed. "I never see him . . ."

"My husband is away," Eve said. "For the time being."

"Which time?" Mia reached for the translator again.

"We are separated," Eve said.

"I see," Mia said. She said nothing for a moment, studying Eve's face. "You are feeling all right? Not sad?"

"Sometimes sad," Eve said. "Sometimes—happier." The words surprised her. But they felt true. Life with Chuck had become effortful, hard to lift—like living with a chronically unhappy, unruly child. Chuck had begun to trudge through his day, where once he'd bounced so jauntily. He'd looked sad and tired, with lines on either side of his mouth. He watched too much TV. He hid inside the earphones of his walkman.

"You are very excellent teacher," Mia said. "I feel—" she stopped. "When I try say a thing deeply I cannot find Englishy words." She glanced up at the kitchen clock. "Late!" she said.

"Let me know what the Gap say—*says*," Eve

corrected herself. Instead of teaching Mia to speak correct English, she was learning how to speak like a Korean. After Mia had left she would find herself thinking in Mia's voice. The kids did it, too. "Sank you," they would say to each other. Or, "So to say."

Now, Eve sat with the kids, playing Go Fish. When the phone rang, no one wanted to answer it. They all sat for a few rings, looking at it. Chuck never said much about plans anymore, just vague promises for the future. If it was hard for Eve to hear, she knew it was harder on the kids. Noni had begun to suck her thumb again at night, in her sleep.

But it was her mother calling again from Tennessee, which surprised Eve. Charlotte never phoned twice in one night.

"Wow," Marcus was saying weakly now into the phone. "Cool, Gramma."

He sounded too polite. What's more, he had turned his shoulder so Eve couldn't see his face. "No, that's great news. Really," he said again. "Thank you." He always pronounced the *th* with a hard sound, as in *that*. "Thank you so much," he said.

After another minute he handed Eve the phone, keeping his face neutral. *Act surprised,* he mouthed.

"Mom?" Eve said. "What's going on?"

"I was just telling Marcus," Mrs. Dunrea said in

her briskest voice. "I have put my condo on the market. I think you all could use a little extra help and support. I am moving to Binghamton. You don't have to worry that I'll ever leave again."

There was a silence. Eve did not have to feign surprise. She was actually speechless.

"Eve?" her mother said. "Are you there?"

No, Eve wanted to say. *I'm not here, none of us are here, so don't you come, either.*

"Yes, I'm here," she said. "Where else could I possibly be?"

Chapter 10

The Interrupting Cow

Mrs. Dunrea arrived with a single red and green plaid suitcase, a long-lost relic from Eve's childhood. Once there had been a fully matched set of these suitcases—the largest giant size, a medium (the one her mother brought), a garment bag, and a cosmetic case no larger than a plaid pocketbook.

"Where's the rest of your things?" Eve asked. Marcus lifted his grandmother's suitcase off the conveyor and set off down the airport toward the doors. Binghamton's airport was so tiny it seemed like the model of some larger airport to be built in the future.

"They're shipping the rest," said Charlotte. "Besides, the buyers wanted most of my furniture," she bragged. Her condo had sold within a few days of going on the market, and the buyers were so eager, they offered more than her selling price. This probably meant that her mother and the real estate agent—an elderly friend of hers—had priced it too low, but Eve knew better than to even suggest such a thing.

Her mother went on. "I kept the dining room table for you, because you've always liked that cherry. And a few things, like Mother's chair. I've arranged to have them shipped." She was referring to her mother's old ornate clawfoot chair, covered in livid flowered upholstery. Eve wondered where they could find an unoccupied corner to put such a thing.

"Can I keep the grandma chair in my room?" Noni asked, as if reading her mother's mind.

Grandma Dunrea looked at her curiously. "All right," she said. "That's as good a place as any. I might come and visit it from time to time."

"You want to visit your mother's *chair?*" Noni said. "Weird, but okay."

Eve had fretted ever since her mother called with news of the sale. *Sold.* There was something so final about the word. Then a *closing.* Everything pointed to an ending. Maybe people should never sell anything. They should just loan things to one another, indefinitely.

"I don't care about furniture," Mrs. Dunrea said. "I want to unburden myself." She called after Marcus, "Slow down!" and added, "He's always rushing off."

On the ride home she sat quietly in the front seat, her hands folded in her lap, staring straight ahead. "I see you've already gotten snow here," she remarked. The headlights, sweeping the dark landscape, picked out a snowy rise here, a frozen patch there.

"There was a snowstorm on Halloween," Noni said. "It was awesome. We had our first snow day, November first."

"Well," Charlotte said bleakly. She pulled her light wool coat around her neck.

"You're going to love it," Noni said. "We go skiing and sledding and everything."

Charlotte Dunrea compressed her lips. She tapped her fingers against one another and looked out onto the dark snowy landscape, against which her pale face fluttered like a ghost's.

On impulse, Eve put her hand over her mother's hand. Mrs. Dunrea was not a demonstrative woman. Her mother's hand was soft to the touch and icy cold. "You need gloves and a hat," Eve said.

"If you say so."

Over the next days, Mrs. Dunrea ventured as far as the dollar store, where she bought bags full of autumn decorations—brown and orange paper leaves, a plastic acorn wreath, cutouts for the windows, pilgrims in brown buckled shoes. At least, Eve thought, there were no Indians with feathers. There was a ceramic pumpkin and spice-scented candles. But as to finding a place to live, or calling the senior center to begin making friends and finding activities, she left it all to Eve. "You call," she'd say. "My eyes are bad. I can't read the phone book."

Even after Eve bought her mother a magnifying glass on a gold chain, Charlotte refused to make any calls. Gradually, Eve realized something surprising: her mother, so intimidating and outspoken around strangers, was actually quite shy. She hid in her room when Mia came by for English lessons, though once she saw Mia triumphantly produce a fifty dollar Gap gift certificate and a note of apology from the store manager, she was won over.

Mrs. Dunrea had always championed the underdog. She bullied other people's bullies. The story of the nasty assistant manager at the Gap outraged her.

"I think your mother very intelligenty woman," Mia told Eve.

Mrs. Dunrea and Marcus were debating politics in the next room. Her voice grew loud, while Marcus's rumbled smoothly, without pause, sounding uncannily like his father, Ivan, a natural-born lecturer. Eve knew they were practicing for what lay ahead.

Marcus had written a letter to the *Binghamton Press*, challenging Senator Filliman to a debate before the state senate election in which Filliman was running unopposed. Marcus and his grandmother agonized over every word and punctuation mark in that letter. Eve couldn't imagine why. Even the local Democrats endorsed Filliman. The whole thing was hopeless. But the *Binghamton Press* sent a reporter to interview Marcus. The reporter was young and giggly, in a short denim skirt; she eyed Marcus with the same appraising gaze he was beginning to get from waitresses. The senator finally agreed to the debate as a sort of goodwill publicity stunt.

Between Filliman's PR people and the *Binghamton Press*, the debate got national media attention. One night they even aired the story briefly on CNN. Handsome, towheaded Marcus became a poster boy for "tomorrow's idealistic politicians." Noni and her pals hung posters all over town: LET MARCUS SPEAK.

Close to four hundred people showed up at the Holiday Inn to watch the debate, including his friend Devin MacKenzie, who brought along the raucous football team. They sat in the front row, taking up more space than seemed humanly possible. There were cameramen and reporters from all over the state.

The Butterflies in the Stomach Pre-Event Dinner Party

This works nicely before any public event.

Lay out three wheat thins and a wedge of Laughing Cow cheese. Serves three, or use leftovers for lunch.

Eve, Noni, and Mrs. Dunrea got to the Holiday Inn an hour early. Paper signs pointed the way to the ballroom. Eve had the panicky feeling she'd have before Marcus's wrestling matches, knowing he was certain to end up pinned on his back. Mrs. Dunrea revealed her nervousness by the way she kept twisting the straps of her pocketbook around in her hands. Noni jiggled her feet and doodled. She drew a picture of Marcus in a tie and superhero cape and in a caption beside him wrote, "Leaps tall senators in a single bound!" The Amazing Shrinking Mom cowered in a corner of the comic strip, dressed in a brown paper bag.

In fact, Noni and her mother had forced Eve into a long navy blue skirt and sky blue sweater for the evening. Eve was so used to wearing neutrals she felt conspicuous wearing blue. But every time she looked down at herself, the color cheered her. Never mind that the skirt had to be safety pinned at the waist, or that the sweater was too long and too wide; she felt exotic, like one of those blue butterflies of the Amazon.

They sat and waited as the large room filled with more and more people. At one point Noni got up and said hello to the football players. When she came back, she looked flustered. "Devin MacKenzie *hugged* me," she said. "Oh my gosh he is so cute—but he smelled funny."

"Funny how?" Eve asked.

Noni frowned, concentrating. "Like beer or something." She shook her head disapprovingly. "I wish he wouldn't drink," she said.

Only after the dull introductory speeches and thanks did the debate finally begin, ten minutes late. Marcus was barely recognizable under the glare of the camera lights, handsome in his father's old Brooks Brothers suit. He had combed back his hair. A small pile of note-papers sat on the lectern in front of him. He kept touching the papers with his fingertips, but nothing else gave him away. His voice was vibrant and low; if Eve shut her eyes she could have thought it was Ivan's. Noni sat forward in her seat, gnawing at her upper lip. She hung onto Eve's hand with a death grip.

Marcus reeled out statistics. He quoted senate hearings verbatim. He had researched every vote Filliman ever cast, every reform he'd opposed. The list of Filliman's blunders was depressingly long. He had blocked a program for handicapped children providing wheelchairs and seeing eye dogs. He'd proposed tax breaks for the local Exxon/Mobil stations. On the ballooning size of classes in the state college system, he was quoted saying, "What the hell do they expect for twenty grand a year?" Eve was appalled. This was the man she had voted for and endorsed with a sign on her own front lawn, for heaven's sakes.

Helen Gollow sat a few rows ahead of Eve, her black-jacketed back rigid, her head unnaturally high. She was wearing a feathery purple wool scarf that dragged behind her chair like a tail. When she caught sight of Eve, her expression grew stony, as stiff as a gargoyle's, and she swung around again. Each time Marcus made another point, she shook her head or sighed loudly.

Well, she wasn't going to affect Marcus at the dais, Eve thought. She could see that. He chattered on with his deadly facts and figures, his voice strangely low and sweet, in contrast to what he was reporting: whole programs for the mentally ill wiped out; halfway houses shut down; the Refugee Resettlement Center downtown shuttered for lack of funds, years of late budgets in Albany. "It ain't going to break my heart," the senator had reportedly said of the closing of a local food pantry.

They were all crammed together in a large

banquet hall at the Holiday Inn overlooking the Susquehanna River. Now and again Eve would catch light glinting off the water. There were cameramen on every side. All this was being recorded and aired. She sat in her gray metal chair listening to her son with a mixture of admiration and horror, and saw the same look across Senator Filliman's tanned face, mingled with something like fear and, increasingly, intense dislike.

The senator chewed his lower lip, glanced once or twice at his gold watch.

"Senator Filliman has been the governor's hatchet man long enough," Marcus said.

"*Hatchet* man?" The senator lunged forward. It looked like he was going to strike Marcus. Filliman was a big man, still athletic, shoulders immense in his pin-striped suit. Tall as Marcus was, he was still in some ways a child. He looked at the senator and smiled sheepishly. "Sorry," he said. "I thought it sounded better than bag man."

Filliman jabbed a finger. "We will have civil discourse here!" he roared, to a smattering of applause. The senator signaled to someone at the back of the room. "Let's look at the facts," he said.

A PowerPoint presentation blinked on. A movie screen slid down. Soft music began to play. The fact that the senator's statistics glowed on a lit screen made them seem more convincing. According to Filliman, everything in upstate New York was getting better, stronger, safer, richer. Now all the numbers marched on his side. Patriotic music played in the background.

"We have time for just a few questions," Filliman said, "since our young friend had wasted precious moments with his fantasies and unfounded accusations. I'll do my best to set the record straight."

Filliman allowed for only a few raised hands in the audience. He ignored all the football players wildly waving their hands in the front row. The next three questions were directed at the senator. With a few minutes left, an elderly woman wearing a robin's-egg-blue wool jacket stood up and faced Marcus. "Telling the truth is a thankless job. It has never been easy or popular. I just want to say that I admire your courage, young man!"

Maybe just out of sympathy, Marcus received the most resounding ovation of the evening. Helen Gollow turned and glared at Eve. An instant later she drew herself up and wrapped her scarf more tightly around her neck.

"Mom," Noni said in an urgent whisper, tugging on her hand. "Mom, did you just stick your tongue out at that big woman?"

"Of course not," Eve whispered back. She didn't have to admit it, anyway.

At the end of the debate, Filliman refused to shake Marcus's hand. He walked to the opposite side of the stage, chatting with the voters. He kept his back turned, even when Marcus approached him, hand outstretched.

That was the photo that appeared the next morning in newspapers across the state: SENATOR SNUBS YOUNG HOPEFUL IN LIVELY DEBATE. The name under the photo was the name of the young journalist so smitten with Marcus.

Marcus forgot all about it as soon as the election was over. That was Marcus; what's done is done, and never look back. He received 165 write-in votes, all disqualified because of his age.

The morning after the election, Marcus was wearing one of his satirical T-shirts and a pair of old sweats. His long-boned feet were bare. "I called Filliman to congratulate him, and he wasn't, you know, very nice or anything."

"Marcus has better things to do," Mrs. Dunrea announced. "For instance, working on his college essays. Passing his driver's test."

If Marcus failed again, it would not be for lack of trying. The old lady took him driving every afternoon. They even practiced parallel parking. "I nailed it, mom," he would say, and Charlotte didn't outright disagree.

Sometimes she'd stay for dinner after the driving lessons, but most nights Charlotte was too tired, and besides, she was used to going to bed early. She was on her own now, she said.

Mrs. Dunrea had moved into one of the suite hotels off the Vestal Parkway, which were supposed to be homelike but would only have seemed so, Eve thought, to a homeless person. It depressed her to visit her mother there, to pick her up from the sterile-looking lobby for dinner, or to take her on a round of doctors' appointments. Mrs. Dunrea too now went to Dr. Schwartz, Danny's father.

"He's too short," she complained. "I never liked little men." She needed a dentist, an orthodontist, a podiatrist, an eye doctor, and then a second eye doctor when she didn't take to the first one. There were two or three medical appointments every week.

"Why not stay with us till you find a place to rent?" Eve asked.

"I'm fine here," her mother said. "Just bored."

"You're home all day, why don't you check out a few places on your own? You don't need me along."

"I do," Mrs. Dunrea said. She sagged when she said it. "You should know that. I don't like going into strange situations alone."

They visited at least twelve apartments in two weeks, starting with an upscale condo over the river—nice enough, her mother admitted, but with a high maintenance fee. "I'm not paying top dollar for Binghamton," she said. "Not for this godforsaken place." She said it right in front of the rental agent.

"We'll be in touch," Eve murmured diplomatically. She had spent her childhood smoothing the ruffled feathers of people her mother insulted. It was a familiar, hopeless feeling.

"Oh no we won't. What for?" Mrs. Dunrea said. "The answer is no."

One place was advertised as a "penthouse," and turned out to be above a Subway sandwich shop. Another advertised two bedrooms, but one was a walk-in closet. A bulb hung in the middle, with a dirty white string dangling beside it. "This is nice," the landlord said. "You could fit a cot," he said. "Or a desk, maybe, against the wall."

Sometimes Mrs. Dunrea would turn on her heel and hobble swiftly out while the person showing the apartment was still in mid-sentence. Eve was left to gather up the application forms.

"I'll stay where I am," Mrs. Dunrea said after they had visited a few more dismal apartments.

"You can't live in a motel the rest of your life," Eve told her.

"Maybe I'll get lucky and die soon," Mrs. Dunrea said. "This is a dreadful city, What possessed you to move here?"

Mrs. Dunrea was still living in the motel when Thanksgiving rolled around. Eve had invited

Mia and her family, and Eve's friend Tracy, who was alone except for her aging chow chow. Marcus, oddly, had invited not only Danny Schwartz, but his favorite teacher, pretty Ms. McLain. "She's going through a tough time," he explained. "Divorce."

"*I'm* going through a tough time," Noni said. Her new coach had put her on defense, when she wanted to play wing forward. Offense was what Noni was best at—she was fast and light on her feet, fearless to the point of recklessness. But she had stamina, so the coach kept her where she was. "What about Danny?" Noni pressed on. "He's not getting a divorce, is he?"

"The Schwartzes say Thanksgiving is a Christian holiday, so they don't celebrate it."

"Thanksgiving is an American holiday," Mrs. Dunrea said crisply. "His friend sounds nutty."

She had come to look over some of Eve's recipes, which were mostly Mrs. Dunrea's own recipes, for sweet potato pie, chestnut stuffing, candied pecan and apple salad.

"Don't let the Koreans bring anything," Mrs. Dunrea ordered Eve. "They're terrible cooks, and besides, they can't afford it."

"Mia wants to bring dessert," Eve said.

"She makes good rice pudding," Noni said. "Ask her to bring rice pudding."

Her mother had taken over all the counter space in the kitchen, while Marcus and Danny sat at the table, demanding to be fed. No one had school—not even Eve, though she'd thought she'd go catch up on paperwork. But she had twelve guests coming for Thanksgiving the next day at her mother's cherry table that fit eight comfortably, ten in a pinch. She might even have thirteen if Lev Schooner showed up.

Since that humiliating morning in the coffee lounge, Eve had felt self-conscious around Lev, but he acted the same as ever. He was making bitter jokes about dining with his dog and cats on Thanksgiving—Hannah-Lore was going to the Midwest, along with her girlfriend.

"You're welcome at my house," Eve said. "We've got a crowd."

"Thanks," Lev said, "I'm not keen on crowds —but thanks. I might surprise you."

Eve gave him her address on a piece of scrap paper, the kind she always lost five minutes later. Lev was not a social person; the chances of him showing up were about as good as Chuck coming to carve the turkey.

But they'd have plenty of company. What her children liked to call her "cast-off and hand-me-down friends" had multiplied exponentially. Tracy sometimes showed up with an uninvited friend in tow, a bedraggled ex-addict, strung out and with no appetite, or strung out and starving. Eve would seat Tracy as far as possible from Mrs. Dunrea. Eve's kids were used to her; Mrs.

Dunrea was not. Noni and Marcus loved Tracy as if she were some weird maiden aunt; Mrs. Dunrea would not.

Noni was at work on a new comic strip called Amazing Shrinking Mom's Thanksgiving Adventure. There were Thanksgiving specials from all of the seasons of her favorite sit-com; people dropping turkeys on the floor, one character walking around in a penguin suit.

"Not penguin—I said pilgrim," someone said. The laugh track roared appreciatively. Noni barely wavered long enough to shake her head no when Eve invited her to come for a walk.

Marcus and Danny disappeared into the basement to play video games. Danny could stand for hours behind Marcus, watching over his shoulder, his arms beating up and down.

Chuck finally called that morning. It had been a long time between calls. He needed to get his act together, he said.

"The kids already *have* their act together," Eve said. "What am I supposed to tell them?"

"Just say—tell them I've gone on a long hike. Into the woods. That would be good."

"Noni would worry you'd get eaten by bears," she said.

He laughed. "Yeah," he agreed. "I dunno. Make something up. You're the smart one."

According to Chuck, she was the responsible one, the good, the smart one. She didn't remember asking to be any of those things.

"I met a guy says he can set me up welding. Remember when I used to do welding?"

"That was before I met you."

He loved risk and speed—cliff diving, bungee jumping, loud grunge rock. He had wanted them to get married in a hot-air balloon. They were mismatched from the start. He'd wanted to be a race-car mechanic, and got an offer at the Penn Yan Speedway—and then she got pregnant with Noni. Instead he took the job at Diute Ford.

"How've you been, anyway?" he said. It was always the last thing he asked.

"I fit into all my old clothes," which was true. Altogether she had now lost almost thirty pounds. Of course, nothing looked right—the skirts were too short and boxy, the jacket lapels too wide—had she ever worn any of it? But she wasn't about to spend money on new clothing, not with four years of Marcus's college costs ahead. Instead she just dressed in layers of old clothing, figuring one of the layers might look all right.

Letters from universities and small colleges all over the country came every day now, three or four a day, sometimes twice a day from the same colleges. Noni sorted through them, organizing them into piles, finding something wrong with each one. "Frat school," she'd grumble. "Too small. No Art Department. No decent gym." Marcus had an almost perfect score on his SATs, higher than anyone would have guessed from his grades. He'd already been offered scholarships at two small schools, and Notre Dame offered to fly him out for an interview.

"I don't play football," he told the recruiter. "Let me put you in touch with one of my football buddies." He was surprised when the recruiter was not interested in his friends. "Some of them are very smart," he told the man. "Smarter than me, for sure. This friend, Devin MacKenzie, he's wicked smart, and fast. Dev could run the track three times and I'd still be tying my sneakers."

One thing about being a single parent: it left little time for brooding. Some days Eve could barely squeeze in a shower, or skim a magazine. If one of your children needed to be driven, you got in your car and you drove them. If you needed laundry detergent, you went out and bought it, and then came home and did the laundry, no matter how late it was or how tired you were. She'd had practice at this before, as a young widow. It was like riding a bicycle—you discovered that you'd never forgotten how.

Chuck had been gone for three months, a whole season, a quarter of a year. She hadn't moved any of his things out of her closet. She told herself that she wore the same things over and over partly because she couldn't even make room to slide the hangers down and see what was in there. Her life felt simultaneously cluttered and abandoned.

Mrs. Dunrea took up all the space in the kitchen when she cooked, and she got rattled if Eve said more than three words to her. "I can't keep anything straight if you keep interrupting me!" she cried.

"Hey," Noni called from the next room. "Do you know the Interrupting Cow joke?"

Mrs. Dunrea put down a spatula in exasperation. "If this doesn't beat all," she said.

Eve raised her eyebrows in warning. "Tell us," she called back.

"Knock, knock," said Noni.

"Okay. Who's—"

"The Interrupting Cow!" Noni shouted.

The dogs were half asleep, but when they heard their leashes, they rushed to the front door. Eve felt almost giddy to be out of the house. She liked walking the same familiar streets, past the same familiar stoops and sagging porches and cheap holiday window displays. She relished her slight flirtation with Jonah, who made her feel brave and clever. Besides, she was feeling claustrophobic.

"I'll be right back," she called.

Noni grunted, or maybe she was laughing at

something on one of her idiotic shows. If she didn't watch them, she told Eve, "I'd have nothing to talk about with the other kids in school." Television was what the university art students talked about, too, not to mention the staff, even faculty. Only Lev kept out of it; he didn't even own a TV set.

The dogs picked up speed the closer they got to the park. They dragged her across Beethoven Street and tugged her into the depths of the park, like a team of small sled dogs. It was quieter inside than on the street just a few feet back. Rec Park, with its green benches and ancient oaks, belonged to an older era. It would not have surprised her to see a horse and carriage trotting by. In summer, it always felt a few degrees cooler. In winter, it held the last warmth and sunlight.

It was good to breathe fresh air. She could feel the wind blowing her plaid wool skirt around her knees. Eve lifted her face to the autumn sun —and walked smack into Jonah's enormous chest.

"Whoa!" he said, putting up a hand. When he smiled broadly, as he did now at the sight of her, his cheekbones rose up round as a Cherokee's— not surprisingly since, according to Jonah, he was part Native American.

"What you doing sleepwalking? Why ain't you home cooking?"

"I am," she said.

He cocked his head.

"My mother is. I'll start the turkey tomorrow but she's making most of the side dishes today."

"What kind of stuffing?" he asked.

"Chestnut."

"Good," he said. "I'll come by."

"Oh!" she said. "Because—you would be . . . very welcome."

He laughed, pawing at the ground with one boot. "Naw, I'm just kidding you. I got more invitations than I can handle. That's one thing about this job. Everybody knows Jonah Cement."

"Cement?" She'd never known his last name.

"I got teased back in the day. Now nobody don't want to mess with me *or* my name. Whatchoo got going for dessert?"

"Sweet potato and chocolate pecan pie," Eve said.

"Your mama's making that? I got to meet this woman."

"The pecan pie is mine," Eve said, "sweet potato is my mother's."

"I might come try them," he said. He fished out a spiral notebook from the depths of some pocket, and after another moment, fished out a small snub-nosed pencil. "Where you live at?"

She gave her address, feeling a confusion of pleasure, surprise, and dread. Her mother had an old-fashioned view of black people, to put it kindly, and as her friend Tracy often said,

"There's no fool like an old fool."

Eve spoke to Jonah every morning, walking the dogs. Their conversations were brief, but they added flavor to the day. In some ways he felt like one of her best friends. Both of her children knew him—everyone did.

"He is wicked fast," Marcus once told her. "I saw him chasing some kids back to school, and they didn't stand a chance."

"Everyone likes Jonah," Noni chimed in.

Noni and Marcus might be surprised if he showed up at Thanksgiving, but they would take it in stride, along with the rest of her friends they deemed "weird" or "cool" or "pathetic."

Her friend Tracy was a mix of all three categories—weird, cool, and pathetic. She had been on disability since her first husband died playing tennis across the net from her. Eve met her at a bereavement group right after Ivan was killed, and though her interest in the group hadn't lasted, her friendship with Tracy hung on.

When Tracy went off the meds, her weight dropped precipitously. She had manic buying binges, one of which had cost her a beautiful house on Riverside Drive. Now she rented a studio apartment near Eve and lived with her aging chow chow, Capote. She was a fine potter, but most days her hands shook too much for her to work, and she barely slept.

"What do you do in the middle of the night?" Eve once asked her.

"Oh, you know," Tracy said vaguely. "Just prowling about, prowling about"—imitating Daffy Duck.

It was possible, Eve suddenly thought, that Tracy and Jonah would hit it off. Tracy could use an attentive boyfriend for a change.

"Your mother living with you?" Jonah asked her.

"No," she said. "She's still searching."

"Bring her to the Chestnut Arms. Don't look like that. The place is nice. I live there!"

"We'll see," she said. The way Jonah described his residents, he spent most of his time fending off drug dealers and felons.

"First I taste her pie, then I decide if she can stay in my building." He leaned forward and tapped her arm. "I'm just playing wicha!"

He fitted his headphones over his ears. Eve wondered what kind of music he listened to. For all she knew, he was listening to opera. Jonah was full of surprises. He'd been on the Winter Olympics curling team, for instance. He had stolen cars. Someone once tried to knife him on a subway in Brooklyn and he'd broken the man's hand.

"If I don't come by, you have yourself a nice holiday. A safe and happy, *healthy* holiday!" He could have been a preacher, the singsong way he emphasized his words and always left her with a blessing. Eve thought Jonah had missed his true calling. Wasn't that the Bible story? And wasn't it about how you couldn't escape your fate?

"We might have more company tomorrow," Eve announced. She took off her gloves and slapped her cold hands against her sides to warm them.

"Who?" It was Noni who asked the question, but her posture and sharp tone might have been her grandmother's. Noni was helping Mrs. Dunrea make peach cobbler. Down in the basement, Eve could hear the tinny repetitive music of Marcus's video game.

"Jonah," Eve said. She spoke to Noni, which she knew was cowardly of her.

"The big guy who works at the park?" Noni said. "Cool."

"You invited some *park worker* to your home for Thanksgiving?" her mother said. She was holding up both hands, covered with flour. "Do you know this man? Do we know his name?"

"His name is Jonah," Eve said. She tried to sound dignified. "He's a very nice, respectable African American man." Had she just snuck that in there? If Jonah were white, she would not have said, "He's a nice, respectable white man."

"He manages an apartment building. He suggested you come see it," Eve plunged on. Might

123

as well get the whole thing over with.

"Whatever for?" Mrs. Dunrea said.

"Because you are looking, for an apartment." Eve spoke the words too loudly and slowly, as if she were speaking to an idiot. She hated when she talked this way to her mother. She tried to soften her tone, but it came out pleading. "You don't have to live there, but it can't hurt to look."

To her surprise, her mother said, "Oh, I might as well," turning her attention back to the cobbler dough. "If you overmix that, it will be tough, not flaky," she told Noni.

"Okay." The little girl was concentrating so hard her hair was actually matted to her forehead. "We want it flaky, not tough."

Eve snorted.

Both her daughter and mother looked at her as if she were some stranger intruding. "Right!" Mrs. Dunrea said. "Back to work."

Chapter 11
The Feast

Mia's family clustered at the front door, removing their shoes. They made sure each pair was neatly lined up before they could be coaxed into coming any further inside the house. The children stuck close to their parents. Mia and her husband Sook-yun both clutched long foil-covered pans.

"Uh-oh," Noni said in a low voice. "Doesn't look like rice pudding to me."

"Very special!" the young man sang out. "Long times ago, people make this for many weeks in advance."

"I make yesterday," Mia said hastily, catching the look on Noni's face. "Not worry." She looked like an exotic orchid, wearing an exquisite pale pink suit.

"I'm sure it's delicious," Eve said. "Do I need to put this in the oven?"

"In oven?" Mia echoed. Her two eldest children, four and seven, were hiding, one behind each of her legs. The baby was still parked in his infant seat next to the front door, lined up next to the shoes.

"What a cute little baby!" Noni said. "Look at this cute little baby, Grandma!"

Mrs. Dunrea emerged reluctantly from the kitchen, both hands still inside pot holders. The two children looked at her as if she were a giant old lobster, waving her claws around.

"Welcome, y'all!" Mrs. Dunrea crowed. The more nervous her mother was, the more pronounced her southern accent. "We are so glad you all could come heah!"—acting like she was the hostess, which Eve resented, ridiculously, like a sulky teenager.

"You didn't have to bring anything," Mrs. Dunrea said. "We've cooked enough to feed several armies. Didn't I tell you Tuesday night? You didn't have to bring a single thing."

"Candy jin-jin put in," Sook-yun said. He and Mia were still hanging onto the aluminum pans for dear life.

"Put in . . . ?" Eve asked. "Put in the oven?"

"What kind of candy?" Marcus said. "Hey, Mia," he said. "Hey—" Marcus was never sure how to pronounce Sook-yun's name, but he seemed to find something vaguely obscene about the possibilities. ". . . how ya doing," he trailed off.

"Candy jin-jin," Mia said. "You like?"

"We surely will," Mrs. Dunrea said. She shot Eve an I-don't-have-the-faintest-idea look. The Korean couple made no move to let go. They clung to the pans, and their children clung to them.

"Do I put it in the oven?" Eve said again. "Cook it?"

"I cook," Mia said. "Little bit sweet, little bit spicy. Not too."

"Okay!" Eve said cheerfully.

"Maybe you warm, a little bit later," Mia said.

"Okay, but what is it?" Noni asked directly. "What is jin-jin?"

"Candied ginger pudding," said John, the seven-year-old. He spoke loudly in his high voice, as if

126

everyone else in the house was deaf or just stupid.

Tracy stepped in. A few more guests, Eve thought, and they could have a basketball game. Tracy had just gone back on her meds, so she was bony and wan, her eyes shiny. As always, she came empty-handed. It was hard for Tracy to buy things for other people. Eve had once gone with her to buy a birthday gift for Tracy's sister. At the end of the day, Tracy had a shopping bag full of things for herself and nothing for her sister, not even a card. Eve thought it was a starvation mentality.

Maybe it had to do with the deprivation of living alone so long, never getting treats from anyone else. Tracy ate most of her dinners at restaurants, using coupons she printed off the computer, taking home leftovers, and the rest of the time her refrigerator was bare—a few bottles of water and an apple. When Tracy said, "There's nothing to eat at my house," she meant it.

Eve, Noni, and Marcus had once gone to Tracy's for dinner. Tracy arranged one small piece of chicken and one spoonful of green peas on each plate. "Isn't there any gravy or anything?" Marcus asked, and Eve shook her head at him. For dessert there were two chocolate chip cookies, which Tracy carefully broke in half, a half cookie for each guest. Marcus studied his half in something close to horror. After they had polished off everything on their plates, the children sat there, looking at Tracy.

"Didn't I make enough food?" she said. "The cookies were so enormous. I could never finish one by myself."

"I'm stuffed," Marcus said.

"Should I have brought something?" Tracy asked now. "Oh," she murmured, looking at the large pans the Korean couple were still holding. "Should I take my shoes off, too? I might have holes in my socks."

"Gross," Danny said.

"Danny," Eve warned.

"What? It is gross to have holes in your socks."

The doorbell rang. Ms. McLain stood on the front porch, her cheeks pink from the cold, her gold hair prettily windblown in strands against her face. The dogs, at the doorbell, became hysterical inside their crate. Mia was terrified of the dogs. Eve tried to introduce Ms. McLain around but could barely be heard above the din of the shih tzus, leaping and crashing now against the inside of their crate. To her amazement, Ms. McLain said something in Korean to Mia and her husband, and when Sook-yun answered, she understood him enough to continue. Then she broke off, laughing. "My Korean is pretty bad."

"Very good!" Mia said enthusiastically.

"Excellent," Sook-yun agreed.

"I studied it in college," Ms. McLain said, and, "please, call me, Kimberly. Not you," she told Marcus. "I'm still Ms. McLain to you."

"How about me?" Danny asked. Tracy had sagged visibly as soon as Ms. McLain walked in. She stood with her arms at her sides, her head hanging down, her lank hair hanging in a dark curtain across her face.

Noni took Tracy's hand. "I want to show you my art project for school," she said.

Tracy perked up. "Great!—Hi, Mrs. Dunrea," she said. "You look elegant tonight."

Mrs. Dunrea had removed her apron. She wore a trim black lamb's wool cardigan buttoned over a print dress. On the cardigan she sported a large silver pin in the shape of a swan; its eye glittered with a red stone. Eve was in slacks and a long-sleeve T-shirt with brown leaves printed all over it. She felt like she was dressed for kinder-garten.

"Thank you," Mrs. Dunrea said coolly. Tracy was not Mrs. Dunrea's "type of person." Mrs. Dunrea liked only two kinds of women—the very elegant, famous ones, or the very sweet and subservient ones. Eve supposed that the ideal female friend would somehow combine all four characteristics: elegant, famous, sweet, *and* sub-servient.

Noni took charge of the coats, marching up-stairs with her small brown head barely visible above the highest jacket. Tracy followed behind.

A little later they were finally all settled at the

dining room table—the kids drinking ginger ale in fluted glasses, the grown-ups toasting with champagne—when the doorbell rang again. Eve did a mental sweep of the table. Mia's two older children were crowded on the little piano bench. The baby, eyes solemn, was taking turns in Mia's arms and on Sook-yun's lap. Everyone else sat close together—not quite crammed in.

Maxine Schwartz had offered to "drop by for dessert," though Eve hadn't invited her. First she'd invite herself over, then she'd show up early. Heart sinking, Eve walked to the door. The dogs yipped madly inside their crate.

Lev stood with a large soup tureen in his arms. It hid most of his head. "If I'm too late I can go home," he said. There was something different about him—his face or his hair—that made him look like a stranger. Then Eve realized what it was. He had dressed up. He was wearing a suit, the sport jacket like a boy's private school blazer, navy blue, with narrow lapels. "I made butternut squash soup," he told her.

"How lovely. Thank you," she said. "We're just sitting down. Come on in. Marcus!" she called, in a voice she hoped didn't sound panicky. "Pull another chair from the kitchen!"

Marcus scraped back his chair. "Okay," he said. Noni gave Eve a little puzzled frown.

"This is Lev," Eve said. "He's a colleague at the university, in music.—Lev, everyone." She could not bring herself to do the full round of introductions. She was sure she'd forget someone. Probably this made her a terrible hostess. Mrs. Dunrea seemed to think so.

"I am Eve's mother, Charlotte Dunrea," she drawled, frowning, holding out a hand. "I'm sorry, I am too old to rise."

As if on cue, Sook-yun jumped to his feet. "You sit here!" he said, jabbing at his own seat. "Have seat!"

Noni tried to coax Lev out of his sport jacket. "I'll keep this on for now," he said. He stood looking at Noni, smiling awkwardly. She was only a few inches shorter than he was. Marcus was standing at the doorway to the kitchen, holding a chair. "Where do you want me to put this?"

"Right here," Eve said. She seated Lev between herself and Tracy, bumping her own chair right up against her mother's. Her mother grimaced. Eve hurried into the kitchen for a soup ladle.

"The soup is vegetarian," Lev explained. "I hope that's all right."

"Thank God!" Danny said loudly. "Something I can eat!"

"Are you vegetarian?" Lev asked.

"No, but I'm Jewish."

"So am I," Lev said. He was looking at Danny, puzzled. People often did when they first met Danny.

"Yes, but I am a real Jew," Danny said. "So I can only eat kosher. Are you kosher?"

"Sadly, no," Lev said, just as Mrs. Dunrea jumped in.

"And what do you teach at the university, Lev?" she asked.

"I don't teach," Lev answered. "I'm in administration, like your daughter." His way of speaking to older people was habitually kind and solicitous.

"You're a secretary?" Mrs. Dunrea asked. "Isn't that unusual for a grown man?"

"Not exactly," Lev said. "And we aren't secretaries, as a matter of fact."

The oven timer buzzed just then, and Eve hurried off gratefully to check the turkey. Noni helped her carry out the side dishes, her small hands enormous in the pot holders. Eve lowered the oven to 250 and set the ginger pudding inside to warm it.

"I made all this!" Noni announced, carrying in one of the casseroles. "Me and Grandma are the real cooks of the family."

"Thank you so much," Eve said.

"Everything looks delicious," Lev said. His chair was crammed at an awkward angle to the table. To Eve's relief, Tracy began plying him with questions about music and concerts. They shared some of the same favorite singers, and rattled off names and dates and albums at each

132

other. Mrs. Dunrea looked affronted. In her silent way she insisted all conversations be about or directed toward her. Mia and Sook-yun, when they weren't speaking to their children in Korean, were focused on the old woman. Mia would not take any food until Mrs. Dunrea had been served and acted aware of everyone's needs at the table but her own. She didn't even seem to mind; helping came as naturally to her as breathing. Meanwhile, Marcus was busy trying to make Ms. McLain laugh, and Danny kept interrupting Marcus.

"Kennedy deserved to be shot!" Danny announced. "He had it coming."

"Shut up," Marcus said.

There was a volley of Korean back and forth across the table. John, the seven-year-old, trotted into the kitchen behind Eve. "May I have a glass of water for your mother, please?" he asked.

Eve poured him the water and handed it to him. He took it with both hands and looked at it as if the water might explode. "Thank you for having us to your home," he said in his grown-up voice.

"You're welcome, honey," she said.

Marcus and Danny were on third helpings and Mia had barely touched her food. She was too busy serving everyone else. The doorbell rang again. This time it would certainly be the Schwartzes, Eve thought. Her head swam. She'd ask everyone to move to the living room where she could serve buffet style. But she heard an unfamiliar deep voice at the door, and Noni, calling back into the kitchen. "Mom! More company!"

His spicy-sweet cologne preceded him. The room fell silent at the sight of Jonah in the dining room doorway. He took up all the space in the archway. The uniform was gone, along with the work boots and gloves. He was dressed in a double-breasted dark suit, with a rose-colored shirt and striped tie, and because he was so large and dark-skinned, he looked twice as exotic in his conservative attire. He dwarfed everyone else in the room. He was holding a bouquet of fall flowers and smiling down at the top of Noni's head.

"Hey, Jonah!" Marcus sang out, and Ms. McLain chimed in, "Happy Thanksgiving, Jonah."

"How y'all doing?" Jonah said.

Eve made the introductions. This time she got flustered and mispronounced Sook-yun's name. Then she got Ms. McLain's first name wrong, calling her Kirsten instead of Kimberly. Noni set Jonah's flowers in the middle of the table, completely blocking one side of the table from view of the other.

Eve was tempted to leave them there. She ushered Jonah into her own chair, the only place open. From now on she would stand.

Jonah and Lev appraised one another.

"Aren't you the guy who works at the Y?" Lev said.

"You use the ellipticals," Jonah said. "Very quick. Very hardworking." He waved away Eve's offer of turkey. "I want to try some of your mother's famous pie," he said, leaning close to Mrs. Dunrea, who was, in any event, only a few inches away.

Mrs. Dunrea seemed to wilt back in her chair. "It's just ordinary sweet potato pie," she said. She seemed almost frightened.

"Ain't nothing ordinary about sweet potato pie in Binghamton," Jonah said, and laughed.

"Aren't you kind to say so," she said stiffly.

"I understand you are looking for a place to live," Jonah went on. "I hear you're going to come on over and take a look at the Chestnut Arms. Is that correct?"

Mrs. Dunrea looked to Eve for help.

"Isn't it all black over there?" Danny said. "That's what my mother says."

"Danny, Marcus! Help me clean the table— now!" Eve barked from the doorway.

"We got all kind of people," Jonah said. "We got black people, white people, blue people, green people . . . "

"In that case," Mrs. Dunrea said with a weak smile, "I'll certainly have to take a look."

When the doorbell rang yet again, Eve jumped as if jolted by an electric shock. She simply could not imagine adding Maxine and Joel to this mix. Maxine's political opinions ranged from right to ultraright wing to liberal, and flopped back again in the same sentence. Maxine didn't call black people black or African Americans; she used the old, dismissive Yiddish word: *schvartzes*. "Too many *schvartzes* moving into Binghamton." Too many s*chvartzes* who didn't want to work.

As Eve made her way to the door, some part of her brain noted that the dogs were barking in a new way, almost joyfully.

And it wasn't Franny and Joel Schwartz standing at the door.

Chuck swung his motorcycle helmet in one hand. "Hi," he said. "Hope I'm not too late for turkey."

Chapter 12

Time Out

"I just don't get it," Chuck kept saying. "Who were all those people?"

They were watching some silly comedy that Marcus and Noni had seen a dozen times. Mrs. Dunrea had put on her red wool coat right after supper and asked to be driven straight back to her motel. Lev drove her.

Chuck's arrival threw the meal into instant turmoil. Noni jumped up screaming with joy as soon as she spotted her father, which frightened the three Korean children into shrieking, even the baby, his mouth twisted in a figure eight. Only Jonah took it all in stride, shaking Chuck's hand, giving up his own seat at the table. Before he left, he reminded Mrs. Dunrea about the Chestnut Arms.

"Bring along your nice daughter, too," he told her.

Chuck turned his head sharply at this, but Mrs. Dunrea said sweetly, "Thank you, she is nice."

Lev and Tracy hit it off so well they'd made plans to go to a jazz club. Tracy was supposed to have been interested in Jonah, Eve thought irritably. Not Lev. She felt a twinge of annoyance when she overheard them making plans, their two dark heads nearly touching. They looked like brother and sister. Lev scribbled Tracy's phone number on the back of his hand. It looked like a blue tattoo.

Lev had never once—not in the thirteen or fourteen years she'd known him—invited her to any music event. Of course it was true, she had to admit—watching Tracy tilt her head and smile, her dark eyes shining, looking young for once, looking beautiful—that she had been married all those years. But she wasn't sure she'd ever even made him smile, and he had been laughing at Tracy's stories all through dinner—the time she ordered a truck full of ceramic tiles by mistake and had to sell it off her back porch; the night she drove the wrong way on a four lane highway.

"Sounds like you need glasses," Eve said to Tracy, rather peevishly. She didn't know what had gotten into her.

"Who were all those Chinese people?" Chuck asked. His long feet, clad in cowboy boots, were propped on the coffee table. Eve resisted an urge to swat his legs back down.

"They're Korean," she said. "They're friends of ours."

"How could they be your friends?" Chuck said. "They don't even speak English."

"Dad!" Noni said.

"Well, they don't," he said. "And who was that big guy, Jonah? I didn't like how he was looking at you."

"Which was how?" Eve said.

"Like he was going to swallow you," Chuck said. "Like in the Bible."

"You've got the story backward," Eve said, "for a change."

"Well." Chuck smiled good-naturedly and reached for another handful of popcorn. "Now he knows I'm here."

"You're staying now, right?" Noni said, voicing what the rest of them hadn't been foolhardy enough to ask. "Now you're back."

"Mm," Chuck said. He was nibbling popcorn from his cupped hand, hunching to make sure he wasn't spilling. "Till you guys go back to school, anyway."

Eve's stomach had felt tight ever since she laid eyes again on her husband's sharp, handsome face. His hair had grown long; he looked younger than when he left. He looked in fact almost like a stranger.

"That's only till Monday!" Noni said. Her large brown eyes immediately filled with tears. They spilled over onto her hard, high little cheeks.

Noni, normally so brave, was crying. It shocked Eve into speaking. "Your father will probably be back at Christmas," she said.

"Back to stay, though?" Noni said. She was wiping her tears with the backs of both hands.

"Sure," Chuck said, at the same time Eve said, "We'll see."

Noni blew her nose into a tissue Marcus retrieved from the bathroom. He patted her on the back without a word, reaching behind Chuck to do it.

" 'We'll see' means no," Noni said bitterly.

" 'We'll see' means we'll see," Eve said. "Now it's late and I want you in bed."

Marcus stood without argument.

"But the movie isn't over!" Noni protested.

"We've seen it a million times," Marcus said. "It'll be on again, I promise. We can TiVo it next time." He bent to kiss his stepfather and instead halted, then straightened, patting him awkwardly on the shoulder. " 'Night, Chuck," he said.

But Noni wrapped herself around her father. She rocked in his arms and planted a kiss on each of his cheeks. "Daddy," she said. "I missed you so much!"

"What were you thinking?" Eve asked Chuck wearily, as they put the leftovers away.

Her guests rushed off so fast the candied ginger pudding had been abandoned in the warm oven. It was hard as a rock by now. She took out the two pans and looked at them. She'd never be able to salvage any of it.

Chuck dried the dishes, circling the cloth around and around inside the same bowl, till she finally plucked it out of his hands. Then he started on the glasses. "I hated the idea of you all being alone on Thanksgiving."

"We weren't alone," she said.

"Well, I see that," he said. "*Jeez.* Practically the only ones I recognized were Tracy and that short guy, Louis."

"Lev," she said.

"I didn't know those two were going out," Chuck said.

"They aren't going out," she snapped. "They just met."

"All right, all right." Chuck set down the last of the glasses and put up both hands as if she was about to shoot him. "They seemed to be hitting it off. Tracy could use a guy."

Eve tossed a pillow at him. He caught it neatly. "You can sleep here on the sofa bed."

"I figured," he said. "Truth is, I should really get going by Saturday, Sunday at the latest. I've got this welding job set up out West."

"And then what." Everything came out sounding flat, like one of those science fiction stories where characters suddenly enter a different dimension. She had gone from three dimensions to two.

"I really don't know," Chuck said. "You look good," he said. "Thin. Sexy. Like when we first met."

He came around behind her and put his arms around her waist. She tried to free herself but he just held her tighter, leaning his jaw into the side of her neck. He nuzzled her ear. He smelled so new, so masculine, it made her head reel. His cheek softly scraped the side of her face. Calm down, she told herself. It's just some new after-shave. But he smelled sharper and sweeter, almost smoky. Only his voice, right against her ear, was familiar.

"I've really missed you," he said. "Don't think I haven't."

He did not sleep on the sofa bed that night, and the next morning he bought her a dozen red roses from the Price Chopper, but by Saturday he was gone. As painful as breaking a bone the second time.

That morning, Eve woke with the bed empty and Noni's voice traveling through the house. Noni was opening and closing doors, her voice growing louder and more frantic. By the time Eve got her robe and slippers on, her daughter had already pulled on her winter coat and was struggling with the front door. Marcus was still asleep.

"Where's Dad?" Noni cried. "Where'd he go?"

Eve could have wept to see her sensible Noni so worked up, her long brown hair sticking up in all directions, her legs still in flannel pajamas under the winter coat.

"He'll be back soon," she said.

"*How* soon? Soon, like he went to the CVS, or soon like we won't see him for another three months?"

"He'll be back for Christmas—maybe even earlier."

Noni sat outside on the front stoop, bundled up in her winter coat and pajamas. She refused to come back inside. "I'm going to sit here and wait for Daddy," she wailed. She clutched a flower-like crumple of tissues in her hand.

Eve went into the kitchen and put on the water

for cocoa, then came out to the steps again with two mugs, one in each hand. She sat beside Noni, who edged over to make room. The girl had already stopped crying, and was gazing out at the snow with a disconcertingly adult look of resignation. The tissues were in her lap.

"I made it with extra marshmallows, the way you like it," Eve said.

"Thanks," said Noni. She set the mug down on the step beside her and blew her nose into the least crumpled tissue. Then she picked up the mug of cocoa.

It had snowed lightly that night, but now the air was too cold for snow. Everything had iced over. Cars spun their wheels, moving so slowly down the road they looked like they were skating.

"Why'd Dad come home if he was just going to dump us again?" Noni asked.

"Your father has not dumped you," Eve said. "He needs time to think."

"You mean like a time-out?" Noni asked.

"Sort of."

"You put Dad in time-out?" Noni said. There was a hint of reproach in her voice but her nose was buried so deeply in her cocoa mug it was hard to tell.

"Let's say he put himself there," Eve said. "He needs to figure out what kind of work he wants to do, where he wants to live. Things like that," she finished lamely.

"What's wrong with Diute Ford?" Noni asked. "He loves cars. They have cool vending machines and things. He can drink all the sodas he likes, all day."

"He's got to figure it out for himself," Eve said. She felt as if they were talking about somebody else's husband. Maybe they were, really. Maybe when she cleaned out the house that summer she had actually carved out space for him to exit.

Noni sipped daintily at her cocoa. "I miss him, though."

"Of course you do." Eve put one arm around Noni, and the little girl snuggled closer, cupping her mug in both hands. They sat companionably in the bitter cold a few more minutes, watching the cars slither up and down the street, an occasional pedestrian pick his careful way, feet high, in black rubber boots. Summer was a dim memory now. The wind kicked up leaves at the base of the bare maples. Beside her, Noni shivered.

"We're freezing," Eve said. "I challenge you to a game of Scrabble."

"I accept," Noni said. "Prepare to lose." She held out one small hand. It was cold and red. She shook the hand at Eve impatiently.

Eve let Noni help her up and together they went inside.

Chapter 13
The Chestnut Arms

The Chestnut Arms sat at the corner of Chestnut and Main, a squat red brick building a few doors down from Kensey Fried Chicken, a sad imitation of a Kentucky Fried Chicken that was nearly always empty. At that end of Main Street there was also a health food store, a gas station, a Hallmark card store, a music store, and two competing pharmacies across the street from one another. There was a supermarket where the customers inside always seemed transient: old men buying a few cans of soup, big black women buying boxes of cereal and milk. Even the shopping carts were old and rickety. It was a borderline part of downtown, between the posh mansions close to Riverside Drive and the drug dealers who bicycled up and down Main, so broke they couldn't afford cars.

As Jonah had promised, it looked spotlessly clean—at least from the outside. The evergreen bushes were closely trimmed, the front walk swept bare. Not a speck of snow remained. Even the parking lot blacktop looked as if someone had just vacuumed it. They rang the buzzer beside the front door. A moment later Jonah's voice crackled over the speaker and the door was unlocked. The entryway was dark. Shards of colored light poked through the stained-glass panels.

A few doors had small holiday wreaths up, or cut out paper turkeys. There were pairs of boots slumped out in the hallway, but the carpet looked new. There was a distinctive, Binghamton smell —old wood, cooked onions and cabbage, cedar chips, lemon furniture polish.

"At least it's clean," Mrs. Dunrea said.

An elderly black woman with a frizzle of white hair opened her apartment door, peeked out at them, and shut it again.

Jonah invited them into his place, but Mrs. Dunrea said, "I came to look at a vacant apartment, not to see where you live." Jonah was wearing olive-colored pants and an olive shirt —the kind of outfit that Dr. Schwartz wore, but with an entirely different effect, more dashing— dangerous. GI Joe goes *GQ*, Eve thought. "How do you like it so far?" Jonah asked.

"It's not air-conditioned," her mother said.

"Not in the halls this time of year. But your apartment is. Nice and cool. Got three big air conditioners."

"It isn't mine," she said.

"No." Jonah laughed. "Not yet, it ain't."

Eve feared it would be as it had always been when she was a child, when her mother was offered a room in a motel she didn't like. That she would back up frowning, turn around, say, "I don't think so," and out the door they'd go.

But her mother said, "Has the building got an elevator, at least?"

"Two of them." Jonah led the way.

The same little old woman poked her head out her apartment door as they passed. Eve's mother jerked back as if she'd seen a snake. The woman glared at her.

"Get you to run an errand for me?" she said to Jonah. Her voice had a high, peculiar whine like a mosquito.

"Maybe in a bit, Mrs. Ritchie," he replied. "I'm showing these people the apartment on five. This is Eve and her mother. That is—I don't know your first name," he said.

"Mrs. Dunrea will do," her mother said.

"I got a dollar here for you," the old woman said. She waved it.

"Okay, well, I'll be stopping by for it," said Jonah.

Eve and her mother stood in stiff silence inside the elevator. Someone had painted chubby angels on the ceiling—a long time ago, apparently; most of the gilt had worn away. Still, they all cast their eyes heavenward, as if praying that the elevator would rise. Jonah reached forward and pushed a button with his index finger. The elevator jerked and ascended. "Lots of the older folks ask me to run their errands. Got no one to look after them."

Eve was thinking about what he had once said, in the park. "The only color I care about is green."

"I do a lot of running around. A lot of running around."

The two women stared at the elevator doors. "A-course, I don't ever take any money." The elevator stopped with a slight jerk at the fifth floor. "She been waving that same old dollar bill at me I don't know how long."

Jonah took Charlotte's arm and led her off the elevator. Eve realized she had been holding her breath. She let it out and followed them.

The vacant apartment smelled of fresh paint. Its three rooms were painted beige. Eve suddenly envied her mother this chance to start over from scratch. The rooms were deliciously empty. A new gray-specked rug covered the floor. The windows looked into the back of the parking lot, but beyond that, one could glimpse the Susquehanna River, moving slowly, sulkily.

"It's what you call a winter water view," Jonah said. "You can watch ducks. Geese. All kind of things."

A few winter flies buzzed near the glass. There was a window seat underneath, also beige. Eve wandered into the small beige kitchen. Two fan-shaped windows arched over the living room. It was a bright day.

"This is nice," she said.

"Not bad," Mrs. Dunrea said grudgingly. "It's better than nothing."

"That's right," Jonah said. "You bring in your nice things, furnish it up, it'll look like out of a magazine. That's my opinion."

"Thank you," said Mrs. Dunrea. "I hope I won't spend too much time waiting for the elevator."

"No ma'am. Half the residents never go out anyways."

"I suspected as much," Mrs. Dunrea said dryly. "Of course, where would they go. There is no place to go."

Jonah introduced them to all the residents on the fifth floor, one apartment at a time. Eve doubted her mother had ever spent this much time with a neighbor, potential or real. Mrs. Dunrea was not a friendly woman. She discouraged chitchat. Eve thought of the exchanges she had overheard at the condo in Tennessee. "How are you doing?" an old woman would ask. Her mother would clamp her lips together. "Not well."

"Oh, I'm sorry to hear that." That was how every exchange with her mother seemed to end.

"How was the visit to the doctor?"

"Not good."

"I'm sorry to hear that."

And so on.

They went in and out of apartments. Eve was

surprised by how many people were sitting at home in the middle of the day. It moved her, this glimpse into other people's lives, other people's space. In nearly every apartment the TV was on. Some residents ran to turn it off when they let them inside, others left it blaring. Some kept their eyes on the set, out of habit, nodding to them and then to the TV, their eyes shifting back and forth between the two. No one seemed to mind the interruption. Four of the residents of the fifth floor were black. At least three old ladies seemed to Eve to be Jewish, and one couple, the Goldensohns, no question. There was a tiny old Asian man, who collected bird statues in his apartment. One woman opened the door of her cluttered apartment, a wailing child in her arms, a toddler pushing like Samson at the twin columns of her legs.

"Babies, no less," Mrs. Dunrea murmured to Eve. But to every resident, she said, "Pleased to meet you," and, "This is very nice," even as she rolled her eyes at her daughter.

They were trotted into bedrooms with unmade beds, rooms where smelly dogs slept on the sofa, draped over the arms like furry white shawls. They saw chamber pots left out in the open, piles of old magazines, lunch leftovers, oil paintings, collections of geraniums, American flags, old beer cans, and the Asian man's birds, carved from celery-green jade. Eve was fascinated. Who,

150

she had always wondered, actually bought the things she saw for sale; the Hummel figurines and beer steins, the crystal bowls, wax fruit, and indoor fountains. Now she knew.

Her mother said, "Enough—Is there a place I can sit?"

Jonah led her to a wrought-iron bench between two elevators.

"All those people." Mrs. Dunrea waved one hand. As if on cue, the Goldensohns tottered down the hall, leaning on each other, taking baby steps. Mr. Goldensohn clutched a wrinkled paper bag. He held it out to Eve's mother.

"To welcome you," he said. "Some delicious plums."

"I never said I was staying," Charlotte Dunrea said. "But thank you." She unrolled the bag and looked inside. "These look very nice."

"Jonah takes care of us," Mrs. Goldensohn said. "Not like a son. But he does a . . . very . . . good job." She said the words carefully, as if writing out a recommendation.

"Oh, now," Jonah said. "Thank you."

"He always clears the snow and ice from the front stoop—you know, the stairs," Mr. Goldensohn said.

"I know what a stoop is," Mrs. Dunrea said.

"You do," Mrs. Goldensohn said. She and her husband exchanged glances. That had been a test, Eve realized. More subtle than saying, "So,

151

what are you doing for Hanukkah?" or, "Do you go to temple?"

"You don't have to worry about falling," Mr. Goldensohn went on. "That kind of tsuris you don't need."

Mrs. Dunrea hesitated only briefly. "Certainly not," she said.

"Anything goes on the fritz—plumbing, electric. Jonah takes care of it. You don't wait around."

"Just doing my job," Jonah said, smiling.

"We don't have the garbage sitting out like some of the other places."

"Doing my job," Jonah chanted.

"Once he drove Sidney to the hospital. In the middle of the night.—Not that we count on it," Mrs. Goldensohn said.

"Well, we'll leave you alone, to make up your mind," her husband said. The two of them turned, bumping shoulders, and shuffled away.

Her mother was looking pale. She handed the paper bag of fruit to Eve wearily, as if it was too much to take care of.

"How are you feeling, Ma?"

"Not good."

"You're making friends already!" Jonah said. "Look, Mrs. Dunrea, if you can move in—or make your deposit before the first of the month —I can let you in on the old rate. Otherwise the rent is going up, I know. By thirty dollars."

"Don't rush me," Mrs. Dunrea said. "I'm an old lady."

"Take your time," Jonah said. "I just don't want you to pay more than you have to."

"Why are you so eager to have me?" she said. "I'm a pain in the neck. Believe me. I'm not easy."

"That's the truth," Eve put in.

Jonah laughed. "Oh, I don't know. You got you a sweet daughter . . ."

"I'm the one who's going to be living here, not my daughter." She gave him a hard look.

You could not tell much from Jonah's eyes, Eve realized. He was always polite, calling everyone "Miss so-and-so," or "Mr. or Mrs. so-and-so." Still, there was something arrogant in his sheer size, the way he held himself. He took up space. He let you know he was there.

"You ready to sign?" he said.

"Oh!" Eve thought her mother would blow up. She got to her feet with difficulty, but her face looked angry, energetic. "Oh. All right," she said.

Later, back at Eve's house, Mrs. Dunrea said, "I think you should watch out for that big black man. That Jonah." As if there were other big black men around.

So her mother had noticed, too—the way Jonah looked at her. The way he always moved around to be standing right next to her.

Eve said, "Watch out for what, Ma?"

But her mother said, "I think he steals. Did you see that big ring on his finger? He didn't get that ring from managing an apartment building."

"He works two jobs—he lives alone."

Her mother just said, "Well, there's something funny about him. Maybe he's gay. He dresses too nicely. How old is he, forty, forty-five? Not married. That could explain the jewelry."

Eve couldn't tell if she felt disappointed or relieved. Her mother had noticed nothing. "Maybe so," she said.

Eve flew down to Tennessee with Marcus and drove back her mother's little red Ford Escort filled with the few remaining items Mrs. Dunrea still wanted. Noni stayed home with her grandmother and promised to keep a diary, reporting on everything exciting that happened. She stood in the big picture window making the two dogs wave good-bye with their paws.

Marcus drove most of the way home, as long as the daylight lasted, since he only had his learner's permit. But he drove with more concentration now, and considerably more skill. Other cars on the road no longer rattled him. He had loosened his death grip on the steering wheel. Watching him, Eve felt her heart rise and fall, rise and fall, like a tide. No question, he was growing up. Even his profile seemed more serious these days, his eyebrows darker and thicker, his hair a darker shade of gold. They loaded a few boxes into the back of the car, knickknacks that Mrs. Dunrea had set aside and stored with the realtor, her former neighbor.

"We'll miss her," the woman said tearfully. "Your mother is such a dear, kind person."

"Thank you," Eve said, surprised. It seemed insufficient. She must not be as dear and kind as her mother, or she'd have been able to think of just the right comforting thing to say. Instead she said, "Thank you for storing these things."

"No problem, dear," the woman said. "It really isn't much."

It really wasn't. Mrs. Dunrea was as good as her word. "A clean sweep," she had promised.

This had been her parents' retirement home— but truly, her mother's last house, close to the town where she'd spent her childhood in her first. Her father just went along for the ride. He'd been doing that most of his life.

A few years after the move to Tennessee, he died suddenly, out in the garage puttering around with lawn tools. That's where her mother found him, lying on the cement floor as if he had suddenly fallen asleep by the lawn mower.

"There's nothing I could have done. I ought to have been there. Maybe to catch him, when he fell. That's what a wife is for."

Mrs. Dunrea was braver than she was. Like her father, Eve believed you had to put your head down and keep it there. But even that didn't always work. Look at Helen Gollow.

Just the week before, Helen had yelled at her in front of everyone over a typo in a departmental memo. Finally, Frederick stumbled out of his office, his hair rumpled. Eve couldn't tell if he'd been drinking or napping.

"What's going on?" he demanded.

"Look at this!" Helen shook the memo in his face. "It *says* that students are '*requited* to buy their own art supplies.' Requited instead of 'required.' "

Frederick said, "Calm down, Helen," and, "Everybody makes mistakes," and finally, "It's just a goddamn typo!" snatching the paper out of Helen's hand, crumpling it into a ball and firing it at the recycling bin. It bounced off the rim and lay on the floor. Eve resisted the urge to get up and place it inside.

"I am an artist! " Helen fumed. "Accuracy matters to me. Disorder offends me. *Laziness* offends me." She sailed out of the office, all in black, her limp more pronounced than usual. She reminded Eve of the Spanish Armada.

"You don't have to put up with that," Frederick told her.

"I know," Eve said. "It didn't seem worth the fuss." That was the phrase that would end up on her gravestone, she thought.

She could have talked it over with Lev, but

Lev and Tracy were becoming good friends and she felt outside of a magic circle. Every time she talked with Tracy, she had just come from having breakfast with Lev, or was just going out to see him.

"Tracy is so great," Lev said. "I wish she had more confidence in herself." He talked about her the way he talked about his cats, two strays who had showed up on his doorstep. "She's not the kind of person you meet every day."

Lev would have been ashamed of her cowardice, Eve thought. Her mother would have been furious. Noni would have turned it into a comic strip.

It was better not to talk about it at all.

Mrs. Dunrea insisted on renting furniture instead of buying it.

"But they have terrible stuff, those rental places."

"It's good enough for me," her mother said tartly into the phone. "Besides, I'm planning to die soon. Hopefully before Christmas."

"That doesn't give you a lot of time," Eve said. "Better get a move on."

"I mean it," Mrs. Dunrea said.

"Then I'm returning all the presents I bought you," Eve said.

"I'm not buying you anything."

That brought Eve up short. "You're not?"

"Well, I am really," her mother said, in an almost meek voice that made Eve realize her mother had not in fact planned on buying anything. "I'm an old woman, it's not easy to shop. But you're my daughter, of course I'll buy you something—and the children, of course. Better yet, you should go out for me. I can't fight the crowds. Get anything you like."

With Chuck gone, and nothing to suggest another visit anytime soon, Eve figured the holidays would be a disaster this year. Especially for Noni.

Noni was making something at school for Chuck—she wouldn't tell Eve what it was, but she stayed late after school a few times to work on it. "It's going to be amazing," Noni said. "That's all I'm going to say."

"Is it a time travel machine?" Marcus asked.

"No," Noni said.

"Is it a trapeze?"

"Shut up, stupid."

"Then what's amazing about it? It's probably a house made out of macaroni. Or a bird-feeder."

"It is *not*."

"Okay, okay," Eve broke in. "Noni wants it to be a surprise."

"The surprise is if Chuck shows up at all," Marcus said. He was friendlier these days with tough kids like Dev and Skip Russell. Kids who drove their own cars to school, cut school, and drank on the weekends—Marcus confided that much. Devin talked about dropping out of school altogether, though he was a smart boy, good around people, with a friendly, open face. Eve remembered him at eight or nine, dropping off a box of frozen popsicles after Marcus had his tonsils out. She'd thought Devin would become some sort of a counselor, maybe a therapist. He was a good listener. He was patient, and kids adored him. Noni thought the sun rose and set on Devin.

Her mother had just finished saying something about Noni and Marcus over the phone, but Eve couldn't remember what they were talking about, she hadn't been paying attention.

"Hello?" her mother said. "Did you hear me?"

"Yes," Eve lied. "How do you like your apartment?"

"It's not Tennessee, I can tell you that."

"I could have told you that before you moved here," Eve said. "In fact, I believe I did tell you that."

"Never mind," Mrs. Dunrea said.

"How's the TV working?"

"Not good," Mrs. Dunrea said. "That Noah keeps saying he'll fix it, but he never does."

"Jonah," Eve said.

"He puts on a good show before you move in, but once you're here—Wait," her mother said.

"What?"

"Hang on." There was the sound of her mother putting the phone down. Eve could hear voices in the background. "He's here," Mrs. Dunrea said, coming back on. "To fix the TV. Took him long enough."

"Try to be nice," Eve pleaded.

"Nice is overrated," Mrs. Dunrea said. "You're nice enough for both of us."

"Okay, okay," Eve said, but then Jonah was on the phone, his voice unexpectedly loud and low in her ear.

"Taking care of business," he said.

"Thank you so much," Eve said.

"I wanted to wish you a happy holiday—in case I don't see you at the park." The mornings had grown so bitter, the thermometer needle on her back porch seemed stuck below zero. The dogs looked unhappy when she got out their leashes, and Refrigerator, the larger dog, sometimes balked at the corner, refusing to go another step.

"Thank you," she said. "Same to you." She made a mental note to tell her mother to give Jonah money for Christmas. If her mother refused, then Eve would give him fifty dollars of her own.

Mrs. Dunrea was back on the phone now. "Some of the residents don't like it that a black man is superintending the building," she said.

"Please tell me Jonah is not still in your apartment," Eve moaned.

"Of course not. I'm just saying, some—"

"Ma, don't start," Eve said.

"Why can't they find a nice white man for the job?"

"Because they found a nice black man."

"Well, I don't think it's so nice. It sets a tone."

"How are your eyes?" Eve said. "You were going to see a new doctor."

"It's not just me," her mother said, immovable. "The Goldensohns, too."

"Yes," said Eve. "Let's work on that relationship between the blacks and Jews."

"It's not only the Jewish residents, believe me. That little Chinaman is beside himself. He can't speak a word of English, of course, but he's always making faces."

"He's not a Chinaman. He's Chinese."

"I was raised the way I was raised. Let's change the subject," she said. "How are things going for you? Have you found a new husband yet?"

"That is a—a—macabre joke," Eve said.

"I'm sorry. You got nasty with me, so I got nasty with you."

"Well, we can stop now," said Eve. "How are you doing?"

"Not good."

"Are you making friends?"

"Who makes friends at my age? Don't be ridiculous."

"It's a hard adjustment," Eve said, determined to keep trying.

"You don't know how hard," her mother said. "I'm lonely. I'm bored. I never should have moved."

"Maybe not," said Eve.

"I'd be better off dead." Both women sighed. "Let me get off," Mrs. Dunrea said. "Aren't you at work? Do they let you spend this much time on the phone?"

"It's my lunch hour," Eve said. "The office is closed."

"Well, *Oprah* is coming on," her mother said. "I'd better go."

As if on cue, there was a loud rapping on the glass of the Art Department door. It was Helen Gollow. She had the dean with her, and the two women were peering in through the little glass window at Eve, with her half-eaten lunch still in front of her.

Gollow rapped harder. She had an intent, half-wild expression. Maybe she had one of her heavy rings on—she always wore a lot of jewelry —it sounded as if she might actually break the glass.

"I'll call you back later."

"After *Oprah*," her mother said. "Not before."

Chapter 14
The Booby Hatch

Eve unlocked the door and Gollow pushed her way inside. "*Now* do you see?" she asked. "Do you?" Gollow's large eyes were fixed. on the dean. She was panting, as if she had run to the office.

"Do I see what?" the dean said. For once, her coldness seemed to Eve like a gift. She kept gazing over the top of Eve's head, taking in the notices and art posters on the bulletin board behind her.

"Just look at this! It's revolting." Helen Gollow waved her arms, taking in the lunch on Eve's desk, its open carton of orange juice, and a salad from the Chenango Room, in its little tin square. "And she was on the departmental phone."

"It was a local call," Eve managed. She started to gather up her napkins and utensils, but the dean put up a hand.

Her fingernails were manicured, with square white tips.

"Don't," she said.

"We are paying for this!" Helen cried. "Why, when we are short on faculty, when we can't offer our MFAs a decent stipend, why in God's name are we still paying for *this*?" She pointed at Eve. Her hand was shaking. It looked like a claw.

"Calm down," Eve said.

"Don't you dare tell me to calm down! You have no right to speak to me like that. You have no right to speak at all!" The print teacher's voice was shrill.

"Was this what you wanted to show me?" the dean said. "That a staff member is eating her lunch?"

Eve's hands were trembling. She put them in her lap, to hide the evidence of her fear.

"Oh my dear God!" Helen cried. "Please! Are you all too dazzled? Am I the only one who has eyes to see this tricked-out piece of work?"

Is she talking about me? Eve thought.

Two students stood in the open doorway, their mouths open. One was an Asian work-study student, a painter who hardly ever spoke.

"Should we come back later?" the taller girl asked. She, too, was a grad student in the MFA program.

"If they haven't dismantled the program and left us stranded here with nothing but—but this!" Gollow jabbed a finger in Eve's direction.

"They're firing the faculty?" the tall girl asked.

"No," said the dean.

"Who's getting fired?" the girl insisted.

164

"*She* is!" Gollow screamed. "This floozy! This tool! This—"

"Come with me," the dean said quietly.

Helen Gollow began terrifyingly, raggedly, to weep. Her shoulders heaved inside her black dress. The students stared at her, aghast. Eve's hands seemed frozen to her desk. She felt—not furious, not humiliated, but guilty. She must have done something terrible. Something to have earned this kind of fury.

The dean led Helen away, one arm firmly across the other woman's back.

"Wow," the Asian work-study student said after they were gone. Her T-shirt was paint-spattered, the badge of honor of all the art students. "Are you okay?" she asked Eve.

"Oh yes. I'm fine," Eve said, sweeping the remains of her lunch into the trash can under her desk. She could feel how hot her face was, her cheeks burning, as if she'd been slapped.

"Jeez," the tall girl said. "Gollow's totally lost it this time."

"I'm glad," the work-study girl said. She looked defiant. "She told me I should give up art and work in a laundry. A *laundry.* Get it? Because I'm Chinese."

"Oh no," the other girl said. "That's awful." They began to giggle.

That afternoon, Eve went through her filing cabinets like a machine, throwing out outdated papers and memos, alphabetizing everything. Frederick offered to let her go home but she refused. It was the kind of mind-numbing work she normally hated. Leo Basilica, the senior painter, the star of the department, came by and patted her roughly on the back. The taps were like small blows. "Don't let the bastards get you down," he said in his hoarse, husky voice. Eve would not have believed he knew who she was. She nodded, ashamed, keeping her face toward the papers in her hands.

Later, she walked downstairs to Olivia Zarembo's dark basement office by the permanent art collection. Olivia's family, who were Muslim, had escaped Croatia by way of Romania. She was the most soft-spoken person Eve knew. She quietly went about her business, in the bowels of the Fine Arts building, among dusty ancient vases and furnishings. She arranged for an occasional special exhibit; one on Persian miniatures, art by local school-children. Her tiny office was about the size of a supply closet, but she was always calm, always in a good mood.

"Here's the list," Eve said, handing it to Olivia. There were forty-five faculty works this year. Sheryl Stoddard, the director, never allowed the faculty the use of her main gallery space. She reserved this for strange exhibits with a barely peripheral relationship to art. "The Art of

Microscopes," for instance, was the current semester-long exhibition.

"Good," Olivia said, pushing the dark bangs away from her white forehead. Eve wondered if she was naturally fair or had gotten that way from spending the past six or seven years below ground level. "I am happy with how things are taking shape."

It was an underground world, separate from the rush and buzz of the students, the nervous energy of the university. Here, everything moved at a slower pace, like a stream that met a boulder and meandered as it trickled downstream.

"I heard the sad news about Professor Gollow," Olivia said.

Things were pretty bad if word had already descended this far. Eve tried to shrug it off.

"That must have been painful." Olivia's face was serious, a perfect pale oval, like a Botticelli painting.

"I think it was more painful for her," Eve said.

"That's good," Olivia said, smiling again.

Lev made her tell him the story three times, though each time he would interrupt her furiously, right in the middle. "There's where you should have got her! That's where you should have told her off!"

"I was too surprised to say anything," Eve said.

Lev wasn't listening. His dark eyes flashed.

"And the administration is worse," he said darkly. "Always looking to get rid of people."

But it was Helen Gollow who left that same week. The terse note from the dean said she was pursuing her research, but Harry Dunsk pulled Eve aside and explained. "She's in the loony bin at Binghamton General. We have to thank you," he said. "Ding dong the wicked witch, etcetera."

One evening, after she fed the kids, Eve climbed into her rusty old Citroen—the last working remnant of her life with Ivan—and drove to Binghamton General. It was only seven o'clock, but the sky was black, the air felt brittle. Many houses had already put up their Christmas lights, and they twinkled forlornly, like chips of colored ice. She had skipped dinner to do this.

Dinner on the Go

Designed for the busy woman: paper cup of coffee, and the half-eaten granola bar your child left on the car seat.

Eve bought some flowers in the gift shop, which was getting ready to close. There was the usual sad assortment of stuffed animals and cards, T-shirts, mints, and candy. She chose the least dead-looking flowers and a small glass vase to put them in, and rode the elevator to the fifth floor.

A small group of men and women sat in a lounge on sofas and chairs intently watching an old black and white movie. They shared a bowl of popcorn. Eve realized with dismay that she was dressed a lot like these people. An old woman in a baggy blue sweater asked her for a cigarette.

"I don't smoke," Eve said. "I'm sorry."

"Go downstairs and buy some for me?" the woman asked.

"Alice," said one of the nurses. "Go back in your room. You know you don't have any money."

"Because my damned husband spent it all!" the old woman snapped.

"You know you don't have a husband," said the nurse.

"Because my sister stole him from me," said the old woman, but she tottered down the hall in the opposite direction.

Helen Gollow sat alone in her room, her hands folded in her lap. There were art books on the table beside her bed. In a sky-blue chenille robe, she looked younger. Her gray hair was pulled back.

She gestured at the only other chair, by the other bed. "You can pull that around," she said. "I have a roommate, but she's in the lounge watching TV."

Eve said, "These are for you." She held out the flowers inside the vase. They looked smaller and less healthy than they had moments ago.

"Thank you," Helen said. "How kind." She set the vase on a brown swivel-arm table beside the bed. The flowers toppled to one side of the vase. The room was warm and dry. Eve felt thirsty. The carnations, dyed in unnatural shades of purple and pink, looked like they were already dying of thirst.

Eve said, "Shall I put some water in the vase?"

"No, that's all right. I can do it later."

As if she hadn't heard, Eve filled the vase with tap water from the bathroom. There was underwear hanging from the doorknob, beige and loose-legged. She felt as if she had seen something secret and shameful.

"Thank you," Helen said, with what sounded like mockery. "You were always so helpful."

Down the hall some man was yelling. "Get your hands off me!"

"How are you?" Eve asked.

"I feel like I have a touch of the flu, to tell the truth. I hope insanity is not contagious." Helen turned her head and looked out the window. The drapes were open; reflected in the glass were the lights from the hospital room, and a vague blackness shimmering beyond. "It will be Christmas soon," she said.

There was another, longer silence. Helen spoke in a deep, vibrating voice, as she always did, but in the tiny room it seemed magnified and mysterious. "Do you have any messages?"

The way she asked made Eve think she meant something supernatural, messages from above. Then there was an angry shout down the hall and a door slammed. There were running footsteps, and then a voice over the loudspeaker, "Code Red! We have a Code Red."

"Keep your hands to yourself or I'll drop-kick you!" the man shouted.

Helen dismissed it with a wave of her big hand, freckled and ringless. "He used to be a minister. Of course."

"Messages?" Eve said.

"From the department. From Frederick, for instance."

"Oh!" said Eve. "No . . . but I'm sure everyone sends their best."

"Yes, I'm sure," Helen said. "However, you are my first visitor. That is ironic."

Helen turned her head again to look at the flowers, this time reaching up to touch the dry, ruffled edge of one carnation. "I've been needing a rest. My doctor is trying to convince me I'm a lesbian. I keep telling him I am too old to change my mind."

After another moment she said, "I owe you an apology."

Eve's hands fluttered. "Oh . . . well." She half rose from her chair, as if her body wanted to escape the room.

"I didn't say I was ready to deliver it yet."

171

Helen looked at her without blinking. "Give me time."

Eve was determined not to lapse back into that strange, deep silence. Nonetheless they sat there without a word, their knees practically touching. Someone laughed in the next room. The man cursed again, seemed to struggle—for a moment it sounded like he would come charging through their door—and then he began, in the midst of all the chaos, to sing. He sang, "O Come, All Ye Faithful."

"Oh Lord," said Helen Gollow. "This is my punishment. I hate Christmas carols, and they sing them all day long.

"They give me sleeping pills if I ask nicely," she added. "Pills and chocolate bars."

"Milk or dark chocolate?"

"Milk," Helen said. She looked interested for the first time since Eve had arrived. "Dark chocolate tastes like ashes to me."

"Me, too," said Eve. "I don't need my chocolate to have eighty percent cacao. Just give me the sugar."

A young woman shuffled in, wearing a pink cotton robe untied over elastic waisted pants, the belt trailing behind. She wore pink furry slippers. One half of her hair was shoulder length, the other half was shaved off. Her skull looked blue. It gave her the exotic aspect of some foreign princess.

"Chatty Cathy," Helen said. "Eve here works in the Art Department. Which I do not, any longer. Eve, Cathy."

"Pleased to meet you," Eve said.

The young woman appeared not to hear them. She shuffled to her night table, opened a drawer and began to paw through it agitatedly. She took out a comb and brush, and a watch. None of this, apparently, was what she was searching for. At last she removed a candy bar and sat down with a sigh on her bed to eat it. She did not look at either of the two women.

"Cathy never speaks," Helen said. "No matter how engaging I am, how amusing, no matter how much I insult her, not a word. Not since I arrived. Not one bleeding word, morning, noon, and night. One of these days I shall probably murder her in her sleep." Helen rose, tottering, to her feet, and compared to the girl, who was small and squat, she looked like a giantess. The girl stared at Helen Gollow in what might have been terror or awe. She tugged at a piece of her hair as if to hide behind it.

"Well? Do you have nothing to say, you miserable little goat?" Helen demanded.

"I—I . . ." The young woman looked all around the room, as if for an escape route. "Had . . . a . . . good dinner," she said slowly.

Helen Gollow smiled. It was a broad, beaming, warm smile such as Eve had never once seen on that stiff face. She supposed it explained why certain of Gollow's students were so devoted to her. "It's a start," Helen said.

Chapter 15

Merry Christmas

Chuck did not make it home in time for Hanukkah. He did not make it home in time for Noni's winter concert, either, in which she sang a one-line solo, which Mrs. Dunrea sat through as transfixed as if Noni were debuting at the Met.

Eve didn't know why they bothered to call it a "winter" concert—the children sang nine Christmas carols and one obscure song in Hebrew. Noni's choral teacher was a born-again Christian. Her husband was a pastor. The spring concert would doubtless run the same way—seven Easter songs and one song about flowers and rain.

Chuck finally called on Christmas Eve, his voice fuzzy and faraway.

"He's been hitting the Yuletide cheer," Marcus whispered, handing the phone to Eve. "Want some cocoa?" he asked his sister.

"I want to talk to Daddy," Noni said. She had been tearful and irritable ever since the end of the fall soccer season, when her team lost the county championship by one goal. All the girls cried hysterically, holding one another as if someone had died. That was nothing compared to how the other parents reacted—booing, cursing at the refs and the opposing team.

"Don't shake their hands!" one father screamed at his daughter. "Don't touch them, the dirty, cheating bastards!"

Noni had been carving a wooden dove at school, but the shop teacher called Eve at work to say that she had beheaded it the week before Christmas vacation.

"Chopped its head right off. I'll have to fail her for the project," the teacher said. "Can't let the kids waste materials."

"Is Noni all right?"

"She's fine. It's the bird that lost its head."

"Talk when he's done talking to Mom," Marcus said now, tugging Noni to her feet. "Besides, we've got to leave some crackers for Santa Claus."

"I don't believe in Santa anymore," Noni said, her voice trailing away downstairs. "I'm not a baby, you know."

"Yes you are." Marcus's voice trailed after her.

"There's change coming," Chuck said to Eve. His voice did sound thick. Bar music played in the background. He was probably out drinking with his welding buddies. The pay was good, but the work was tough. Chuck said his arms hurt at the end of each day, his back was killing him, his eyes stung.

"It's Christmas Eve," Eve reminded him. "Were you planning on sending anything for the kids?"

"Oh God!" he said. "How did I forget?"

"Never mind," she said. "I bought some stupid things, wrapped them badly, and said they came from you."

"I'll send a check," Chuck said. "I'll send an extra five hundred."

"You said change is coming. What kind of change?"

"Don't want to spoil a surprise."

"You've surprised us enough for one lifetime," Eve said. She raised her voice to be heard over the din at his end, but it wound up sounding like she was yelling at him. "Should I be filing for divorce?" She had not intended to say this. Least of all on Christmas Eve. The words came flying out of her mouth. She wished she could call them back.

"Oh, no," Chuck said, to her relief. "No!" he added. "—Don't we need a legal separation first?"

She felt the words slam into her and descend like snow. Christmas Eve. The happiest night of the year. So the songs would have you believe. That hadn't been the case since she was six years old. "I'll call Ted," she said. Ted was their family lawyer—more Chuck's than hers.

"Hey," Chuck said. "Let's not spoil Christmas."

"What was the surprise?" Eve said, her voice weary.

"My hair," Chuck said. "I dyed it. You know, with peroxide. Like a surfer. Very cool."

"Noni!" Eve yelled, straight into the mouthpiece. "Phone!"

Eve woke in the gray half-light of Christmas morning. It felt as if she had never slept. She'd stayed up till two o'clock wrapping last minute presents and arranging them, filling the stockings. Then, after she went to bed, she dreamed that she was wrapping the wrong things, putting the wrong names on the tags, throwing them under the tree. In her dream she had forgotten to buy anything at all for her mother, and was trying to gift-wrap an old nightgown.

The kids had gone holiday shopping on their own. They took the bus to the mall—getting a driver's test for Marcus during the holidays proved impossible, the next available date wasn't till February—and were acting mysterious about whatever they'd bought her.

In addition to all the things she'd gotten everyone—too much, as always—Eve bought Marcus a blue sweater, to bring out his blue eyes, and taped a gold gift tag with TO MARCUS LOVE GRANDMA DUNREA on the package. She'd done the same with Noni's skates, and

177

bought a violent video game for Marcus and a twelve-pack of tacky sparkle nail polishes for Noni—from Chuck.

Chuck. There was her lump of black coal. When she remembered last night's phone call, she slumped back onto her pillow. She'd half hoped it was a nightmare, like gift-wrapping her old nightgown. She tried to lie flat again. It was only seven o'clock. A few minutes later, though, she heard Noni stirring, the girl's bedroom door open and close, the creak of light footsteps on the stairs, and her daughter's soft "Wow!" as she peered into the living room. That sound suddenly made it all worthwhile.

"Mom? You awake?" Noni tapped at the bedroom door.

Noni had spent her allowance and birthday and occasional money earned from raking leaves in the neighborhood all on gifts—a portable CD player for Marcus, a robin's-egg-blue angora scarf for her grandmother, and something in a small box for Eve, which Noni snatched out of her hands as Eve was absent-mindedly picking things up off Noni's dresser one day.

Marcus bought a gift for a girl this year. He had his eye on an exchange student at school, a girl from Denmark. Her name was Astrid; she was spending the year at Devin MacKenzie's house.

"Isn't that odd?" Eve asked. "A foreign girl, staying at the home of a boy?"

"Devin's got three sisters," Marcus reminded her. "And two parents. It's not like Astrid's alone in the house with him—though that would be sweet," he added. "Maybe next term you and Noni could move out and I could have her."

Eve noticed that her son combed his hair in the mirror these days, and wore button-downs to school. He'd even asked her to iron his slacks. "Can you put a crease in it?" he said. "Astrid said I looked sharp in those pants."

Ms. McLain paired Marcus and Astrid for an end-of-semester project. "Astrid knows more American history than I do," Marcus told Eve. "All we ever learned was George Washington, Abraham Lincoln, and the Great Depression."

"I know about civil rights," Noni put in. "I know about World War One. Some of us pay attention in class."

"Geek," Marcus said, pretending to cough the word. "Excuse me—geek," he coughed again.

"I'm a jock," Noni said calmly. "You can't be both."

He'd bought Astrid a scarf exactly like the one Noni picked out for their grandmother. "If you tell Astrid we got Gramma a scarf like this, I'll kill you," he warned Noni. It did look strangely old-ladyish. Eve pictured a younger version of Mrs. Dunrea, wrapped up in a wool coat, with sturdy shoes.

Eve had tried to talk her mother into spending

Christmas Eve at their house, so they could all have Christmas morning together, but the old lady said, "I like to watch my own TV programs. None of those crazy cartoons and things. I'm too old for all that fuss on Christmas morning. Besides, it's not our holiday."

"But we always celebrated Christmas," Eve protested.

"That was a mistake," Mrs. Dunrea said. "I realize that now." She went on, "I wish I'd been born Christian. They seem so sure of things. And they all go to church together."

"You can go to church," Eve said. "You're old enough to do what you like."

"I don't believe in God," Mrs. Dunrea said. "But it wouldn't kill you to take the kids to synagogue once in a while."

Noni pressed up against Eve's back now, full of the rapture of Christmas morning, and listed all the presents she thought she'd gotten. "Skates," she said positively. "And a new soccer ball, because I saw the bag from Dick's. I hope you remembered new knee pads." She nudged Eve.

"I'm still asleep," Eve lied.

"And my friends got me movie passes, and I know what Marcus got me because I picked it. You promised you'd get me lip gloss this year."

Eve stiffened.

"You forgot!" Noni said.

Eve wondered if she had any unused lipstick

lying around, anything a girl could use. "You're too young to be wearing makeup," she said.

"I'm not too young for nail polish," Noni said. "You let me paint my toenails any color I want."

Eve rubbed her hand over the top of Noni's silky head. Her daughter smelled like chocolate, a little girl smell that soon would disappear. "Let's rest here a little while longer." She inhaled deeply, but Noni wriggled impatiently out of her arms.

"Mom! It's Christmas morning! Time to get a move on."

Noni had to sit on Marcus before he'd open his eyes. He squinted and waved them off. "Go away," he said. "I'm Jewish."

"I'm only half," Noni said.

"And half moron," Marcus said.

Noni punched him in the arm.

Marcus swung his long bony legs over the side of the bed and moved them around under it, looking for slippers. He settled for socks discarded by the bed the night before. One had a hole in the toe and he looked at it ruefully. "Maybe Santa got us new socks," he said.

Marcus was right—it was socks this year. Each year, Eve wrapped one extra present and disguised her handwriting with elaborate lettering:

To Marcus from Santa. To Noni, love Santa.

Usually it was something practical, like gloves or socks. And a box of dates. Marcus had long ago loved a Christmas book that showed a picture of a boy opening a box of chocolates from Santa. When he asked, Eve lied and said it was a box of dates. She was strict in those days—no candy, no television. Since then she always filled little gift boxes with dates. One year she didn't realize that they were out of dates and substituted prunes instead. The kids would never let her live it down.

"Prunes!" Marcus cried. "Santa's getting old!"

It took the kids fifteen minutes to tear open all the presents. As usual, it never seemed she'd bought enough till the gifts were torn open, and then it looked like way too much again. They made her open her gift last. The small box sat inside a sky-blue Van Cott Jewelers bag, with little white handles. Eve opened the velvet ring box and stared uncomprehendingly. It was a gold band studded all around in a circle with bright red stones, the color of pomegranate seeds.

"They're rubies," Marcus explained.

"Do you like it?" Noni asked.

Eve held the box out to them. It hung open like an astonished mouth. "I can't accept this," she said. "Did you spend all your babysitting money?" she said stupidly. "Did you rob a bank?"

"I cashed in one of my savings bonds," Marcus said.

"You're supposed to be saving those for college!" Eve said.

"I have nine more," Marcus said. "I'll get a scholarship. I've been writing those stupid college essays all vacation. I'm brilliant. Try it on."

"Put it on, put it on!" Noni sang. "I know it'll fit, because we took one of your rings to the store to make sure."

"A woman of virtue, who can find her?" Marcus said. "Her price is above rubies . . . Hebrew class, fifth grade," he added.

"It's too much," Eve said, putting it on her finger. She closed her other hand around the ring, clasping it, holding it tight. The ring dazzled in her swimming eyes.

At noon it began snowing in thick, angled drops you could have photographed, they came down so slowly. Soon the road in front their house was covered in a slick coat of white. Eve phoned her mother.

"Isn't it too early for dinner?" Mrs. Dunrea asked. "They're having a special on sterling silver on QVC I wanted to watch."

"It's snowing pretty hard," Eve said. "I don't want to wait till the roads get bad."

"My God!" Mrs. Dunrea cried. She hated bad weather. "I hadn't even looked outside.

183

Are you sure you still want to come?"

"Mom," Eve said. "You live half a mile away. Of course we'll come."

"Wear boots," Mrs. Dunrea said. "And a hat. And don't let Marcus drive in this weather. Come alone. It's so dangerous."

"Right. If I die," Eve promised, "I die alone."

The Goldensohns were perched on her mother's rented living room furniture, looking as if they might fall off onto the floor. The furniture never looked quite real to Eve. It looked as if the men who'd moved it in could show up any minute to move it back out again. None of it suited her mother's taste—everything was heavy and floral, in navy and greens and cranberry reds. The Goldensohns sipped their tea. They sat quietly, not saying much. Her mother offered them cake, cookies, fresh fruit, all of which they refused with dismay. "Oh, no," Mrs. Goldensohn said. "No! We couldn't possibly!"

Mr. Goldensohn patted his belly. "As soon as the holidays are over, we're going on a diet. I'm still carrying around a few extra potato pancakes."

Eve looked at her watch and pretended to be surprised by the time. She had more sense than to mention that it was Christmas in front of the Goldensohns. Nonetheless the old couple rose instantly. Mr. Goldensohn's face was pasty white, as if from some disease. His skin was as loose as pudding. Mrs. Goldensohn wore her hair in a short bob, and she sported sweatshirts with childlike decorations on the front—teddy bears or hearts. Today it was snowflakes.

"We didn't mean to keep you," she said. "You should have said."

"You know you're welcome any time," said Mrs. Dunrea. But as soon as they'd tottered out the door she said, "I thought they'd never go."

It took forever for Mrs. Dunrea to get dressed. She fussed over one sweater after another. Nothing was quite right. "I'm particular about what I wear," she said. "Not like you." She had to sit down to put on her boots and then had trouble lifting her feet so she could tie them. One of her winter gloves was missing. Eve called home to check on the kids. They were watching a cartoon special and making chocolate chip cookies.

"From scratch," Noni told her proudly.

Eve had hunted all through the apartment but still held the one unmatched glove in her hand. "You can wear my gloves," she said for the fourth time.

"Never mind," her mother said. "It'll turn up."

On the way out of the building several residents wished Mrs. Dunrea a Merry Christmas, and one young Latino woman said she'd baked some cupcakes she would be bringing up with her three kids.

"Aren't you sweet!" Mrs. Dunrea exclaimed. "Better wait till tomorrow. I'm going home to my daughter's." She announced it proudly.

"Isn't that nice." The young woman beamed at them. Her three children circled around her, like cats. One kept sticking out his tongue and making faces. "Tomasito, stop that," she said, batting at him, hitting the air. "They love to visit your mother," she said to Eve. "They're always begging to go to the fifth floor."

"Don't let them ride the elevator alone," Mrs. Dunrea said. "It's not safe."

"No, no, they're not allowed," the young woman said.

Jonah's doorsill was piled high with presents. Eve had sent a check with a card signed in her mother's name, hers, and the kids.

"He doesn't do as much as he claims," her mother said grudgingly, "but he's better than nothing."

"I'm sure he'd be happy to hear that," Eve said, sure that he wouldn't be.

"That woman and her three kids," her mother went on, once they were out in the cold. Snow fell all around them, sticking on her mother's wool hat, a vivid shade of violet. "I wish they'd stop dropping in on me. I don't like surprise visitors. Why doesn't she call first? That way I could pretend not to be home."

"Why do they want to come so badly?" Eve

helped her mother down the stairs, carefully, pausing at each step.

"Kids just naturally like me." Mrs. Dunrea added, "And I made the mistake of giving them some candy the first time they came. Now they expect it."

"So stop giving them candy," Eve said.

"I tried that. They looked so disappointed. She can't afford much. Of course there's no husband. I just go to the dollar store and buy whatever junk they have. Little cinnamon buns, Twinkies, candy bars."

"And you're surprised they keep coming? *I'd* come by, Ma."

"Well, it wouldn't kill you to visit more often." Her mother talked about how some daughters went absolutely everywhere with their mothers, how they were inseparable, like twins. Some women even dressed like their mothers.

"You want to start dressing like me?" Eve asked.

"No," Mrs. Dunrea said. "All your clothes are so baggy. And you wear too many at once. I wish you'd buy a new suit at Bon Ton's."

"I will, Mom."

"Have you been to a doctor?"

"For what?" Eve was walking her mother with infinite slowness across the Chestnut Arms parking lot. In her ankle-high boots, Mrs. Dunrea wobbled like a shopping cart with a broken wheel. It took fifteen minutes just to get near Eve's car. The old Citroen was sprinkled with snow.

"Losing weight could be a bad sign. Cancer. It could mean something's wrong—not that I think there is," Mrs. Dunrea said. "Where's a piece of wood?" She stopped, put one hand out and rapped a dead tree branch. "Knock on wood."

Eve unlocked the Citroen and helped her mother slide both legs inside. The inside of her car was messy with Marcus's old school papers, empty candy wrappers, and spring-water bottles or empty Gatorade. Both kids treated the car like a giant moving garbage can. She wished, not for the first time, that she could have one clear space she could claim as her own.

When she put the key in the ignition nothing happened.

"Oh God," her mother groaned. "I can't make it back across that parking lot."

"Hold on," Eve said. She turned the key again. She was sweating inside her wool coat. "Sometimes it takes a minute."

"You need a new car," her mother chanted. "You need a new winter coat. You need a new hat. What is that, Noni's old hat?"

Eve peeked in the rearview mirror. She was in fact wearing a pink wool hat with a white pom-pom and a picture of Cinderella on the front inside a pink butterfly, a discard of Noni's.

"I have other hats," she said.

"How can you go out looking like that?" her mother said. "I see how people stare at you. It's terrible."

"Ma," Eve said, angling sideways in her seat. She could barely move because of the heavy sweater she had on over her turtleneck, under the wool coat. To her relief, the car finally started, leaping to life under her sweating hands. "It's Christmas. Give me a break."

Her mother gave her head a little shake. "You're right," she said. She planted a sharp kiss on her daughter's cheek. "Merry Christmas."

Chapter 16

The Fall

The orgy of opening presents was behind them, the wrappings and boxes stuffed into a large black garbage bag near the tree. The house felt chilly, no matter how many layers she put on or how high she turned up the heat, and the kids were bored and antsy, which in turn made their grandmother nervous.

Helen Gollow sent an enormous fruit basket. The basket contained pears and apples, jams and nuts, cookies and candies. "You have great enemies," Noni said. "There's a girl in my class but all she does is give me dirty looks. Soccer envy," she added.

"Can I call Danny?" Marcus asked.

Danny's older sister and brother were away—his sister in law school, the brother in residency near Joel's brother, in Pittsburgh. The Schwartz family was filled with doctors and lawyers. "They need an Indian chief," Marcus joked. But now, on the phone, his voice went up at the end, higher than normal. "Really?" he was saying. "Did you tell them? . . . Really? Okay," and he hung up.

"Danny can't come over," he said. "Not unless we take down our tree."

"What?" said Mrs. Dunrea. She'd been hiding out in a corner chair with a new book of cross-word puzzles. She pushed her reading glasses farther up her nose. It gave her a strict school-marmish look.

"The Schwartzes say it's a crime for Jews to have a Christmas tree in the house. They don't want him to see it." Marcus sounded upset. "Now we won't be able to hang out all vacation."

"Tell them it's a winter tree," Eve said.

"I can try." He looked hopeful, and dialed again. "Dan," he said. "Tell them it's a winter tree . . . Okay." He looked at his family. After a minute he started nodding again. "—Mom, are we going to leave it up till spring? Mrs. Schwartz says if it's a winter tree we have to keep it up till spring."

"Let me," Eve said, holding out her hand for the phone.

"I'm sorry." Maxine's voice was brisk. "We have to hold the line."

"It's not your tree," Eve said. "It's not your business." Her mother was looking at her, nodding emphatically.

"That's right," Mrs. Dunrea said. "You tell the little bitch."

Noni looked shocked.

"I've paid a fortune on a Jewish education for my kids," Maxine said. "Do you know the statistics on intermarriages? You don't understand—"

Eve interrupted her. "How about if we cover it up? With a blanket."

That brought Maxine up short. She said, "Let me ask Joel." It was a good start. Joel was far too reticent to meddle in someone else's domestic affairs. "Okay," Maxine said, coming back on after a minute or two. "But keep it covered whenever Danny is in the house."

"Right," Eve said.

"I made an extra pot of soup," Maxine said. "And some potato pancakes. I'll send them over with Danny."

"Thanks, but no."

"Don't get mad," Maxine said. "I'm just doing

my job as a parent. You have to respect that."

Marcus looked so hopeful, Eve didn't have the heart to say, "I don't have to do anything of the kind." She wasn't sure what she believed in, but it didn't depend on rules and regulations. She liked to think of God as evolving along with the human race. But Maxine would have found the idea ludicrous.

The kids helped her drag an old quilt over the tree. It kept knocking the Christmas tree over, till they finally had it balanced upright. It looked like a body was hidden under the blanket, right in the middle of the living room.

"This is so ridiculous," Mrs. Dunrea said, but she tugged one side of the quilt to straighten it.

"You have the weirdest friends," Noni said as the doorbell rang.

It wasn't Danny, however, but a beautiful teenage girl. Noni snatched the blue scarf from Grandma Dunrea's neck just as the young woman stepped into the living room.

"What is the matter with you people?" Mrs. Dunrea cried. "Scarves aren't allowed now, either?"

The girl was dressed all in black—black leather jacket, black velvet pants, high-heeled black boots. Her hair looked like spun gold. "Wish you a Merry Christmas," she said. The words seemed to catch in her throat as she caught sight of the blanketed Christmas tree with everyone gathered around it. She turned to Marcus. "This is a special custom?"

"Not exactly," he said.

She was holding out a slim package wrapped in silver and blue. "Happy holiday," she said. "And thanking you."

"Uh . . . okay," Marcus said. "I've got something for you, too. Why don't you come into the kitchen? Um, Mom, Gramma, Noni, this is Astrid." He flapped a hand at all of them and dragged Astrid into the kitchen, holding her by the wrist.

"I bet he's going to kiss her," Noni said.

"Let's hope," Mrs. Dunrea said. "I want great-grandchildren. Not right away," she added quickly, and a little too loudly.

"What's that, Gramma?" Marcus called from the kitchen.

Marcus and Astrid soon wandered back into the living room holding mugs of tea. They had no sooner settled on the sofa than Danny barged into the house with his jacket flapping open and his eyes squinted shut.

"Is it covered?" he yelped from the doorway.

"Yes," Marcus said. "Danny, you know Astrid, don't you?"

"Mm. Are you a German spy?" Danny said.

"I am from Denmark," Astrid said coldly.

"I heard you were a spy," Danny insisted. "You look like a spy."

Luckily, Devin MacKenzie showed up behind Danny with one of his sisters in tow and a few friends from the football team. Devin always traveled in a small crowd, never alone. He looked just as Eve remembered him from grade school, with his short blond hair, snub nose, and freckles. He still looked a lot like Dennis the Menace.

"How ya doing!" Devin said, punching Marcus on the arm. He caught sight of the blanketed tree. "Wow. It looks injured," he said. He looked to Eve for help. "Is this a Jewish thing?"

"Never mind," Marcus said. He was tugging on Devin's arm, but Devin leaned the other way, laughing. "Come downstairs to the basement," Marcus said. "I've got the new Dark Empire game."

"I've got other games we can play," Devin said. "Way more fun." He pulled out of Marcus's grasp and banged against the stair banister. Astrid stood looking at him, dismayed.

"C'mere, dog," Devin said to the older shih tzu.

He crouched down to pet him, and Refrigerator leaped up, knocking him backward. Devin sprawled flat on the floor, laughing. Toaster was yapping madly. Refrigerator licked Devin's face. Noni was trying to pull the dogs off him. Her face was red.

"I think your dog just tried to French-kiss me, man," Devin told Marcus.

"Dev, come on," Devin's younger sister said. "Downstairs," and the other teenagers whisked him out of sight.

What was left behind, however, was the distinct smell of alcohol.

"Has that boy been drinking?" Mrs. Dunrea said.

"Yes," Noni said.

"I hope not," said Eve, but a few minutes later she headed into the basement to check. The boys were playing the Dark Empire game, while Astrid and Devin's sister sat on the sofa talking quietly. Devin sat between them, his blond head back on a sofa pillow. He was asleep.

"He's fine," his sister said. "He's just tired."

"He's not driving anywhere, is he?" Eve asked.

"Nah," said one of the other boys, a big kid named Ryan. For years, he and Marcus had wound up in the same elementary school class. Ryan had been a small, quiet kid. He must have grown a foot that year. "I've got the car keys." He patted his red and white varsity jacket pocket.

"Okay," Eve said, and went back upstairs, still troubled. Should she call Devin's mother? Devin's parents had divorced a few years ago, and he spent most of his time living at his father's place. Eve didn't really know Mr. MacKenzie. She wasn't sure she'd recognize him if she saw him on the street.

"Stop worrying," Mrs. Dunrea said. "It's not your problem."

"They're children. They're all my problem."

There were six different MacKenzies in the phone book. Eve remembered that they used to live on Matthews Street. She dialed the number but it rang and rang. No answering machine picked up.

By the time all the teenagers had trooped upstairs to raid the refrigerator, Devin seemed himself again, only a bit more rumpled and chagrined. He had always been a cheerful child. He'd never sulked or cried, or got into fights with the other kids. He asked Eve, diplomatically, whether she found it hard, being alone on Christmas. "My mom hates the holidays now," he said. "She just pretends they don't happen. I guess for her they don't."

"I don't really feel like I'm alone," Eve said. She wondered if this sounded strange. In fact, she often felt pressed and crowded on all sides. But that wasn't what he meant. And the kind of alone he meant wasn't anything she was going to discuss with the kids, not on Christmas day. To change the subject, she asked, "What are you taking next quarter? Any interesting classes?" She asked it casually, busy wiping down the counters. She felt rather than saw the sudden stillness in the room.

"None," he said. "I'm done."

No one spoke, but they were all looking at Devin, except for his two sisters, who looked away.

"I'm out," Dev said. He scuffed one sneaker toe along the linoleum. "My dad got me set up working full-time at the Galleria." The Galleria was the upscale end of the MacKenzies' carpet business.

"I'm nineteen," he said. "School is just a waste for me. I've been working over the holidays. One of the salesmen is retiring."

"I see," Eve said. None of the other kids said anything.

Noni stuck her head into the kitchen. "Who wants ginger cookies?" she asked.

Mrs. Dunrea insisted they eat dinner early. It was pitch-dark now at six o'clock, the streets looked shut down for the night. Snow had fallen into the afternoon, but cars had been swishing up and down the streets all day, and it was a wet snow, easily cleared from the windshield.

"The shortest day of the year is behind us," Eve said, trying to think of something cheerful to say. She'd been feeling melancholy all day, even worse since Dev announced he was dropping out of school. Soon all the kids would be moving off in different directions, to colleges all over the country, or to jobs, to wives and families, their own divorces . . .

"I'm getting old," Mrs. Dunrea said. She shut her eyes and leaned her head back against the headrest. "I'm starting to feel my age."

Eve walked her mother back to the Chestnut Arms; first the long slow walk across the parking lot, then up the elevator to the fifth floor, clutching a small shopping bag. Inside were the gifts for her mother: the blue scarf from Noni; a nightgown, robe, and pair of cashmere-lined gloves from Eve; the crossword book and a gift certificate to a bookstore from Marcus.

Later that night, much later, when Eve and the kids were sitting around trying to toast marshmallows in the fireplace—they kept catching fire and burning and falling into the flames—Mrs. Dunrea telephoned to say she had fallen down.

"How?" Eve asked. "Where?"

"I don't know," Mrs. Dunrea said. Her voice sounded tight. "My hip, I think. I hope I didn't break it. I was making myself a peanut butter sandwich and somehow I slipped and fell. I must have turned the wrong way."

"Can you move at all?" Eve asked. "Shall I come get you?"

"I can move a little," her mother said. "There's no need to go back out tonight. It's snowing again. This will wait till morning."

"Are you positive?" Eve asked.

"Of course," Mrs. Dunrea snapped.

"Well, then, I'm sure you didn't break any-thing."

"Let's hope not," her mother said, and hung up.

But she called again just after six the next morning, sounding weak and frightened. "Something's really wrong," she said. "I'm sorry to wake you. I was up all night. I dragged myself into the bathroom. That's where I slept."

"You slept in the bathroom?" Eve said.

"I slept on the bathroom floor," Mrs. Dunrea said. "Do you think Marcus is strong enough to carry me?"

"Why didn't you call me?" Eve asked. "Why didn't you call Jonah?"

"I don't have his number," her mother said. "I don't even know his last name."

It was infuriating and terrifying to think of her mother lying there all night.

"Why didn't you call 911!" she cried.

"It never occurred to me," Mrs. Dunrea said. "Stop yelling."

"I'm coming now," Eve said.

She woke Marcus and made him put on his boots and his coat over his pajamas, and then woke Noni to explain where they were going. "I want to come too," Noni said. She sat up in bed, her eyes closed.

"No," said Eve. "You stay here. I'm taking Grandma to the hospital. And if it takes more than an hour, I want you to go to Anna's house to play. Okay?"

"Okay," Noni said, and then she was asleep again.

"Come on," Eve said. The keys to the Citroen shook in her hand. Marcus took them from her.

"Let me," he said. "You're way too upset to drive."

The front door of the Chestnut Arms was locked. She had a key to her mother's apartment, but not to the building. She rang the bell for Jonah's apartment. "Stupid, stupid," she kept muttering under her breath. "Stupid!"

"Mom! Calm down," Marcus said. "I'm sure Gramma is fine." But he looked relieved when Jonah came down the hall, walking jauntily, wearing a sweater with reindeer dancing all over it. His face lit at the sight of Eve and Marcus, but his lips parted when he saw her expression, and he yanked open the door.

"What's wrong?" he asked.

They rode up the elevator in near silence. When they reached the fifth floor, Eve said, "She fell last night, but she waited till this morning to tell me to come." Tears were dripping down the sides of her face, and she wiped them away with both hands.

"She should have called me," Jonah said.

"She didn't have your number," Eve said. "I should have made sure she had it."

"It's printed right on the phone," Jonah said. "Right underneath her own number. I put it on all the telephones." He used the master key to unlock the door, and pushed it open, calling, "Mrs. Dunrea? Where you at?"

"In the bathroom," Mrs. Dunrea called back. Her voice sounded weak. "I feel so helpless," she said. "So foolish." She was lying on the floor, looking almost as palely translucent as the shower curtain beside her head. She was still wearing her new Christmas nightgown and robe.

Jonah bent down and scooped her up in his arms. "Which hospital?" he said to Eve.

"Lourdes." It was closest.

"We'll go in my car." Jonah was already heading back out the apartment door. "She's going to be fine. I've seen lots worse. Mrs. Dunrea, you're going to be all right. But this ain't no way to be spending your holiday."

Mrs. Dunrea had her eyes closed and her mouth pinched tightly shut.

While Eve filled out the paperwork, her mother lay on the hospital gurney, where Eve could still see her, like a package someone was about to roll away, wrapped in white. After an impossibly long while, the emergency room aides took her mother away down to the X-Ray Department, and from there back up to a room separated from all the others by a thin white curtain. Eve followed her mother from place to place, while Marcus and Jonah stayed in the emergency room waiting room decorated for Christmas with one anemic tree that kept blinking red and green.

Mrs. Dunrea said little, kept dozing and then waking with a whimper. "All I did was turn around," she told Eve. "I lost my balance and fell."

"She was lying on the bathroom floor all night," Eve explained. She felt the need to confess this to everyone she saw—the admissions woman, the orderly, the attending nurses, other patients in the waiting room.

"Your mother is a brave lady," the doctor said. She was a young woman named Dr. Jadhur, with a crimson dot on her forehead. She was tiny, not much bigger than Mrs. Dunrea, but arrow-straight in her slim white lab coat, and white leather clogs. "Mrs. Dunrea, you are a very courageous lady," she added. "She lives alone?"

Eve nodded as if admitting a crime.

The doctor turned away, handing her clipboard to a nurse. "We will take some further X rays and then speak. Now your mother should try to rest . . . Is the pain medication helping?" she asked Mrs. Dunrea.

"A little," Mrs. Dunrea said.

Within minutes she was asleep. Someone had removed her partial plate, the upper denture. Without it her face looked wasted, as if her whole body had caved in. Jonah stayed in the waiting room till Eve looked at the clock above the line of orange vinyl sofas. It was almost noon. "You're missing work," she told him. It was a Tuesday.

"This is my work," Jonah said. "I phoned the Parks Department. They understand we had an emergency over to the Chestnut Arms."

The young doctor surveyed the three of them, the large black man in his reindeer sweater, the pale teenager, and Eve, still in the gray sweats she had slept in. She said, "You should all go home and get some rest."

"But—"

"We will call if there is any need. Certainly the hip is broken. We will see how fractured, maybe a clean break. The radiologist will call me. But for a few hours now let us do our work. You are tired."

Jonah he put one hand on Eve's back and the other on Marcus's and steered them back to his big sedan. The heat blasted on, and so did the radio, some man singing in a low sexy voice. Jonah shut it off.

"I want to go back to bed," Marcus said. "Is that okay?"

"It's fine, sweetie," Eve said.

Jonah dropped Marcus at the house. The Citroen was still parked back at the Chestnut Arms. Eve's head throbbed. Dr. Jadhur, the emergency room physician, had said Mrs. Dunrea would likely be in the hospital for a week to ten days. Then another month or so for rehabilitation. Her voice had been so musical that she made it all sound like a pleasant rest. But now the grim reality was sinking in. Her mother might never really recover. That's how it went when old people broke their bones. They ended up in wheelchairs and nursing homes.

Eve shut her eyes, and Jonah said nothing till they pulled into the parking lot. Her Citroen sat in the lot, looking lost. She needed a few things to bring to her mother—a change of clothes, medications. She dreaded having to rummage through her mother's things, searching for clean underwear, her mother's toothbrush, like someone poking around after a funeral.

"How about you have a cup of tea first?" Jonah suggested. "You got a little time."

He unlocked his door. There was a red glass vase on a shiny black desk in his front hall. Its handles were yellow. It startled her—the vase looked like something you'd find at a museum.

He saw her looking at it. "I got that at an auction," he said, "on public TV. You like it?"

"It's surprising," she said. "I mean—it's beautiful."

"Come all the way in," Jonah said. "Let me show you."

His living room opened directly into the bedroom. A red beaded curtain separated the bed-room from the rest of the apartment. A lamp was on. The bed was covered in a red quilted bed-spread. It looked like a football field. It seemed to be pulling all the energy of the apartment into itself. Jonah turned on his stereo. She thought of it as ghetto music. It was foreign, like visiting another country. He changed the station and lowered the volume.

"Don't you want to see the rest?" He turned on the gas flame under a teakettle in the kitchen.

"I can see it from here," she said.

"The bedroom's the best part." He grinned.

"I'd better go," she said.

"I got another vase in there," he said. "Same artist, I think. Same auction, anyway. Come see." He took her hand, and a confused thrill went through her. It was all like a dream, taking her mother to the hospital, her mother's mouth open as she slept, the phone call with Chuck, every-thing mixed up together. She was aware that Jonah's palm felt dry, that his skin was warm, that he smelled like candy. Her heart was pounding so loudly in her chest it felt like a gong. She took a few steps forward, enough to see inside the bedroom. There was indeed another glass vase by the bed, this one vivid green.

She said, "I'd better go," and pulled her hand free.

He looked at her and his brow furrowed.

"Aw," he said. "You don't have to leave. You're tired. You haven't even had your herbal tea." He pronounced the *h* in herbal, breathing into it.

She could not explain how or why, but he seemed to grow younger by the minute. He looked like one of the college kids who were always hanging around the Art Department, cocky and nervous.

"You sure you don't want to stay?" he said. "You seem to me like maybe you want to." His voice was coaxing, a kid Marcus's age, high school, or even younger, one of those elementary school kids hanging around the playground. "Don't you want to stay?" He leaned forward and his chest brushed against her. He smelled of cinnamon. He was going to kiss her.

"Wait!" she said. She put up one hand.

She never knew which one of them moved first. He gathered her into his arms and his lips pushed against hers, soft and heavy and slow. His mouth tasted like a spiced gumdrop. Her legs actually felt weak. She pulled away, dizzy from it.

"Hang on," she said.

He was still bending over her. She rested her hands against his chest, balancing against him. He was square and muscular. She could feel his muscles through the soft sweater he wore. He felt so solid and real. He was wearing work boots, the dark tanned leather the color of oak leaves at the park. Just then his phone rang, three shrill phrases repeating.

She stepped back.

"Yeah," he said sharply into the phone. It was a different voice from any she'd heard him use, "I got it . . . Yeah. I got it. In the toolshed . . . Okay, see you."

She was still looking at his boots, for some reason. What was the matter with her, kissing some man at a moment like this? Was she out of her mind?

"Chuckleheads at the park," he said. He lifted his hands. "They need me for everything."

"I have to get going anyway."

He stepped toward her, but she sidestepped away, behind the sofa table.

"Really, I need to go," she said.

He sighed. Then he grinned. "Give me your phone number. I promise not to use it right away. You going to be busy, I know. I'm going to tuck it away, and one day let me buy you a nice dinner."

Eve was conscious all at once of the sweats she was wearing, her old sneakers on her feet. She hadn't had time to comb her hair or brush her teeth. She realized with horror that she wasn't even wearing a bra. She folded her arms across her chest, dictated her phone number—he wrote it on the pad by his phone—and then, arms still crossed, edged around the table toward his front door.

"I, um. I want to thank you—" she said.

He raised one big hand, stopping her. "Do that over dinner," he said. "Tell your mama, she need anything whatsoever, I'm right here." He tapped himself on the shoulder.

Chapter 17

Broken

The hip had fractured in two places. Mrs. Dunrea's doctors wanted to operate right away, putting a pin in, setting metal screws against the fractured bone.

"Oh, I won't like that," Mrs. Dunrea said. "No. That doesn't sound good at all."

Eve tried to explain that there wasn't a choice. Her mother seemed to think if she just waited there in the hospital, holding still, the bone might heal itself. Eve half believed it herself. The doctors shook their heads and smiled as if at whimsical children. They went over the X rays again, pointing at the images with little sticks that looked remarkably like magic wands.

Mrs. Dunrea, they explained, had suffered two femoral neck fractures that were minimally displaced. That was the good news.

"I didn't break my neck," she insisted. "It's my hip."

"A femoral neck fracture is what they call it, Mom," Eve said. The orthopedist and orthopedic surgeon were dressed in nearly identical gray suits. The surgeon wore a brighter tie, with musical notes all over it in red and blue. The orthopedist wore a plain blue tie. The surgeon was nearly a foot taller than the doctor, so they looked like a pair in a comic strip, except that neither one said or did anything funny.

The surgeon was using the wand to demonstrate something across a cartoon drawing of the human body. Again, this was a cartoon without humor. The man in the picture had open, pinkish-red muscles and exposed bone across half his body, and one staring eye socket. The surgeon explained that he would make a few small incisions on the outside of the thigh—he slashed again—and then, using an X ray and computer imaging as guide, he would pass several screws across to stabilize the broken bones. He hoped that would be sufficient. "You may need a partial hip replacement down the road," he said.

"There may not be any down the road," her mother answered.

"I'm sorry," the orthopedist said. "I know this must all be a terrible shock."

"It could be worse," Mrs. Dunrea said. "I could be dead."

They met later with the anesthesiologist, named Dr. Lee. He knew Mia and Sook-yun from the Korean Baptist Church. At that moment of connection, a smile passed briefly over his blood-less lips. He was so thin that his skin stretched across his teeth, his cheekbones narrow. He explained that Mrs. Dunrea had choices.

"Not a general anesthetic," Mrs. Dunrea said. "I don't want to go under." She spoke like a swimmer who was afraid to drown.

"You want spinal?" Dr. Lee said. He made a note on his clipboard.

"I don't want any of it. Can't we just wait and see?"

"Wait?" Dr. Lee drummed his pencil against the paper.

"Mom, you need the surgery now," Eve explained. "The sooner the better."

"Maybe not," Dr. Lee said. "Not good to hurry. Wait two days." He held up his fingers as if offering them a secret formula. The two women looked at him, mesmerized. He briefly tapped Mrs. Dunrea on the back of the hand. "Not worry. Strong constitution. Like Hercales." He flexed his nonexistent muscles.

After he left, Mrs. Dunrea asked weakly, "Which one of us is Hercules?"

"I think you are," Eve said.

"I certainly am the better candidate," her mother said.

• • •

Eve spent nearly a week at the hospital, before and after the surgery. She came home only to check on the kids and to shower. Tracy stayed over to keep an eye on things. She brought her elderly chow chow along, which made Toaster and Refigerator bark all night long, Noni informed her. Most of the time, Mrs. Dunrea dozed, or lay still with her eyes closed, dazed from the pain medication.

Eve slept in a vinyl armchair beside the thin white curtain that separated them first from a woman who had suffered a stroke, then from an old woman dying, it sounded, from emphysema. The noise from her breathing machines, the loud, intermittent hiss and click of the oxygen, kept Eve awake, so she sat in the vinyl chair and read a book of short stories, or just sat with her hands in her lap and watched her mother sleep. She ran trips to the ward's refrigerator for watery cranberry and apple juice. She smuggled in a few contraband Tylenol. Sometimes she brought plastic cups of Jell-O for her mother and for each of her mother's roommates, who never seemed to have any visitors.

Hospital time ran twenty-four hours in a continuous loop. The bright fluorescent lights glared down day and night. Four A.M. felt like 4:00 P.M., only quieter.

Eve learned to recognize the names of the

211

doctors paged over the intercom. The day nurses were brusque and efficient, the night nurses tender and tired and kind.

When Mrs. Dunrea was first wheeled out of surgery, she seemed to have shrunk, and her chin was tilted sharply upward, like the face in a coffin. But within a day they had the old lady out of bed and hobbling to the bathroom, complaining loudly.

Eve finished her book of stories, then went right back to the first story and read it straight through again, amazed at how much she had already forgotten. The author, on the back cover, looked happy and beautiful, her blond hair swept back from her forehead. She lived in Ohio with her husband and three pet beagles. Eve devoured every word, the author's bio, even the dedication page. The book was like a giant pacifier she clung to, holding it in her lap or keeping it on the table beside her. Its voice kept her company during the endless night. Sometimes she and her mother watched TV, but the programs tired Charlotte, and Eve generally ended up watching the shows alone before switching them off.

Even as her mother began to recover, Eve noticed that the doctors seldom spoke directly to Mrs. Dunrea. They chose instead to speak to her. Mrs. Dunrea said, "Talk to *me*. I'm right here," but after a few seconds the doctors would shift position and address themselves again to Eve.

"Please talk to my mother," Eve insisted. It was useless. They spoke as if Mrs. Dunrea was in another room. Her mother was making reasonable progress. She was slated to spend a few weeks in rehab at Marywood. After that, they would see.

Eve called the assisted living facilities in town. She knew that Frederick Cummings's mother had lived for a time in Emerald Gardens, a place with large light atriums filled with plants between the wings. Mrs. Cummings had liked it there. Eve made the necessary phone calls and filled out application forms. Her mother would not even consider a return to the Chestnut Arms.

"I can't," Mrs. Dunrea said. "I'm afraid to fall again."

Eve wore a pair of loose black flowered pants when she came to the hospital. By the time her mother came out of intensive care, she was so sick of the sight of those flowers against the black background she would have burned them, but they were made of rayon and probably would have melted.

New Year's Eve barely registered in the hospital, with ginger ale fizzing in their small paper cups and a rock music special saluting the Queen of England—of all people. Eve hadn't spent this much time alone with her mother since childhood. They played gin rummy and go fish. They ate sandwiches from the cafeteria, each woman eating half, doling out an equal number of potato chips from the bag. Mrs. Dunrea didn't have much appetite, but neither did Eve, on the Hospital Diet. They lived like two children.

It seemed as if it would all last forever. But on the tenth morning, Eve wheeled her mother downstairs and out to the curb where the Marywood medivan already waited, its engine running, puffing blue fumes. The fresh air felt foreign, as did the sight of the cold sky, bare trees, and buildings. Two men loaded Mrs. Dunrea into the white van.

Eve felt a tug in her chest like a kite string, close to the pang she'd felt after giving birth to Marcus and the maternity nurse first came to listen to his heart with a stethoscope in hand. Not through Eve's belly, after all those months, but across the room from her, there in his own bassinet.

"Go on now," Mrs. Dunrea said firmly. "Take care of your children. Go back to work. I'll be fine."

But when Eve arrived home, Tracy and the kids were nowhere around. She wandered through the house, straightening sofa pillows, stacking magazines. After the hospital room with its narrow twin bed, single chair, and table, her house seemed cluttered with unnecessary, useless objects: paperweights and dried flowers; glass balls and magazines, baskets, boxes of CDs no one bothered to put back into their cases. The garage sale had barely scratched the surface of the chaos. She began carting things into the living room and stuffing them into garbage bags—some for charity, the rest for trash. Maybe she could carve out a space, she thought, some breathing room. Just then the phone rang.

All the warnings from the hospital brochures came rushing back. Twenty-five percent of elderly patients who broke their hips died within six months of injury. More than half went into nursing homes. There was a decrease in life expectancy and what one brochure described as "a meaningful decline in the overall quality of life." Eve's heart was pounding so hard she could barely hear.

"Eve . . . Eve, are you all right?"

She hadn't even recognized Lev's familiar voice.

"How's your mother?" he said. "I called and left messages for you. Did Tracy tell you?"

"I don't remember," Eve said. "I don't think so."

She took down a message for Tracy and hung up. Why hadn't she heard yet from her mother? Fingers trembling, she called Marywood. They told her they were just settling Mrs. Dunrea into her room. "Give it a little time," the woman said.

"She's fine. Her phone will be turned on in an hour."

Photographs of her two children hung on the wall, in pairs, looking like the faces of beautiful strangers. She began to tidy up the piles of dishes and cups on the coffee table; neither the kids nor Tracy had bothered to clean since she'd been gone.

But it was more than facing the clutter and the mess, this grip of cold gloom that surrounded her. She had never been prone to depression, not even after Ivan died, but what she suffered now felt like a disease of the soul. She wandered aimlessly around the house. The flowers in their clay pots out on the front porch were long dead and withered. A few brown leaves stuck out from the stems. She seemed to be staring at the demise of everything. Everything she'd already lost, all the losses still to come. It all headed toward grief in the end. Humans were soap bubbles, clinging to any solid surface. They rested briefly, then were gone. Her mother would be gone soon, and not long after, it would be herself, and one day even her own children . . .

A chill stabbed her heart. Why on earth bother? Why clean, take out the trash, make the beds. Why not let it all alone to rot? She went to the front door and gazed out.

The Binghamton sky was the brushed gray-blue of steel wool. The winter sun glimmered weakly between the houses. Shadows on the street appeared to be breathing. Across the way, her neighbors had not yet taken down their Christmas lights, and as Eve stood watching, the small white-gold lights suddenly blinked on. They fluttered off again, then came back on more brightly. It was amazing how gay and delicate the lights made the plain house look, strung along the wooden trim, twining around the columns of the porch. Through the leaded glass panes of her front door, sunlight bloomed an instant, casting a prismatic ribbon over the back of her hand like a many-colored bracelet.

The two dogs groaned, leapt heavily off the sofa and came to stand behind her. It was beauty that dragged you back into the world. The pine trees dripping with snow, branches curved downward like wings; or that deep electric blue the TV shimmered between stations, so vibrant a blue it aspired to something beyond color. It was all like some message she could not decode —the fairytale gold of the Christmas lights across the street, the rainbow on the back of her hand. A maple tree holding onto a few last spiky leaves. The dark macadam of the street shone like iron.

Both dogs looped around her legs and then Toaster let out a short, sharp bark. And that was the thing: you couldn't just stand there gawking at the world. A car slipped by. Then another. It was as if she'd stood frozen by the river of the world and gratefully stepped back into it, resuming her place. Change was the only constant. The rest was mysterious. Maybe that was why people loved mystery novels and detective shows, loved trying to solve crossword puzzles. It was time to walk the dogs, lift their leashes from the hook behind the door, put on her winter coat.

The world waited, cold, grim, alive, beautiful. There was no saying no to it.

Chapter 18
The Furies

Air slowed as soon as it hit the Marywood lobby, filled with plastic plants and plastic flowers and old people in their wheelchairs. There was a smell of urine and mashed green peas no amount of disinfectant spray could mask. Her mother holed up in her room, or went to Occupational Therapy. She refused to eat in the dining room. She took all her meals in her room, like someone riding a train.

For the first time Eve could remember, her mother became anxious about her health. She worried about the smallest things—whether she would remember where she'd put her slippers, if the aide would bring her eyedrops. She looked smaller, sitting in bed with the enormous white cast on her leg. The cast dwarfed her. Her doctors stopped by twice to see her. They appeared to see only her leg. They spoke to the leg, they looked at the leg. Her mother said, "If they chopped off the rest of my body, they would only recognize the leg."

People believed bad things came in threes. Eve thought they came in packs, like wolves. The week that Ivan was killed, someone had stolen Marcus's new skateboard out of the driveway. The Citroen had needed a new clutch. She'd torn her stockings just before the funeral, and just after, opening the sympathy cards and letters, she got a paper cut, a small stinging pain to remind her of the larger one that would not be so quick to heal.

That week her mother went into Marywood, the kitchen sink began to leak. They mopped up with towels and hoped for the best. The toilet in the downstairs bathroom overflowed. A pipe broke and needed to be replaced.

"These pipes are antique," the plumber said, tapping on them like he was playing percussion. "You never even see lead like this anymore."

"Lead?" Eve said. "As in lead poisoning?" This would have been the icing on the cake, she thought.

"You've got copper pipes coming in. But we'd

best replace the lead anyway." The plumber had an old-fashioned way of talking. The first time he tried to solder a pipe without success, he walked upstairs, calling, "Wherein have I failed?"

He set to work, laying out tools, going out to his truck for more materials, in and out of the house like a squirrel all morning. Eve knew women who could fix things by themselves— Tracy did all her own yard work and house painting—and then she knew other nincompoops like herself. How, for instance, did a furnace in her basement heat the second floor? What made the car brakes work? How did the water get from the Susquehanna River to her faucet?

Mia tried to explain it to her. The young woman, it turned out, was one of those who understood how things worked, and better yet, how they ought to work. She persuaded Eve to switch the downstairs bathroom and laundry room, as long as plumbing work needed to be done. The laundry room was much larger than the bathroom, and got more light. "Why waste so good space?" Mia asked.

She was absolutely right. Suddenly, Eve and the kids had a downstairs bathroom that felt spacious, with room for spare towels and all the bottles and jars they'd been cramming onto one tiny glass shelf. Mia helped her arrange an airy pyramid of green plants by the bathroom window. They bought window shades made of crinkled white rice paper that let in the light. There was still plenty of room in the smaller room to do laundry. Eve was amazed that she had not thought of it herself. The plumber was untroubled by such mysteries. Eve spent mornings with the calm plumber, her afternoons with her mother.

Charlotte was anxious, moody and withdrawn. She came to life only when the occupational therapist came around, a perky blonde named Cindi, who'd once been an aerobics teacher. The cheerleader quality of the aerobics instructor still lingered in her voice and manner. She tied her long blond hair back with a pink ribbon, and wore small dangle earrings, with pink crystal stars.

Cindi said Mrs. Dunrea was her hardest worker, her favorite patient. "We're going to strengthen these muscles, get you back on your own two feet."

Mrs. Dunrea was touchingly earnest about her rehab exercises. Even sitting alone in the room with Eve, she would swing one foot out from her chair, hold it straight for ten seconds, then put it back down. Then the other foot.

Still, she said, "This is the beginning of the end. People my age don't bounce back. I want you to be prepared."

Eve was arranging flowers on her mother's bedside table. There wasn't much she could do to brighten this room, but she brought fresh flowers. Cries of the other patients floated down the Marywood halls. Their distress was pitiful. Unlike Mrs. Dunrea, most were there permanently. Some had Alzheimer's. Others were just too old to do anything but sit tucked inside their wheelchairs, blankets over their knees, parked by the elevators in groups of three or four, waiting to ride down for meals. Eve had seen a line of seven women waiting, their hair lit by the wintry light of the window. The elevator rode up and down without them, the doors opened and closed like hungry mouths. The seven old women sat looking out the picture window like people in a theater waiting for a show to start.

"And these are supposed to be the golden years," her mother went on. "Just look at this place. These people. Terrible."

The plumber was a gentle, tall, dreamy man who wore cowboy shirts and boots and talked about the true nature of time, which wasn't real, he argued, not clock time. He liked to talk about God, and the universe. He was an optimistic man who expected the Messiah to return any day now, a visionary sun-lit version of Lev. One morning he hung a homemade coffee can bird feeder in Eve's backyard and left her an extra bag of birdseed before he left off work.

Mia dropped by with pans of macaroni and cheese, homemade gingerbread. Even her cooking was becoming more American.

"Why don't you take a few classes at BCC?" Eve had suggested. "I think you'd like it."

"Oh no," Mia said. "Not ready. English not good enough now."

"Yes you are. Yes it is," Eve insisted, and to her surprise Mia came over a few days later, her face pink with excitement, clutching a course catalogue.

BCC offered an Associate's Degree in Interior Design. Sook-yun agreed to watch the children two nights a week while Mia took a class. She had already studied design back in Korea. Mia faxed her old school for the transcripts, and Eve found someone in Asian Studies willing to translate them and send them to the Registrar's Office. She called the Dean of Students. She was dogged. The two women worked their way through the application and registration forms and the red tape.

"Class looks so hard," Mia fretted, studying every nuance of every word in the course descriptions. "I think I will fail." It wasn't till her translated transcripts arrived that Mia finally admitted to a 4.0 GPA back in Korea, one perfectly earned A after another, even in classes like Calculus and Higher Physics. She had graduated high school at sixteen. What else was she hiding? Eve wondered. Mia had only told her she'd worked as a stewardess in Korea. It was Ms. McLain who explained just how hard those jobs were to come by, how prestigious.

"They go to the top one or two percent of the female students," she said. "It's not the way we look at stewardesses here—you've got yourself a prodigy."

As soon as the plumbing was fixed and the bathroom and laundry room switched, Noni came down with a stomach flu. She kept running to the new bathroom to be sick. Eve held the hair back out of her daughter's face, dabbed at her mouth with clean washcloths. She brought her Dixie cups of ginger ale to drink, but Noni couldn't even keep the ginger ale down.

"I want Daddy!" she wailed into the toilet.

Nursing was Chuck's greatest strength as a parent. He calmly removed splinters. He sat by the kids' sides when they threw up, brought in the nighttime cough medicine, fetched juice and water and Tylenol. He could go on two hours' sleep and still head into work alert and cheerful. When Marcus needed stitches near his eye, Chuck sat next to him and held his hand without flinching, chatting good-naturedly with the doctor who did the sewing.

Noni knelt on the tiled bathroom floor and moaned for her father. She was just beginning to absorb the fact that this was not temporary, this was their life.

Eve did her best to make up for it. She bought Noni the teen magazines she normally poked fun at, and a set of lip glosses that looked like a tiny plastic painter's palette. Still, she knew she was hopelessly second best at this. To her eternal gratitude and relief, Marcus stepped in.

"Okay, deep breaths," he told Noni, holding back her hair while she hung over the toilet. "You'll feel better soon." He read chapter books. He told her stupid jokes that made her forget how bad she felt. He slept with his door open so he could hear her when she cried out for him at night. It brought back memories of Ivan in the nursery, pacing up and down for hours with Marcus in his arms.

Meanwhile, Mrs. Dunrea barred Eve from Marywood. "Don't come," she said crisply. "Those stomach flus are highly contagious."

Eve offered to send Tracy, but her mother said no, Tracy might be a carrier, and there was no need to baby her.

"I don't want you to feel all alone," Eve said.

"I am all alone," her mother told her.

The day Noni could finally keep down a little dry toast and rice, Marcus came home from school with stomach cramps and chills. Eve's Citroen, which had begun emitting a strange dark blue smoke, was making ominous whistling noises. Someone broke a window in the front of the house. The Furies were after them again.

Chapter 19

Saturday Night

Eve knew it was childish the way she snuck back to her mother's apartment, coming only when she was sure Jonah was at the park. She walked the dogs after work, when he'd already left for the day. She left a message on his answering machine explaining that her mother was moving to Emerald Gardens and mailed a check for the last month's rent. But when her mother needed an extra pair of pajamas, Eve tiptoed into the Chestnut Arms like a third-rate spy.

She had replayed Jonah's kiss in her head too many times to count, but each time it frightened her, her breath seemed to rush out of her body, she felt like someone about to be pushed into the deep end of the pool.

The company that rented Mrs. Dunrea the furniture showed no interest in her current condition or in anything that had happened to her. If she didn't need the furniture anymore, she had to get it moved back to the rental store. They charged an astronomical fee for this service. This fact was in tiny print at the very bottom of the rental agreement. Eve arranged for local movers, feeling that they were dropping yet another level;

her mother would no longer be needing even rented furniture.

Emerald Gardens offered fully furnished rooms. Mrs. Dunrea had a choice of medium-size and large rooms, they told Eve. The medium rooms were tiny and the large ones medium, like fancy cups of coffee—tall and grande, never small. There was something so American about this. In fact every room at Emerald Gardens was furnished in Americana—heavy, polished oak bed stands and white coverlets, with lacy white curtains to match. In the dining room, a huge American flag blanketed one wall.

Residents were encouraged to bring their trinkets from home, the woman in Admissions explained, and opened the door to a room where two old women sat at opposite ends. A soap opera was on the TV set, parked in the middle. One bed was covered in a crocheted afghan, green and purple and red. The other appeared to be a spotless white shrine for teddy bears. Some of the women shared rooms, the Admissions woman explained right in front of these two, to save on expenses. This looked like the room of two sisters who would never get along.

Mrs. Dunrea refused to take part in any of these decisions. "Just put me somewhere," she said. She was sick of Marywood. Anyplace would be an improvement.

One woman at Marywood kept climbing into

other people's beds. Mrs. Dunrea had found the woman asleep in her bed and didn't have the heart to wake her.

"She's always putting her head down right on the dining room table," she said. "You need to get me out of here fast. My own mind is beginning to slip."

Eve chose a large corner room for her mother that overlooked a field. The room felt narrow, but it would have to do. This was the new life. Beyond the field was the local Jewish community center. A few residents from Emerald Gardens walked over on Wednesday afternoons to have lunch, Eve was told, or on Mondays to play Bingo.

"Bingo," said Mrs. Dunrea. "Just shoot me in the head."

The moving company consisted of a father and son, working together wordlessly, almost without equipment. They strapped the furniture to their bodies with what looked like giant rubber bands. They did not use dollies or lifts. The father was in his early seventies, and the son almost fifty, he told Eve, ready to retire. The father had something wrong with his neck, so he always seemed to be looking off to the side, his head bent. He moved the heaviest furniture without complaint. He directed his son, and walked backward down the stairs of the Chestnut Arms, carrying the back end of the ugly rental sofa, when Jonah showed up.

"Moving day," Jonah said. He folded his arms and looked at them, but when the two men moved toward the car, staggering under the weight of the sofa, he stepped in to hold up the middle.

"That was the heaviest piece," the father said placidly. "We can git the rest ourselves."

"You gentlemen are doing a good job." Jonah looked at Eve and curled one hand into the shape of a telephone receiver, next to his mouth and ear. *I'll call you,* he mouthed.

Eve felt the movers looking at her with a mixture of curiosity and what seemed like pity. She nodded, looking at her feet. Of course, she was wearing her worst clothes again, for moving day. She had on her old black stretch pants and a sweatshirt that had belonged to Marcus. She was wearing her grass-stained sneakers, the heavy running kind that made her feet look like two toadstools. Jonah would never call her.

He called that same night as they were sitting down to dinner. Marcus answered. He handed the phone to Eve, eyebrow raised. "It's Jonah from the Chestnut Arms," he said. "I thought Gramma didn't live there anymore."

"She doesn't," Eve said. She took the cordless phone out into the hall.

"How about dinner this Saturday?" Jonah said. "You hungry yet?"

Saturday night, she thought with a pang, almost a feeling of doom. It seemed so . . . datelike. It had been years since she she'd gone on a date. Decades. Her last real date had probably been back in college, freshman or sophomore year.

"Are you busy Saturday night?" she asked Marcus, stepping back into the kitchen. She was half hoping he would say yes.

"No."

"Can you stay home with Noni?"

"No one needs to stay home with me!" Noni chimed in.

"I'm not a baby. When you were helping Grandma, I did all the grown-up things."

"Like what?" Marcus challenged.

"Well, I took showers, for one. I changed the sheets."

"Saturday's fine," Eve told Jonah. "Six o'clock sounds great." The words came out automatically. Inwardly, she was filled with doubt. She might as well have been going out on a date with one of the two moving men, that's how well she knew Jonah. What did they know about each other, really, when you came right down to it, except a handful of stories they had shared in the park, passing remarks on the dogs or weather or the leaves?

What's more, she thought, fighting down panic, she had nothing to wear. She peered into the cavernous chaos of her closet and quickly retreated. Half her clothing was still wrapped in plastic from the dry cleaner's.

Valerie, from the drama department, perked up when Eve told her about the closet. "Hey, I can fix that for you," she said. "Please. I love that kind of thing. It's what I do best."

Eve shook her head. She wasn't ready yet.

Valerie offered to go shopping with her instead. "Clothing is what I know," she said. It was true, she had run the costume shop for years. She practically lived there. What's more, Valerie was nonjudgmental. "A date? Cool," was all she said.

Val was tall and slightly punked, with her feather-short hair sometimes tinted pink, other times blue or peach. Her face, fine-featured and aristocratic, reminded Eve of photos she'd seen of the writer Virginia Woolf. To distract from that impression, Valerie wore three or four earrings in each ear and a small silver stud in one nostril. She had given up smoking for two months now, she told Eve, so she'd put on five or ten pounds. She'd taken up running and working out. Thin as she was, she was athletic-looking, so it looked as if an all-American had been kidnapped by a rock band.

Sometimes Valerie dated other young women, sometimes men. It had been a while since she'd been seeing anyone. "I think I'm giving up on romance," she said.

Val tried on shoes while Eve stumbled off to the dressing room, loaded down with an armload of clothes Valerie had picked out for her— all of it wrong, Eve thought, all of it costumey —flirty skirts, flared pants with multiple pockets, and cropped sweaters in vivid shades of orange or green.

When Eve emerged from the dressing room in one outfit, the salesgirl arched one eyebrow. She was standing next to Valerie, who was admiring a pair of forest-green loafers she'd slipped on.

"Cute. They really look sweet on you," the salesgirl said. "Look, they go with what you're wearing right now." Valerie wore a fawn-colored corduroy jacket, greenish-gray slacks. She looked like a wood sprite.

"They're so comfortable," Valerie said. "Eve, you should try them." They wore the same shoe size even though Val was three inches taller.

Eve dutifully tried on the green shoes. They looked all wrong on her feet.

"Hmm," the salesgirl said. "On you I think I prefer the black—or try these." She proffered a pair of sensible-looking black pumps. They looked like something her mother would wear.

"What do you think of this skirt?" Eve asked.

"I like it," Valerie said.

"Too short," said the salesgirl. Eve was beginning to actively dislike the young saleswoman. "Have you looked in the Career Department?

They have more options for older women. "

Valerie shrugged into a red velvet jacket with pleats at the back, on sale from the holidays.

"It's adorable!" the salesgirl exclaimed.

Eve went back to the dressing room and changed back into her own clothes. *Cute. Adorable.* These were words that no one would ever say about her again. Maybe if she lived to be one hundred, in a nursing home, with a big bow in her hair.

She looked into the three-way mirror. She looked even worse from behind. A person could lose a lot from a dressing-room diet.

Carry lunch into dressing room. Eat in front of three-way mirror. Take special care to look at the rear view. Your lunch will look better than you do.

Eve ended up buying a jar of expensive moisturizer at the cosmetics counter. Valerie bought the green shoes, and a pair of flats as pointy as cowboy boots, and the red velvet jacket. Back in the car she said, "Can you believe it? That salesgirl gave me her phone number." She eased out of her parking space. "She was cute, though."

When Saturday came around, Eve put on lip gloss, a smudge of eye shadow to highlight her brown eyes. She swept a brush over her cheeks to give her face some color. She considered perfume and decided against it. Noni and Marcus would smell it and think she had completely lost her mind.

She wasn't sure if they thought of this as a date or some other weird anomaly.

The Pre-Date Diet

Put the usual serving of food on everyone's plate, including your own. Contemplate borrowing something from your nine-year-old daughter's closet.

Now imagine sitting across a restaurant table from a stranger, trying to make conversation. To practice, try making similar conversation with your family. Introduce interesting and amusing subjects. If no one responds, try rapping on the table loudly with your fork. Do not repeat this while on actual date.

Jonah was wearing enough cologne for both of them. Marcus actually stepped back for a minute, shaking his head. Then, recovering as quickly as possible, he said, "Phew! It's cold—come in."

The night before, Eve hung a dress from her closet door, a black knee-length chiffon. Looking at it this afternoon, it seemed ridiculous, impossible. The dress even had a rhinestone buckle at the waist. She thought she had probably worn it twenty years earlier to the opera, with Ivan. Everything in her closet looked equally ludicrous or worn-out and exhausted. She finally settled for what she'd worn to work that day, a black turtleneck and a pair of corduroy slacks. Protective layering. A black zippered cardigan over that, and a scarf. At the last minute she took off the cardigan and scarf. She felt naked without them.

Marcus fetched her suede jacket from the closet, and Jonah helped her into it, the cloud of his cologne surrounding her. "I won't be back late," she said to Marcus.

"Take your time," her son said. "No rush."

"Have fun!" Noni chimed in. She fluttered nervously around Eve, patted her mother's hair in place, and kissed her good-bye three or four times.

Jonah kept up a steady stream of one-way conversation in the car. Eve felt like a boulder planted in her car seat. It was all she could do to nod or say uh-huh. Jonah didn't seem to notice. "I'm not here to discriminate," he said. "I'm here to participate." The words sounded rehearsed. Then he frowned, his gloved hands tightening on the wheel. "Gotta watch my back. One man, approach me in the park and ask for five dollars. An hour later he asks again. Informs me he's on coke, been coked out for two years. That's sad but I got to protect my people, which are the good people. I tell him if he need help I'd be glad to make a phone call on his behalf. He just pull his arm away and walked off.

"I didn't come here to be no statistic," Jonah said. "Do you want to visit the graveyard? Hell no! I'm here by the river. I'm listening to my mama. I *like* where I am."

The last time Eve had been on an actual date, she'd been eighteen or nineteen. She had no idea how to behave, if Jonah's monologues were normal behavior now. No clue. She'd met Ivan in college. "Introduction to Philosophy." He was her graduate teaching assistant till she changed sections. Ivan had spotted her in the hall and asked, half kidding, "Did I scare you away?" After that he sat next to her in the large lecture once a week. It had been as easy and natural as breathing.

Even Chuck was someone she'd seen around town—the friend of friends. At holiday parties, touch football games, he'd been in plain sight. Handsome enough to take your breath away, always with a clutch of people around him, laughing. He loved telling jokes and knew dozens of them. It was nothing like this, sitting in a strange car, with a strange man. Jonah parked the car downtown, by the HSBC bank and the dollar store.

"I got ambitions." He still had not told her where they were going. "Got to get me some money," he said.

Eve thought he meant it in a general way, till he steered her toward the bank, guiding her around melting puddles. They were in the midst of a February thaw. Everything had been dripping and melting for days. Strange things were revealed—an old boot in the street, a child's crayon drawing curled like a giant leaf.

Eve had noticed pink buds forming on her tulip magnolia tree, but it was too soon. Weeks of winter lay ahead, snow, but now, just for the moment, it felt like May was around the corner. There were other couples lined up in the cramped bank vestibule, waiting for a turn at the automatic teller. One of the couples was dark-skinned, with an impoverished, downcast look. The woman nudged the man and whispered something. Her feet, even in the damp weather, looked naked in open-toed shoes. She wore bright red toenail polish, chipping. The man said something to Jonah that Eve didn't quite catch, but she felt Jonah stiffen, and then he stepped in front of her as if to block her view.

"What you looking at?" the man said to Jonah.

"I ain't looking *at* you, I'm looking *through* you," Jonah answered.

His gold medal glittered on his shirt like something a knight would wear. A heavy gold bracelet encircled his wrist, and a large gold ring with a seal on it sat on the middle finger of one hand. The letter *J* looked almost like a dragon, a live thing, writhing in gold.

"Trash," Jonah murmured to Eve. He was standing very close to her. She could almost feel the words come out on her face. His breath smelled fruity. "Look at that man's shoes. They practically made out of cardboard." The shabby couple was at the ATM machine now, having some problem.

"Damn machine is broke," the man said to his girlfriend. She was leaning against the wall of the bank's foyer, one knee bent, foot flat against the wall. Her skirt was very short. She was looking at Jonah.

The man blinked at a piece of paper that slid out of the ATM. He shook the slip of paper in the air as if to dry it off. "Must be they forgot to put my money in again." The man punched some more numbers, jabbing at the buttons. "Lemme try once more."

The machine beeped and spat out a second slip of white paper. "Damn!" the man said in a high voice. "They done forgot to put my money in."

The girl said, "Leroy, try it again."

Jonah turned to Eve. "I know where my money is. Every dime."

"Lemme try one more time," the man told his girlfriend.

"Get off the line," Jonah ordered. He seemed to puff up to twice normal size. The others in the vestibule shrank away. "What kind of fool don't know where his own money is? Get out the line, I said!" He looked gigantic and menacing.

"Come on, Leroy," said the girl. "Less go. Leave this loser be. I got my own money out in the car."

"You ain't even got no car," Jonah said. "Not even a hoop-dee. I know. I seen you walk up. "

"I know something," the man said, but he stepped out of Jonah's reach. "I know the difference between black and white."

His girlfriend laughed shrilly. "You tole him."

"The only color I know is green," Jonah said, but his mouth was set in a tight line.

Jonah was silent at his turn at the bank machine, silent as they left the bank and as he steered her by her elbow up Court Street. Just outside the restaurant, a little Cuban place that looked more like a check-cashing store than someplace to eat, he stopped and looked squarely at her. "That all bother you?" he said.

"A little," she said. She felt it was useless to lie.

He rolled one shoulder as if easing out a cramp. "There's people all over this town call me a sucker, because I work for white folks. I got friends black, white, Chinese, Puerto Rican. The richest man in Binghamton is my friend." He looked at her intently. "I grew up in the

239

projects in Brooklyn, but I come up here, started working for Animal Control. Stood on the back of a truck. Got promoted to the Parks Department. I ain't going nowhere. I like it here."

"That's good," she said. "Now can we eat?"

His laughter seemed to break the spell. He opened the door, which jingled from a bell overhead. A woman sat by the restaurant cash register with a baby in her arms. Two children played behind her. She searched for two menus but only came up with one. The children recognized Jonah. He produced a stick of gum for each child.

"My great-grandmother was Cherokee Indian," he told Eve over their dinner of chicken and rice and beans. "She could tell you the weather. She could tell your fortune. My daddy's people came from Cuba." He nodded at his plate. "Maybe that's why I like this food." It tasted to Eve like something she might cook at home on a bad night. There was a scoop of rice, a scoop of red beans, a chicken breast, none of it very seasoned. There was an empty paper napkin dispenser on the table, a salt and pepper shaker, and a bottle of ketchup.

Jonah asked how Mrs. Dunrea was doing. "Do you know the Goldensohns had tea and pastries at her place every afternoon?"

"No," Eve said. Her mother never told her that kind of thing. Charlotte made it sound as if she did nothing, saw no one. She'd acted that way when she lived in Tennessee, too—as if she lived in a vacuum till Eve came around with the kids.

"Tea, cake, and cookies.—You need something?"

"Sugar for my tea," Eve said. "I'll get it." She got up and retrieved a round canister from the next table. When she noticed Jonah looking around for a napkin to wipe his hands on, she went and got those, too.

"You never let anybody get you nothing?" he asked.

She thought about that. Just at the very end of the meal, while he was eating some sort of custard dessert and she was drinking strong, sweet coffee out of a tiny china cup, he finally asked about Chuck.

"Look, you don't have to talk about it," he added, "if you don't want to."

"No," she said. "I don't mind." But then she didn't say anything else.

He sat there looking at her for a long time, and finally he smiled, a wry smile. "Guess maybe you'd rather not," he said.

Eve took a deep breath. "Here's something I've never told anyone," she said.

Jonah leaned forward, resting his elbows on the table.

Eve kept her gaze on the cross-hatching of the

place mats. She focused first on one slanting line, then another. "My first husband died in a car accident when he went out to buy something at the store. I had said, 'Gee, I wish I had some chocolate ice cream.' And Ivan said, 'You want me to go get some for you?' He was that kind of husband—so sweet, you know? I said, 'Well—if you're sure you don't mind.'" She finally let out the breath she'd been holding. "He was killed driving back from the store."

Jonah folded his arms across his chest, the heavy gold bracelet sliding down on his arm. He said, "That's a heavy cross to bear." He bowed his head, he said, "Lord, Lord," like a man in church. "I suppose it does you no good to tell anything about that."

She smiled ruefully. "Nope," she said.

"What you felt was deep down. I can see it all over your face. I never felt that way about a woman," he admitted. "I'll bet you don't eat no chocolate ice cream," he said.

"Can't stand it—anyway, maybe that's why I never let my kids do anything for me. If someone offers, I say, 'You stay where you are, I'll take care of it.' I wish to God I'd gotten my own damn ice cream."

She had told no one about this—not the grief counselor, not even her own mother. It had been years since she talked at all about Ivan's death. Around town she still sometimes saw the name-

242

less police officer who had come to give her the bad news. His melancholy Irish face, like a bulldog's, in a way almost handsome. His hair had gone from black to gray. He'd said what he had to say so quickly, delivered the devastating news in an instant. She would always be grateful to him for that—the way you feel about a childhood friend with whom you once shared a secret no one else on earth still knew or cared about.

"It's strange," Jonah said. "Strange how the mind will fix things in place."

"I certainly am a delightful date," Eve said.

"Date ain't over," Jonah answered.

After they finished their meal, Jonah asked if she'd like to go out for drinks. She said yes, though she was feeling tired, the long week catching up with her, the strain of trying to do and say the right things. The bar they went into was noisy and crowded and smelled like beer and peanuts, which sat in plastic bowls at every table. You were supposed to toss the shells onto the floor, but Eve couldn't bring herself to add to the mess. She piled her shells in a pyramid beside her drink. It was too loud to make conversation. Jonah nodded and smiled and shouted her name to the customers he knew. He knew a lot of them. All she could do was call, "Nice to meet you!" and then cup her hand over her ear.

She and Jonah sat at a table with three chairs,

and at some point someone asked to borrow the third chair and pulled it up to an already crowded table of six or seven college boys. Without the third chair their table seemed deserted.

Finally Jonah shouted, "You ready to go?" and they escaped into the cool air. It was a relief to leave the noise, the smell of beer. "You want to come back to my place?" he said.

This of course was where the date had been leading all along. Yes or no. At some level she had known that. Yet she felt unprepared.

"You know what?" he said. "You should look at my coin collection." He held up one hand, palm out. "I know it sounds like some kind of line. But I been collecting now five, six years. I think you would be interested to see it. I got some ancient coins."

Now that they were back in his big, warm car, she felt safe, glad to be out in the world, gliding over the little bridge that went across the river, looking at the white lights strung along the arches.

"You ever go to the jazz on the river?" Jonah asked her. "They do it every month."

Lev always went, she knew. But she'd never gone.

"Maybe we could go sometime," Jonah said.

Up in his apartment, he brought two large albums into the living room and set them down on the coffee table in front of the sofa. He opened the first.

"These are commemorative quarters," he said. "I got all the states. In fact, doubles of all the states." He flipped through a few heavy pages. "Then I got some silver quarters—these are older, see?—and silver dimes. All pure silver. There was one man at the Treasury proposed to make coins out of plastic." He shook his head in pure disgust.

Next came pages of pennies, going back to 1910. Some had sheaves of wheat. Some had Indian heads. "I like the heads the best," Jonah said. "I buy a lot on eBay. You never know what you find. One time I was bidding on an Indian head penny, I ended up with a pair of leather boots from the same seller. Brand new, still in the box."

He opened the second album, holding coins dating back to the 1800s. There were shillings and half-crowns and British pence—coins from the Mughal Empire and British India, and Canadian pennies, American gold coins—"very valuable," he told her—and Mexican silver dollars. "I like history," he said. "I like old things. Always have."

That must be why he liked her, Eve thought.

Abruptly, she asked, "How old are you?" She had no idea. Jonah could have been in his late thirties. He could have been fifty.

"I'm forty-two," he said, "and I won't ask you. Don't care anyway." He held the book gently, like someone opening a baby's photo album, and leaned back. "Take a look," he said. "I'll be right back."

He returned with a third album, heavier, more ornate, filled with ancient coins under protective plastic. This album held Spanish gold coins from shipwrecks, English doubloons, Greek Ionian coins. There was a gold Roman coin from the era of Tiberius, with a portrait of the emperor, a female figure seated to his left. Jonah pointed to each with one broad fingertip.

"Wasn't Tiberius a tyrant?" she asked.

He turned his head to glance at her. His attention was still fixed on the coins. "None of them emperors were what you call good guys," he said shortly. "Here's one from Nero. Here's Honorius from about 400 A.D., got his foot on someone's head." He flipped back a few pages. There were Byzantine coins, medieval coins, Islamic gold coins. Each was neatly labeled and covered in its plastic shield. On some you could see people kneeling or fighting. One showed an angel slaying a tiny gold dragon.

"Now wait," he said, "this is the prize of the collection. I got this from a dealer in New York. Drove all the way down to get it and all the way back and I was sweating in my car. Keep this book locked in a safe in my bedroom. Don't *nobody* mess with it."

The last page of the book was devoted to a

single, small gold coin. It looked like a round brooch, in a not quite even circle, with raised figures on it. A man and woman were looking at one another. The features were blurred, yet there was tenderness in their gaze.

"That's from 350 A.D. Think about that," Jonah said. "Gupta dynasty. And wait." He slid the coin out from its holder and flipped it over. The gold shone against his dark skin. On the reverse side sat another female figure, cross-legged. "That's the goddess Ambika, sitting on a lion," he said. "If I have a little baby girl, I want to name her Ambika."

"Well, there won't be two in any of her classes," Eve said.

Jonah closed the last coin album. He studied her, his head tilted. "You are a fine-looking woman."

She felt embarrassed and frightened. At the back of her mind a battle had been raging all night. What was she doing here? She had weighed each sentence he'd uttered in some back part of her brain, to see how it tipped the scales. He was a good-looking man, he made her laugh. Her breath quickened around him. He was also an almost complete stranger.

After spending an evening with him, he seemed no less strange to her—if anything, more so. There was a chasm between them. All her life she had been leaping into the arms of some stranger, she thought. She should stand on her own two feet for once, make a sane decision and walk away. But there was the nagging question of prejudice. She hadn't ever had close friends who were black.

There was an African American dancer in her English class in college and they'd done a project together on King Lear. He decided to do an interpretive dance instead of a paper. At the last minute, his eyes wide with fright, he approached her and said, "I don't even know what this play is about. Help me!"

So she told him the king went mad, lots of people died, there was a big storm. He went out and threw himself around the room, leaping, and throwing himself in the air, landing in a heap at the end. He was a wonderful dancer. She admired his bravado. In the end he'd gotten the highest mark in the class.

Apart from Mia, she wasn't really close to anyone who wasn't white. Did that mean she was a bigot? She was not blind to the color of people's skin; she noticed and thought about it. She felt a separation between herself and people who were black, or Hispanic or Asian, as if they were communicating not only across cultures, but across some secret wordless wide divide. Perhaps only small children, she thought, were completely color blind.

When Marcus was in first grade his best friend

was a round-headed black boy named James, nicknamed Doobie. At an ice-skating fund-raiser, Marcus and Doobie wobbled off onto the ice holding hands. By fourth or fifth grade James moved to a different part of town. In middle school they didn't even know each other's names. By high school Marcus no longer remembered anything about him. Only the athletes mingled regardless of race, culture, money. Noni had every kind of friend on the soccer term. They still played games together, like small children; maybe that was the secret.

None of this was helping. Jonah was looking at her, his eyes the darkest brown she had ever seen, large and liquid. He turned sideways on the sofa and took her hand in both of his. She felt her body straining from the effort of appearing neither to lean forward nor to pull away.

"The time we kissed, I was feeling you," he said. "I'm not sure I'm feeling you now."

She wondered, If this man were not black, would she even have this moment of hesitation? It was not that she didn't want to sleep with Jonah because he was black—just the opposite. She was afraid *not* to sleep with him because he was black. She didn't want to hurt his feelings. She needed to prove it didn't matter. Which seemed like an extraordinarily stupid way to begin anything. She was ignoring her own instincts, common sense. They were different, not just in color, but in the important things. He wanted to have his own children. He cared so much about money. He slept around—he'd told her as much in the park, half confessing it, half bragging. His special weakness was college girls, who, it always turned out, were hitting him up for tuition and books and spending money.

This whole night could lead only to the bedroom and no place else. How much more racist could it get? She had never slept around just for the sake of sleeping around. Never. She wasn't sure she'd ever even slept with anyone she would not have married.

She had heard that people in accidents felt their whole lives play out in slow motion the instant the car spun around out of control: a tree suddenly zoomed up, leaf by leaf, vein by vein, each shape visible on every single branch. She felt the same way as Jonah turned his body to hers.

"I like you a lot, Jonah," she said.

He dropped her hand. "Uh-oh," he said.

"I'm still married. I have two kids. I'm older than you are. I'm tired—I'm sorry. I really do like you, but I think this would ruin everything."

"Okay," he said, raising one hand. He seemed more amused than upset. "I get the idea."

"You're not mad?"

"Hey," he said. "It don't always end up in bed." He had never seemed as desirable as he did that instant, when she could see him clearly; self-possessed and assured, smelling like lemons and cinnamon. His gold chain gleamed against his neck. She second-guessed herself, thought wildly, for one instant, Wait!—wait, maybe I'm making a terrible mistake. Then she steadied herself. Maybe she was making a little progress.

"So," he said, like someone closing the door on something, with a mixture of regret and relief. Had she been so stupid as to think he had no doubts himself?

"Friends?" he asked.

"Friends," she said.

Chapter 20

The Dance

Her mother said almost nothing about her life at Emerald Gardens. Eve wasn't sure if that was a good or a bad thing. "It's an adjustment," was all Charlotte would say.

They installed a safety chair in her bathtub. One of the aides helped her mother wash her hair once a week. She used a walker now, a deep shiny red like Dorothy's ruby slippers in *The Wizard of Oz*, with a lift-up black vinyl seat for storage. Even folded, the contraption barely fit into the back of Eve's car; she struggled each time they went out, sweating over the trunk of the car, the walker half folded like some unsolvable puzzle. "You certainly didn't miss your calling," Charlotte remarked from the front seat. "You would have made a terrible nurse."

Mrs. Dunrea made excuses not to go out. She was gathering in, closing down. She cancelled appointments at the last minute. She refused to go anywhere without the ruby-red walker, even the dining room. Shuffling along behind it, she appeared to have aged by ten years.

"Do you really need it?" Eve asked. She could feel herself whining.

"I feel more secure with the walker," Charlotte said. "I can get around my room with just my cane." She could have gotten around that tiny room by leaning from one piece of furniture to the next, but Eve didn't say that. If her mother felt the room was cramped or small, she didn't complain. Eve bought her a glamorous-looking black cane, lacquered and painted with flowers. She hoped to lure her mother into using it, but the cane stayed in a brass holder.

Mrs. Dunrea was stoic by nature and long habit. Complaints slipped past her lips like confessions that had been tricked out of her. She wasn't happy, but why should she be? "Most people aren't happy," she said. The staff didn't like it at Emerald Gardens any better than she did. They were always leaving. That meant new staff always coming in. One night the new aide could not locate any of her medications. Nobody liked the food.

"I live on Cheerios," she said.

Eve went out and brought her mother two large sacks of food—containers of yogurt she could keep in the fridge in her wing of the building, fresh fruit, breakfast bars and instant grits, mixed nuts, whole wheat pretzels and cheese.

Her mother rummaged through the bags. "Health food," Mrs. Dunrea said disapprovingly. Then, still poking through the bags, "Didn't you bring me any chocolate? I've had such a craving for a nice big Hershey bar with almonds."

Her mother was becoming capricious. She feuded with one woman who wouldn't give up her chair in the activity room. She'd ask for peanut butter cookies, then as soon as Eve brought them say, "No, I didn't mean these, I meant the other ones. With the figs."

"Fig Newtons."

"It's being around all these old people," she said. "My brain is starting to atrophy. All they do is eat. That's why they're so fat." She said this while sitting at the dining room table with two large women, her table companions. Neither big woman looked offended. Eve had stopped by on her lunch hour. She was having coffee, black. She gave her mother a warning look.

"They don't mind," Charlotte said. "It's the truth."

Her mother was also putting on weight. Her face looked softer, fleshier. She complained that her clothes had shrunk, they weren't laundering them properly. Eve and her mother were trading places—Charlotte had always been the thin one, Eve the soft one. Now it was the other way around. Eve wrapped her new angularity in layers of winter clothes. She thought her mother needed physical therapy, but Charlotte refused.

Eve couldn't even get the doctors to back her up. "Your mother's getting on in years," her mother's new G.P. said. He was a man with bushy eyebrows and black hair. He'd once been Ivan's doctor. They had once all been young together.

"But her hip still hurts," Eve insisted. Her mother sat perched on the examination table, lips compressed, refusing to say a word. "Her back aches, she says."

"Try a new mattress," the doctor said. "A new pillow might help." He turned toward Mrs. Dunrea. "Do you snore?"

"There's no one to complain about it if I do," she said.

"Let your mother be," he said. "She's doing reasonably well. She's coming along."

"It's a period of adjustment," her mother said.

Back in the car, Charlotte told Eve about a searing pain in the back of her neck, a numb sensation in her feet, a whole new litany of disorders.

"Don't tell *me* about it!" Eve said. "Tell the doctors."

She dragged her mother to more doctors in three months than she'd seen in a lifetime. They even visited a local Chinese doctor specializing in acupuncture. The acupuncturist was no taller than her mother. There were bonsai trees in his office—but weren't bonsai Japanese? Eve thought. Not Chinese. He offered them a cup of white tea, much better than green tea, he explained.

"The healing has to happen here," he said, touching his own hip bone, "and move outward. The bone is hollow tube. Made up of many more hollow tubes." His fingers opened like petals.

"I'm deathly afraid of needles," her mother said.

"Drink the tea," the man said. "Eat soy, like the tofu. This will help you to remain calm."

"Calm is good," her mother said.

After that visit her mother had said, "No more doctors. I'm an old woman. Stop expecting me to get younger."

"I don't," Eve said. But she realized that in fact she did.

Her mother generally avoided the atrium at Emerald Gardens. The floor there was made of concrete, the air was moist.

It was late February. A watery green light came through the skylight, filtered through the leaves of the plants. An enormous Christmas cactus sat on the floor in full pink bloom. Piano music tinkled down the hall, playing show tunes from the thirties and forties. It sounded unusually energetic, like a real concert.

"Hey," Marcus said. "Want to go?" He was picking things up and turning them over, wandering up and down the halls.

"And making everyone nervous," Mrs. Dunrea claimed.

"It's only Clem," she said. "Clemente Driscoll. He was a famous pianist in his day," she added with a note of pride. "He played all over the world, poor man. Now he lives here. He never goes anywhere."

Eve asked, "Doesn't he have any family?"

"I think a nephew," Mrs. Dunrea said. "He never married. I'm sure he had plenty of opportunities. He's a very handsome man. Tall. Blue-eyed. Distinguished."

Noni was already on her feet. "I want to see this guy," she said.

"Wait!" Mrs. Dunrea called. "—He's very shy."

But Noni was already trotting down the hall.

256

Eve and Marcus followed her. Mrs. Dunrea brought up the rear with her ruby walker. A tall, thin man sat stooped at the piano. His fingers were incredibly long. They flew over the keys. He played, in fact, beautifully.

The man turned his head sideways an instant, taking in their presence, but focused his concentration again on the piano. When that song ended, Eve asked, "Do you know any Gershwin?"

Her mother glowered, but the man nodded and said, "Gershwin, he was the king," and eased right into "Rhapsody in Blue." After that he played "Summertime." It no longer felt like they were sitting in an old age home. They applauded. The old man turned his head sideways again and nodded. He played "Someone to Watch Over Me," singing the words softly this time, and toward the end Mrs. Dunrea joined in. In her day, she'd had a lovely voice. Singing, she seemed to cast off some of the grimness, the weight of years.

When the last song was over, the man pushed back the piano bench and stood to face them. He was at least six-foot-three. His eyes were a snapping blue. He wore a V-neck sweater, cashmere, a hole in one sleeve, the bottom hem unraveling. "And who are these lovely young people?" he asked, bending his head to Noni and Marcus. "Did you enjoy the music?"

They nodded, suddenly speechless and shy. The

man took their hands in turn and gravely shook them. He seemed accustomed to being approached by admiring strangers. He listened carefully to Mrs. Dunrea's introductions, repeating each name as he heard it.

"You remind me of one of my best friends," he told Eve. "A woman named Katherine. Brilliant violinist." He looked as if he expected her to produce an instrument from thin air.

"I just listen," Eve said.

"Well, we need good listeners," he said genially. "And who might this be?" He was peering now at Mrs. Dunrea.

She frowned, deflating visibly. "I'm Charlotte Dunrea," she said. "I live here."

"I'm sorry," the man said. He pressed the heel of one hand to his forehead. "My memory isn't what it used to be. My mind. I can barely play anymore."

"You were awesome!" Noni said.

"Hardly," the man said. "But I love music. That's the thing." He looked at Mrs. Dunrea again. "I do apologize," he said. "Charlotte is such a lovely name. And it suits you. I can remember that."

Back in the room, Noni said, "That old man was so flirting with you. Did you see that?"

"Nonsense," Mrs. Dunrea said. Her color was high. She patted her hair in place, a gesture Eve had not seen for years. "I feel sorry for him," she added. "He has no one." She seemed to consider this. "I should be more friendly," she said.

The next time Mia came over, a portfolio of drawings for her new class under her arm, she told Eve, "I went visit your mother but she was out with some man, they say. To a movie."

"What do you mean, 'out'?"

"Yeah, that's what they say. Out."

"How is that possible?" Eve asked.

But Noni, who was poking around in the refrigerator while this conversation took place, stood upright, excited. "Grandma went on a date!" she said. "I bet it's the piano player. How cool is that?"

"How *weird* is that?" Marcus called.

Noni sang, "Grandma's got a boyfriend! Grandma's got a boyfriend!"

"How could they have gone out?" Eve said. "I'm sure that man doesn't drive."

"Maybe he does," Noni said.

"What did she do with the walker? How did they get it out of the car?"

"Did I say a wrong thing?" Mia asked, her brow wrinkled.

The next day on the phone, Mrs. Dunrea told Eve, "It was *not* a date. I invited the poor man out to a movie. We took a taxi, and the driver was extremely helpful. He certainly didn't struggle over the walker the way you do."

259

"Who paid?" Eve said.

There was the slightest pause. "I did," Mrs. Dunrea said. "I don't think Clemente has any spending money. Which is peculiar, because he earned enough in his day. He has a lawyer who takes care of everything."

The high school Valentine's Day dance had been snowed out by a mid-February snowstorm, so it was rescheduled toward the end of the month. For once in his life Marcus actually cared. He had circled the day twice on the calendar. Eve and Noni helped him pick a corsage for Astrid. It was made of two bloodred sweetheart roses amidst a spray of baby's breath. Marcus stood in the florist's shop and held it in his hand like a bird's nest. "I'll never know how to pin this on," he said.

"You can practice," Eve said. "Practice on Noni."

"Just give it to her and let her figure it out," Noni, the practical one, suggested. "I don't want to try on your stinky old corsage anyway." But when Eve bought Noni her own red rose, Noni rushed to put it in water as soon as they got inside the house.

For the dance, Marcus put on new jeans, a clean shirt—so white it looked fluorescent—and a flowered tie. He pushed his steel-rimmed spectacles up the bridge of his nose and peered into the mirror by the front door. Astrid was picking him up. Eve was praying it would not snow. The weather station had been threatening a blizzard for days. Marcus stood still while she took his photograph, first alone, then with Noni beside him, holding Astrid's corsage gingerly up to her shoulder. When Astrid came to the door, they went through the same thing all over again.

"I wish *I* could go to a dance," Noni said wistfully. Eve had lately caught her daughter posing in front of the full-length mirror in her room, one hip cocked like a model.

Eve watched Marcus climb into Astrid's car, and then watched the car slowly back down the driveway. "Are you just going to stand there by the door all night?" Noni asked her.

"Of course not," Eve said. But she left the drapes open while she and Noni played Boggle. The February night was dark and still, but they were predicting snow, and this way she could keep an eye on the weather without appearing anxious. She barely had time to worry. Marcus and Astrid were back before ten o'clock, happy and as breathless as if they'd run all the way home.

"The dance was a total bust," Marcus said. "Nobody showed up."

"*Nobody?*" Noni said. "You two had the dance floor all to yourselves?"

Eve knew that Noni was fascinated by everything that had to do with high school. She still thought of it as an infinitely exotic and alluring place. This would no doubt change by the time she reached middle school. By the time she actually hit high school, she'd be looking forward to college.

"Nearly nobody," Astrid said. "Is it all right that we came here?"

"It's wonderful!" Eve said, trying not to show her relief. "Would you like some hot cocoa? Cookies? Would you like to play Boggle with us?"

"Mom," Marcus said. "Please. We're going downstairs to play video games."

"Can I—" but Noni caught Eve shaking her head. "Can I offer you some Cokes?" she finished gamely.

"That would be very nice," Astrid said. "Also they had very strange refreshments there."

"Like what kind?" Noni asked. She helped Astrid out of her long wool coat.

Under it, Astrid was wearing a red velvet dress, with a black satin ribbon tied around the bodice. The corsage was pinned to the black ribbon. Astrid touched it with one finger, checking to be sure it was safe.

"God-awful punch," Marcus said. "Some kind of weird lemon-lime stuff. Tasted like Gatorade. You would have liked it, Nonnikin." That was the nickname he used when he was in a good mood.

Noni hung Astrid's coat in the closet. She went to the kitchen for the Cokes, and asked if they preferred to drink it out of glasses or straight out of the bottles.

"Bottle," Marcus and Astrid said at the same instant, then looked at each other and smiled, pleased.

Noni handed them the Cokes, taking as long as she could. She gave them each napkins. Eve watched her daughter hover. She was trying to breathe in the air of what she imagined to be their great sophistication and glamour as long as she possibly could.

When Marcus and Astrid had gone downstairs, she trotted back to the sofa and climbed under the cotton throw. "Must be nice," she said, "to be all grown up like that."

"I wouldn't know," Eve said.

Chapter 21

Corvette

Devin MacKenzie called close to midnight looking for Marcus. Apparently he had left the dance early as well. "Total dud," Devin told Eve. "Plus some jerk tried to kick me out just because technically I'm not in school anymore."

Marcus picked up the phone down in the basement. A few minutes later he and Astrid came upstairs. Eve wasn't sure, but it seemed as if they'd been arguing. Marcus looked unhappy, his jaw set in a stubborn line that reminded her of Ivan dealing with an unsolvable puzzle.

"Mom," he pleaded. "Dev's father just got a new Corvette. He's letting Dev take it out for a test drive, and then we're all supposed to go out to Denny's."

"No way," Eve said. She didn't hesitate. It had begun snowing an hour earlier. The living room blinds were still open, and she had seen the snow lit up and whirling against the streetlight on the corner. She was relieved that Marcus was already safe inside.

"But if we'd stayed at the dance I'd still be out," Marcus argued. "And I've never even been inside a Corvette before."

"No," Eve said. "It's new, he doesn't know how to handle it yet, in bad weather no less. And it's late."

"You see?" Astrid said. "Sensible."

"It is not sensible," Marcus said. "Sensible is not the same as stuffy."

"You are calling me this?" Astrid said stiffly.

"Mom," Marcus said, ignoring her. "All the other kids are going."

"This is not true," Astrid said. "I am not going." She parked her hands on her hips, heedless now of crushing the corsage. "Absolutely not."

"All the normal kids," Marcus said.

"You are not going," Eve said quietly. "And you aren't being very polite to Astrid."

"This is ridiculous!" Marcus said. "You treat me like a baby. I should have just gone out and stayed out."

"I am going home," Astrid said. She had snatched the long wool coat out of the closet and was headed toward the front door. "And maybe I will go in this Corvette after all, with my real friends."

"Oh great!" Marcus said. "That's just great—go!" He yanked open the front door. Eve had never seen him behave like this, not in all the years she'd raised him. Not even when he was two years old.

"I am going," Astrid said with dignity. "Thank you for the sodas. "

Marcus slammed the door behind her, then turned on Eve in fury. "I can't believe you!" he shouted. "I'm going! I don't give a damn what you say."

"You're not," Eve said.

Marcus seemed near tears. "Why can't I go? Give me one reason."

"Well, for one thing," she said. "You can't drive yet. So you have no way to get there."

He looked at her an instant, stricken. "My life sucks!" He thundered up the stairs and slammed the door.

Noni looked bewildered. "What happened?" she asked. Then she added, "Mom, what's a Corvette?"

"It's a car. A very fancy, fast car."

"You mean it just goes fast?—What's the big deal?" When Eve didn't answer right away, Noni said, sounding disappointed, "A car. I thought maybe it was a horse or something cool like that."

Marcus wouldn't answer when Eve knocked, and he didn't respond even when Noni tried talking to him reasonably through the closed door.

His lights were out. Maybe he was asleep, she thought. The room radiated quiet. So when the phone shrilled at two-thirty in the morning, Eve's first waking realization was that Marcus had been out of the house all that time. How and when had he snuck out? Now he was calling for her to pick him up, in the middle of the night.

But she was still asleep when she thought this. She was asleep even when she realized someone else had answered the phone, a voice down the hall. Then there was a panicked confusion of running footsteps. Suddenly, Marcus was standing in the doorway of her bedroom, backlit by the light in the hall, stock-still as a ghost, looking at her, his mouth opening and closing, not saying anything. He was still holding the cordless phone in his hand but not talking to anyone. His shoulders were shaking with laughter.

No, she realized. It took a few seconds to register. Not laughter. A sob escaped. He bent forward.

Her hand went automatically to reach for someone in the bed beside her, to clutch at someone else, a fellow adult. Her hand fell on the cool empty bedsheet.

"Marcus?" she said. "What's wrong?"

He was still wearing the white dress shirt he'd worn to the dance. It glowed in the dark room.

"They're gone," he said. "Devin and Ryan. They crashed the Corvette. They were going one hundred and twenty. The car hit the guardrail and flipped. One of Dev's sisters is in the hospital."

"Gone?" she said.

"They're dead. Both dead. What do you think I mean?"

"Oh Marcus," Eve said, sitting up straight. "Are you sure?"

"Of course I'm sure!" he said. "They rolled the car, Mom! . . . Oh, Mom," he cried. "I should have been there to stop them. I was supposed to be there!"

She threw back the covers and hurried to her son. The floorboards were freezing underfoot. He was taller than she was, but she rocked him back and forth in her arms. He felt like a tree bent by a storm.

"I could have stopped him," Marcus wept. "I could have tried. I should have been there with them!"

Eve felt chilled, her teeth chattering as if she'd been standing on a steep precipice and someone pushed her just a few inches back from the edge. But someone else had plunged below. Devin's face came into her mind, freckled and grinning, playing marbles on their dining room floor. She thought of Ryan in his puffy red and white varsity jacket. "Did Astrid—"

"Astrid stayed home," he said. "She was too mad to go anywhere. That was her on the phone."

The two funerals took place the following Friday. Ryan's was at noon, at a Baptist church downtown. Devin's was at the west side Catholic church later that same afternoon. Ryan's was a closed casket funeral. Devin's was not.

Marcus insisted on going to the viewing the morning of Devin's funeral. "I want to say goodbye to him."

Eve had so many answers to that, none of them good, none comforting. "I'm not sure you should," she said. "A viewing. That might be harder than you think."

Marcus said, "We're doing this for Dev's family. We don't want them to feel like we're just—abandoning him."

Devin's mother had asked Marcus to be a pallbearer. He was honored, Eve could tell, and also miserable and ashamed. He wore his dark suit with a dark tie. He did not check his look on his way out of the house—in fact he had covered all of the mirrors, according to Jewish custom, draping them with tablecloths and napkins, even his old sweaters. You could see a slice of reflection between the hanging sleeves of the sweaters. Marcus must have remembered her doing that, she thought, after Ivan was killed. He was grasping at straws. He had woken her in the middle of the night, twice, to ask if she believed there was really a Heaven. Now he asked her a third time.

"Yes," Eve said, unsure whether she was lying. "How can there not be, when we want it so badly?"

"That's what I think!" Marcus said, pathetically eager to agree. He had always believed in God, even as a child. She wasn't sure why, but she was glad that he did. People who had faith lived happier lives.

"But still. I don't get any of this." He held his head in his hands, staring down, his elbows resting on his knees.

"Marcus, try to eat something," she said. "You haven't eaten in days."

He shook his head, still looking at the floor. "Not hungry." He kept going over and over the accident. He studied the pictures in the newspaper, he looked at the angles, disputing them.

"This should have been me," he said, looking at the two obituaries in the paper with something, Eve thought, almost like envy, like hunger. "I should have been right there." He jabbed his finger at the newsprint.

"No you shouldn't!" Noni snapped.

"Why not?" Marcus asked. It was a real question. He was looking at Noni hopefully.

"Because you're not dead," Noni said. "You're here with us."

The church was packed for Ryan's funeral. Eve had expected as much. She was led upstairs with the others, to the balcony, which was overflowing. People sat in the pews or stood in the aisles, patiently making room, standing up when someone elderly came in. They were all polite today. The high school kids filled the pews behind the families, a sea of black and navy blue clothing. She made out Marcus's gold hair, his bent neck looking fragile. Astrid sat beside him. They were holding hands.

A football player read the poem "To an Athlete, Dying Young," his voice shaking. The minister gave a sermon about Christ. Only at the end did he say a few words about Ryan. He never mentioned the accident, but instead referred to Ryan's "untimely death." Two of Ryan's little sisters sang his favorite hymn,

"Amazing Grace," but they broke down before they got through the first verse, so the minister signaled the organist, and everyone stood and joined in the singing. Eve could hear Marcus's voice, low and booming—Ivan's voice, back from the dead.

Devin MacKenzie's father had grown up in town. He'd been a star athlete in his day, just like Devin. Everyone within fifty miles of Binghamton knew someone in the MacKenzie family. The Catholic church was immense, made of gray stone like a castle, and there was no way to even get near the front door. An enormous crowd stood outside, in the watery March sunshine. No one complained. Two men came out of the church and set up a TV stand, with a TV monitor on top, and explained that someone inside would be filming the funeral for the people outside. They apologized for the delay. Eve stepped away from the monitor to make room for other people who crowded around, some of them already crying.

After a while she could hear rock music inside the church. She heard voices, less clearly. The voices went on for a long while. Then the rock music blared again, then a church organ, and then people came spilling out of the church. The crowd parted.

Twelve pallbearers shuffled out carrying the coffin, made of dark wood. First came Devin's father, looking like a sagging version of Dev, his handsome jaw slack, his eyes swimming. There were three men who looked like they must be uncles—that thatch of bright hair again, the freckles—and several athletic-looking boys, and Devin's two sisters, including Margaret, who had been in the backseat during the accident, her right arm in a sling. She held up the coffin awkwardly with her good hand stuck straight in the air. She kept stumbling; it looked like any minute she would fall. Marcus was just behind her, almost as pale as the snow that clung to the church roof. He stopped when Margaret stopped. He reached forward to touch her shoulder, but she shook him off and screamed "No!" in a high, clear, hysterical voice. The twelve stopped walking.

Lee MacKenzie came forward and dragged her daughter out from under the coffin. She pushed another football player in her place and said to Marcus, "Keep going."

"It was totally and utterly horrible," Marcus said at dinner. He stared at the lamb chops like foreign objects that had landed there by mistake. Noni poked at her baked potato but did not eat.

"Funerals are hard," Eve said, "especially when it's someone so young."

"I mean the viewing," Marcus said. "There

272

wasn't enough pieces left of Devin after the accident to, you know, put together, so they made—a thing. With hair. It was, like . . . a horrible Devin doll. They put a name tag underneath it so you'd know, that's how bad it was."

"People do strange things to comfort themselves," Eve said. "Maybe they needed some image of him, at least."

"Mrs. MacKenzie was so damn pissed," Marcus said. "She pointed across the room and said, 'What *is* that thing?' She wouldn't go near it. She kept apologizing. She told me, 'You don't have to go over there, Marcus. You can stand right here by me.' "

"That's so sad," Noni said. She had put down her fork.

"Her boyfriend didn't even come to the funeral. He must be a real jerk." Marcus poked his fork into one of the lamb chops and lifted it in the air. He floated it around like an airplane, then set it back down, untouched. "I think I'm going to become vegetarian."

Eve wasn't sure who came up with the idea, it seemed to spring out of nowhere. The high school kids decided to hold their own memorial service in Rec Park. Once it got started, word spread quickly. Marcus was on his cell phone every minute, making arrangements. Astrid came over to help. She used her phone while Marcus used his. They bought boxes of white candles to hand out to everyone.

Someone had a boom box so there would be music. Kids were bringing flowers and balloons. Noni wanted to bring something, too. She drew a picture of horses, one blue and one gold. She wrote Ryan's name on the mane of the blue horse, Devin's on the gold.

Eve was afraid Marcus might discourage her, but he said, "That's great, Noni," and Astrid tucked a roll of Scotch tape in her coat pocket, promising she'd put it up.

"Can I go to the park?" Noni asked Eve. "It won't be like a real funeral or anything."

"I suppose so," Eve said. She didn't see how she could say no.

She and Noni walked down together among others headed the same way, friends and neighbors. It was strange to see a crowd swelling and gathering in the park, normally deserted this time of year; strange to be there so late, without the dogs.

Because the two boys had been athletes, high school kids poured in from all over. Everyone had seen them play, or played against them, or heard of someone who had known them. Many brought handmade cards. Some came clutching flowers, heaped on the concrete gazebo with the plaque in the middle of it dedicated to Rod Serling, a native son. The bronze plaque read,

WALKING DISTANCE, named for an episode on the *Twilight Zone.* Silver mylar balloons had been tied with ribbons to the concrete pillars of the gazebo, and they fluttered in the wind, wearing smiley faces or hearts.

Noni found her soccer friends in the crowd. After a while she came back to Eve's side and took her hand again, holding it tightly in her own small, gloved hand. Eve stood shoulder-to-shoulder with fellow parents. There was some comfort in seeing so many familiar faces.

A tall man hung at the edge of the crowd, a stranger, watching. His hair was long and shaggy. His eyes were hooded. Eve pulled Noni closer. The man seemed a dark apparition. He wore a long olive-green coat, the kind you'd find at an Army-Navy store. It was as if Death itself had come to watch. He leaned with one arm slung around a lamp pole, never taking his eyes from the youngsters gathering in ever-increasing numbers.

Finally, Eve saw Jonah approach the man. He tapped him on the shoulder and the man swung around quick as a snake, ready to strike. Jonah caught the swinging arm and set it back in place, like a doll's, then escorted him out of the park. She saw the dark figure go staggering in the direction of downtown and afterward did not know if what she'd seen was real. The man was gone. Jonah had also vanished. She looked at her watch; it was ten o'clock, and there was a stir-ring in the crowd as if something were finally about to happen.

The teenagers shuffled to the middle of the park. Nobody appeared to be in charge of any-thing, they moved together in a silent huddle. A wind was blowing, and it kept putting their candles out. A few of the boys with lighters went from candle to candle like bees among flowers. Finally they stood in an uneven circle, cupping their hands around the flames. Their faces glim-mered, half hidden in winter scarves and hats and hoods. The teenagers shifted from foot to foot. They just stood holding the candles, look-ing at one another for help. They appeared embarrassed. A few began sidling away, out of sight. The event had stalled and seemed in danger of ending right then.

Marcus half circled his head left and right, a nervous gesture he'd inherited from his father. "I'd like to tell a story," he said in a clear voice. "About Dev and Ryan."

Everyone looked up at him expectantly. Even Eve. It was how she always felt when Marcus stepped to the edge of the diving board at the Rec Park pool, vulnerable in his baggy swim trunks.

"I was a very slow runner as a kid," he said. "Still am. Please don't make me prove it." The crowd laughed, out of nerves. "But Devin, and

Ryan, they were fast. Maybe too fast," he said. "But still, they were gifted. And so, when I played softball at school, I'd swing and miss." Marcus swung at the air. "Every turn, every time.—Finally, Ryan, he was pitching, and he came so close to me, he practically handed me the ball. So I hit it. Ryan let it fly right past him. And Dev—"

Marcus's voice flickered for a second. He rolled his head again, right and left. "Dev was on first and he saw me coming, real slow. So when I got to first base, he picked me up and tucked me under his arm, like I was a human football—" The crowd laughed again. "And he ran with me all around the bases. And that was how I made my first and only home run. And I want to thank them both tonight. I would like to thank them for being who they were."

The crowd seemed about to applaud, but Marcus put up his hand, urgently, as if the sound of their applause would break him.

"We could all tell stories," he said. "We all have stories to tell." Eve spotted Jonah at the far side of the circle. He nodded to her solemnly.

One of Ryan's cousins began speaking in a voice barely above a whisper. Then a few teachers told stories about the boys, dabbing at their eyes with crumpled tissues. Church friends. Teammates. Girls who had only seen the boys at games, one who'd gotten locked out of her car.

Dev had borrowed a coat hanger and pried the door open for her.

By the time they got home, it was past midnight. Marcus walked with them. He said he wasn't sure it was safe, so late at night. Noni had fallen asleep standing up in the park leaning against Eve. But she said, "I was awake the whole time. I liked when they played the songs. That Vestal boy who played guitar was good," she added. "But I liked Marcus best." He reached out and ruffled her hair.

After Noni was in bed, Eve made vanilla milk. She wasn't sure Marcus would drink it, but he sipped at it slowly, pursing his lips to blow on the spoon, which he gripped in one hand, so much like Ivan her heart tightened in her chest. The dead visited you in the strangest forms—in the gestures of your own children, or someone in a movie, or the face of a stray cat, yawning.

Finally she stood, collecting the cups. "You made it up," she said. "That story about the softball game. That never happened, did it?"

Marcus gave her a watery smile. "It was in the realm of the possible," he said. "That was close enough tonight."

Chapter 22
Van Gogh in Binghamton

"What?" Eve said.

Olivia was whispering into the phone. Between the office noise, Olivia's strong accent, and the hoarse whispering, Eve could not make out a word.

"Please come," Olivia rasped. "I cannot tell you over the phone."

Eve hurried to her basement office. Olivia gripped her hand and drew her inside. Her oval face was perfectly pale, like a painting. Her black eyes looked feverish. She shut the door, leaned against it. For a moment she did not speak at all.

"They gave me the Van Goghs," she said. "What will I do? Twenty-four landscape drawings. They are going only to seven places in the United States. We have been selected. The museum in Holland phoned."

"But that's wonderful!" Eve cried. "Congratulations!"

"No! Shh—I've been working on this for months, but in secret. Such a mistake. What about the insurance?" Olivia lowered her voice to a whisper. "I never got permission from Sheryl. My God. What will she say?"

In all the years Eve had worked at the university, Sheryl Stoddard had curated only one major exhibition, a collection of Carl Jung's artifacts. She was a small, skinny, nervous woman; she wore beige pants outfits, pale cashmere sweaters with high waisted pants. She spent her days locked inside her office, where she wouldn't have to deal with the foot traffic of the museum. She was famous for never answering her phone. Her answering machine message said curtly, "You know what to do."

"Talk to her," Eve said.

"What if she says no?" Olivia's eyes were dark and wide. "I would have to leave this place. I would have to quit my job."

"I'm sure she'll say yes," Eve said, though she was sure of no such thing.

As it turned out, not only did Stoddard agree, but the president of the university also caught wind of the news. Here was good publicity for free. Word spread fast. The *Binghamton Press* wrote it up on the front page of the Sunday living section. The local TV stations covered it on the evening news. The mayor and state senator pledged their support. *Van Gogh*. The name had a magical quality. Eve heard it whispered in the halls, in the staff lounge, among the students. There were would be Van Gogh posters for sale, as well as Van Gogh T-shirts, sweatshirts, and umbrellas. The exhibit was not only an honor but a gold mine.

In the Art Department, Eve's phone began ringing with calls from all over the state, and from Pennsylvania to Ontario. This commotion was why they all were called into a conference room in the administration building. They sat at a large, rectangular gray table, faculty and staff, with the president at the head. Each of the Fine Arts departments were represented.

She saw Lev toying with a paper clip, straightening and rebending it. The walls of the conference room were gray, the carpeting gray. What little light filtered through the heavy drapes was also grayish. Van Gogh would have hated this room, Eve thought. There were coffee and doughnut holes on a folding table at the far side of the room, away from where anyone was sitting. No one felt comfortable enough to leave their seat and get anything. Eve had peeked, and on her way in noticed that even the doughnuts looked grayish, with a dull white sugar frosting.

Olivia sat with her hands clasped in front of her, like a child, lips parted to catch every syllable. She referred to notes in front of her when she spoke, but her voice trembled with emotion. "Art can save lives," she said. "Van Gogh's failures teach us never to give up hope."

As so often happened at the university, there

was a flicker of interest in these words, which instantly died of embarrassment. People at Chuck's car dealership were more likely to talk about art than anyone on campus. The conversation returned immediately to administrative details. The vice president of External Affairs spoke about insurance issues, the need for extra security. Frederick Cummings announced that Leo Basilica would offer a fall class on the work of Van Gogh.

Basilica was in his seventies, though he looked younger and more vigorous than his age. His voice was rough from smoking for half a century, and when he spoke, he often sounded as if he were shouting. Students either loved or hated him. Leo Basilica was not present at this meeting. He had not attended a meeting in fifteen years. He was the coyote of the department, a wild card.

The president nodded thoughtfully. "A large lecture class?" she asked.

"Senior seminar," Cummings said. "Limited to fifteen."

"How about a larger seminar," she said. "Something the younger students can take. Maybe even some nonmajors. I'll supply an extra graduate assistant."

"We'll need two," Cummings said. "We can discuss it at the next department meeting." His face, Irish, red-toned, scrunched up, merry, was unreadable to anyone who did not know him well. They needed all the graduate assistants they could get. He had already planned for a large seminar.

"Two assistants, then," the president said. "And I'd like Professor Basilica to give one open lecture to the public. Something we can all understand," she added.

Cummings shrugged. Basilica was not a man to be dictated to.

"Do your best," the president sighed.

There was further talk about publicity, receptions. The chair of the Art History Department offered a lecture series on Van Gogh's contemporaries. It would complement Basilica's seminar, he said.

"Wonderful idea," Frederick said jovially. Eve could remember when Frederick had lunged across a table and grabbed this other man by the throat. It was, she thought, a practical demonstration of the benefits of divorce. Art and Art History had split into two departments years ago. Now they lived in peaceful separate worlds.

Olivia looked from one face to the other, as happy as a girl at her own birthday party. The president now invited them all to partake of coffee and doughnuts, waving her hand, and left the meeting, which broke up within two or three minutes.

Olivia gathered up the doughnuts for the maintenance staff. She could never stand waste of any kind. "It's really happening," she said to Eve.

"It's really happening," Eve echoed.

She had yet another meeting to attend later that afternoon, around a smaller rectangular table, in a legal conference room. There was no coffee and no doughnuts.

The meeting took place in the office of Shapiro, Smith and Elias, in downtown Binghamton. Eve sat watching cars and people below. The office overlooked the Susquehanna River and the old courthouse, its copper roof gone green. Its green female figure perched on top, holding a set of scales, clad in flowing green robes, looked more like a mermaid than like Justice.

In the end, Eve had gotten her own lawyer, a woman. Everyone advised her to do this. Sally Midder specialized in domestic law. She was tough as nails.

Chuck's lawyer was there, too; Ted Danziger, the man Eve had always thought of as her lawyer. It felt strange to sit opposite him at a table.

He did not seem to find it strange. "Chuck is not asking for significant alimony," Ted said in the flat even voice she recognized from count-less small transactions. He was far more familiar to her than her own lawyer. He'd once taken them to the sky box for the Binghamton Mets. Marcus had been impressed by the free hot dogs and sodas. "He wants you to liquidate the real estate holdings and divide them equally," Ted added.

Eve's lawyer, Sally Midder, laughed. She wore a cherry-red suit. She was a large woman, but her ankles were slim and she wore high red heels that matched the suit.

Nothing in any of Eve's phone conversations with Chuck had prepared her for new demands. She had expected an amicable proceeding, sliding papers back and forth across a desk. Maybe a few quibbles over who got which Oriental rug, which one got the Beatles collection. He could have it, as far as she was concerned.

"Chuck wants you to sell your house," Sally explained. "Which of course you are not going to do."

"He has equity in the property," Ted said stubbornly. "In fact, my client believes he made the original down payment."

"So you said," Sally answered. "But I have here a copy of a cancelled check for $25,000," she said, waving it. "It is my client's check, from her personal savings account. Dated May first, 1991. Furthermore, she has made all the mortgage payments subsequent to that check."

Ted looked taken aback. "I was under the impression—" he began.

"You were wrong," Sally said. "Sadly mistaken. Now if Chuck has any personal belongings he'd like to take—clothing or music, toothbrushes, etcetera—he's welcome to them. He's not getting alimony. Let's drop that. He left the house, abandoning his wife and child."

"Children," Eve corrected her. "And he didn't really—"

"In legal terms, one child," Sally rolled on. "Of course there is also his stepson—Mark, is it?"

"Marcus," Eve said.

"Let's sign the separation agreement and get it over with," Sally said. She pushed a stack of papers across the table to Ted.

"Did Chuck tell you to ask for alimony?" Eve demanded. Her cheeks burned, hot to the touch.

"I'm not at liberty to discuss that," Ted Danzinger said. "There is a lawyer-client confidentiality—"

"Ask him yourself," Sally told Eve. There was something coarse about her, yet likable. Her face was full and round. She herself was divorced, she had told Eve the first time they met. She'd been married to the son of a bitch for twenty-five years. Those were her exact words, but she tossed them off merrily, as if they were a joke. Only her eyes did not smile.

"All right," Ted said to the pile of documents. He did not look at Eve. His eyes ran over the papers; he read quickly. "Have your client sign them now, I'll overnight them to my client, and we'll file Monday morning."

Sally Midder had gotten up to pour herself a glass of water from a pitcher. "Anyone else?" she asked. "It's spring water, not the Susquehanna River. Cheers!" She lifted the plastic tumbler.

By Monday, Eve thought, she would be on her way to becoming what?—A gay divorcée? It was an expression she hadn't heard since childhood, but it jumped into her head. She would only be separated. She did not feel gay. Sally Midder pushed a pen toward her. Eve barely glanced at the papers. She did not want to read them. Her eyes caught the word "irrevocably."

Sally pushed one finger down on the page. Her fingernails were painted to match her lipstick. There were little sticky yellow tabs on each of the papers. "Sign at the X," Sally said. "Next to the yellow stickers."

Eve signed.

"I swear to you, I didn't know," Chuck said over the phone. "I told Ted to take care of it. I didn't want to know the details."

"Throwing us out of the house is hardly a detail," Eve said.

"You know me better than that," Chuck said. "Believe me. I'll fire Ted tomorrow. I'll fire him tonight."

Eve toyed with the phone cord, thinking it over. She did believe him, that was the problem. "Don't," she said. It would mean starting all over with a new lawyer, a new set of papers.

Maybe they were rushing into this, but it was the way Chuck always did everything—courtship and marriage and buying the house, only the third one they'd even looked at. "Let's take it!" he'd said. He got excited about things. He was a sucker for every infomercial. They had a hall closet full of food dehydrators, miniature grills, fly fishing equipment. Even buying little things, a shirt or a pair of jeans. Chuck was impatient to get it over with. He didn't try things on, and if they didn't fit, they sat in plastic bags next to his dresser drawers, ignored.

Eve said, "Just sign the papers, all right?"

"I will," he said. "But I wanted to tell you something. I'm moving back to town—well, near it. I want to try living more in the country."

"Back here?" she said.

"They want me back at Diute Ford, they were practically begging me. I'm going to be the new service manager. It's a big promotion. "

"But—" She was about say, *But you wanted to leave all that behind. I thought you needed something better.* But she could not think of any way to say it without hurting his feelings. "What do you mean, live in the country?" she asked instead. She pictured him on a farm, in a

288

straw hat, chewing on a piece of hay. Chuck, who always had to be in the middle of everything, going somewhere, doing something.

"Maybe Pennsylvania," he said. "Friendsville. Or Beaver Lake. I've got a buddy who's willing to sell me fifteen acres."

"Acres," she said. "Of land."

"Sure, of land. Then I can put in my own trailer."

"You're going to live in a trailer," she said. "Alone in a trailer?"

"Hey." It brought him up short. "I wanted to talk to you about that. I don't know how to say this right."

"Just say it."

"Maybe not alone."

She felt the air go out of her lungs. "I see," she said. It did not hurt half as much as she expected.

"I definitely did not plan this," he said. "I met Donna a couple of months ago. At the start of my trip," he said. "She was waiting tables in Illinois. Near where my cousin lives. She's from Rochester, originally. Binghamton is practically her hometown. I'm not even sure she'll come with me. But that's not the point. I want to be near Noni."

"Noni and Marcus," she said automatically. She hoped Marcus wasn't within hearing range.

"Of course," Chuck said. "I'm still her dad. I

want to be there for her—and for all of you. That's real important."

"Okay," Eve said.

"Tell Noni I'm going to be there real soon."

"You're sure about this, right? I don't want to tell her till you're sure."

"Well, I don't know. Maybe this spring, I'm hoping. But I've got stuff to do. A lot of loose ends to tie up."

"Look, Chuck," Eve said. "It's fine. Just remember, everything is going to affect her. Your conversations, your actions. You know? It's going to have some effect on her life. So just— think about it."

"So you're saying maybe I shouldn't move back to town after all."

"That isn't what I meant," she said.

She was beginning to see why this marriage had been doomed from the start.

Olivia was making a clean sweep of her base-ment office. "I must get rid of everything inessential," she said. Eve showed up with empty boxes she'd found in the supply closet. "Good, good!" Olivia beamed, and began throwing things into the boxes. There were decorative fig-ures and small vases and paperweights. There were statues, perfume bottles, notebooks, and bowls filled with pinecones and acorns.

"What should I do with it?" Eve asked.

"Give it away, throw it away!" Olivia said.

"Why don't you take some home?" Eve fingered an embroidered Chinese runner made of blue silk. There was a dragon and a phoenix on it in gold thread.

"No," Olivia said. "Out, out, out." Finally, all that was left on the walls were a few children's drawings.

Olivia took them down carefully and laid them into her filing cabinet. "I will put these back up when the Van Gogh is over." She sighed. "I am looking forward to this exhibit so much, but in my mind it is already over, and I am already sad about it."

"Chuck and I are legally separated," Eve said. "The divorce will happen automatically." Olivia was the first person at work she had told. Olivia seized her hands in one of her own small hands. She wore a thin gold wedding ring. They both looked at it.

"Okay, then." Olivia released her hands. "We will go out and celebrate. We can make a toast to your freedom. To your future!" She snatched up a goblet-shaped plastic glass from one of the cardboard boxes and raised it in the air.

Eve dragged everything back to the common room, where art faculty and staff could take what they wanted. Then, after a week, the students would be invited to take what was left. Art students were famous scavengers: they used everything. When they were through, there was nothing left in the box, not even a button.

Eve kept only the embroidered Chinese runner, and put it behind her desk in the office. She, too, was wary of filling up her house. No more garage sales, ever, she thought. She saved a few novels for Valerie, in the Theater Department, who was out sick with the flu. She thought they looked quirky, the kind of thing Valerie would read. One of them had a bright red cover. Val always had a book tucked in her backpack. The art students, of course, grabbed up all the other books, even the ones with torn covers and turned-down pages.

Not many days later, Valerie stopped by Eve's office. She came during lunch, knocking softly on the glass of the office door and signaling to Eve to let her in. Eve unlocked the door. Valerie was gripping a book in one white-knuckled hand.

"How did you know?" she said. She gestured with the bright red book. It was called *Cutting*.

Some instinct made Eve wait for her to go on. She had no idea what the young woman was talking about.

"Was it when we went shopping together? Did you see my arms then?" Valerie pushed up her sleeves. Her arms appeared to be tattooed with some intricately beautiful design, as if she'd been drawing all over her forearms with pencil.

There was a cross-hatching of tiny lines, bluish-gray. It took Eve a moment to understand that she was looking at scars.

"I've been doing it since I was fourteen. I know what you were trying to tell me by giving me this book," Valerie said in a husky voice. "I know I need help."

Eve didn't trust herself to speak. She knew she couldn't say that she'd picked out the book randomly without thinking, that it had been a lucky hit.

"I called someone yesterday, a therapist," Valerie said. Her thin face looked care-worn, her eyes tired, older than her age. She leaned on Eve's desk as if the weight of her own body was too much for her. "A friend recommended her."

Eve said, "That's a first step, that's good."

"I didn't know whether to thank you or just scream at you," Valerie said.

"You don't really have to do either," said Eve.

Chapter 23

Gin

"Cereal again," Marcus said, pushing the bowl away. He said it with disgust. He said it as if he were not only tired of cereal, but of breakfast, of morning, of everything around him. He had not been right since the accident. Now, he went straight to his room after school, or into the basement. He didn't want to exist on the same level of the house as anyone else. And he was dragging home bad grades. Almost every afternoon, Eve came home to the same recorded message on her answering machine. The voice was without human inflection.

"This is Bing-ham-ton High School. A student in your household—" Here, the robotic voice paused an instant. "—Mar-cus, was absent—" Another brief pause. "Period, two. Period, six. Period, eight." The periods varied, but never the voice, the cadence, or the general gist.

"Call the school," Lev told her. "This could be serious."

They had run into one another in the Arts Commons. Out the window, geese gathered on the lawn, a sure sign spring was approaching, if with glacial slowness. Lev was trying to boost Tracy's confidence, he told Eve. She should go back to school, or at least apply at one of the temp agencies. "She has so much to offer, you know?" he said.

"I know," Eve had agreed. "She's really wonderful." Lev had never praised her.

Now he said, "You can't just ignore what's going on with Marcus. You'd better do something fast."

"Like what?" she asked.

Lev blew into his cup of tea. "No idea. That's why I never had kids."

The one person she could really talk with was Jonah. He'd started dating a woman who went to his church, the Beautiful Plain Baptist. Lorena was an excellent cook, he'd told her.

"I'm still getting offers from some of the younger ladies in my building," he said, "but I'm turning them down. I'm learning ma*tur*ity." He pronounced the word with gusto.

About Marcus he said, "You got to have patience. Keep him talking. Long as he's talking with you, he'll be fine. Give him something to be happy about."

But Marcus was not happy about anything these days. He visited the graves of the dead boys more often than was healthy. He went online and looked at the accident diagrams again and again. He reread the police reports. She knew he kept going back to the scene, studying the angles, the trajectories, trying to undo the accident by the force of sheer logic. Finally, his friends refused to take him anymore. "It's macabre, man," she heard one boy say. "You've got to let it go."

He did ask morbid questions, things like, "Where is *our* family buried?" and, "Is it okay to write your own eulogy?" And he was getting fearful. Suddenly he was afraid of germs. He wouldn't use the pen at the bank because he said too many people handled the same flimsy piece of plastic, and how did he know where they had been? He wouldn't walk into a post office to mail a letter. One day, shaving, he cut himself and it took Eve an hour to calm him down.

Mrs. Dunrea wasn't much help, though she tried. "Sit up straight," she scolded him at dinner at Emerald Gardens. "Try to smile. I know this was awful, it's a tragedy—but just be glad it wasn't you."

Marcus poked at his food. Eve and Noni exchanged glances.

"Time heals all wounds. That, and aloe vera. And Preparation H."

Eve looked to see if her mother was kidding. One of the aides slid a tray of baked chicken in front of her and identical plates in front of Noni and Marcus.

"It's hard," Mrs. Dunrea went on, as if they hadn't been interrupted. "But people survive these things. Life can be so full of joy. It doesn't really make sense to waste a single second. Your friends knew that, I'm sure."

Eve looked around the dining room. It didn't look full of joy. The residents sat at their tables and hardly spoke. Their hands shook so hard it was an effort to bring food up to their mouths. Compared to them, Mrs. Dunrea was in great shape. A heavyset woman approached their table.

"Uh-oh," Charlotte said. "I knew we should have eaten faster. Now we're in for it."

The large woman leaned on the back of Mrs. Dunrea's chair. The act of walking across the room had left her wheezing. "It's so wonderful you're here!" she exclaimed. "You must be Charlotte's grandson."

"Yes," Marcus said.

"How lovely! Did you know my Paulie?" she asked, coughing.

"Who?" he said.

"Paul is her husband. No, Marcus doesn't know him," Mrs. Dunrea said firmly.

"Are you sure? He taught mechanical engineering," the woman said, still wheezing with each word. Her chest heaved. "It's too bad you don't have a sister," she said.

"I do have a sister," Marcus said. "She's right here." Noni tried to smile. She looked down at her plate.

The woman threw up both hands in astonishment. "Do you? *Do* you!" she breathed. "Isn't that wonderful! A sister. What is her name—may I ask?"

"Noni," he said.

"An unusual name. It's too bad you don't have a sister."

"I do," Marcus said, puzzled.

"Do you? Isn't that wonderful! Did you know my Paulie?" she asked.

"Let's get out of here," Mrs. Dunrea said.

A tiny old man came up behind the heavyset woman. He grasped her by the elbow. "Come along, Sid," he said.

"Who are you?" the old woman asked.

"I'm Paul. Your husband," the man said patiently. "Come along, now."

"That's ridiculous," the woman said. "I'd certainly know you—"

Back in her room, Mrs. Dunrea said, "It's sad. They had to find her a separate room, she'd get so agitated when he climbed into their bed at night." She laughed. "The poor man."

Clemente Driscoll stopped by. He was holding a half-finished box of chocolates. "I brought these along," he said. "I'd heard there was a Fred Astaire–Ginger Rogers movie on tonight."

Mrs. Dunrea said to Marcus in a low voice, "I bought him those chocolates." Aloud, she said, "I always liked Fred Astaire. I didn't like that girl with the big mouth. Big teeth, dark hair—"

"Leslie Caron," Clem said reproachfully. "She was lovely. Gifted. A beautiful dancer."

"I never cared for her," Mrs. Dunrea said. "My husband was crazy about her, too. I guess she had sex appeal."

Clem looked embarrassed. Marcus and Noni jumped up from the sofa so he could sit down. He waved them off and put one large hand on

Marcus's shoulder. "I'm sorry for your loss," he said, his blue eyes looking almost green, watery. "Somehow we have to move on."

Marcus nodded wordlessly.

Eve had picked up the driving lessons where her mother left off, but getting Marcus into the car became more and more of an ordeal. They had cancelled his driver's test in February; it happened to fall the day after the accident. He refused to reschedule. He made excuses to put off practicing, and then refused to drive because, he said, he had gotten too rusty.

When she could coax him into the car, he kept a white-knuckled grip on the steering wheel. He hung on so tight it was hard for him to even turn the wheel. He moved his head constantly, to check the rearview mirror, both sideview mirrors, twist around, check again. Finally, one afternoon in late March, after he'd grimly negotiated his way around the traffic circle and driven down Riverside Drive, he pulled to the side of West End Avenue, in front of the Armory, put the car in park, turned off the ignition, and handed the keys to Eve. There was sweat glistening above his upper lip. His skin looked greenish-white.

"I can't breathe," he said.

"Calm down," Eve said. "Try to relax. You can breathe."

"I'm dying. My heart is going a mile a minute."

"You're just having a panic attack," she said. "Trust me."

She rummaged around and managed to find a paper bag in the backseat, which she had him breathe into, but even after she'd gotten him calmed down, even after he was breathing normally and his color had returned, he refused to take back the car keys. "I can't do this anymore," he said.

"You can't do this anymore right *now,*" she said. "Let's not push it, then." They switched places and she drove home. He laid his head back against the headrest and put his arm over his eyes. Nonetheless, tears escaped and slid down his jaw.

Now she could no longer tell herself that Marcus would still be home for another year. Now she was counting months. Soon it would be just weeks, then days. Next year he would not be living in their house, his house. The thought made her whole body go cold. How did other parents bear it? she wondered. She saw them at the grocery store, out jogging or walking their dogs, parents of the children one year ahead of Marcus at school. Their faces showed no obvious sign of misery, of longing. But she knew that some of them must be feeling it. She told herself she should start an Empty Nest Club. They could meet once a week and wail together. They could hold up old photographs and baby clothes.

Refreshments for the Empty Nest Club

Sandwiches: forget the sandwiches.
Finger foods: forget the finger foods.
Empty Nest Gin Punch: Skip the soda, lime juice, cranberry juice, and maraschino cherries. Forget the ice. Go heavy on the gin.

Noni tried. She tried to interest Marcus in her homemade comic books, her soccer games, her TV shows. But the longer he shut her out, the more often he turned away, the harder it became for Noni to try again. If she was hurt, she tried not to show it. She threw herself into spring soccer practice.

Noni told Eve she'd been talking to some nice man in the park, after school.

"What do you mean?" Eve said. Her breath seemed to catch in her throat.

"He's lonely. He really misses his daughter, he told me."

"Oh my God," Eve said. "You can't just talk to strangers. Haven't I taught you anything?"

"He's not a stranger," Noni said. "He's just sad. He's a veteran. He's nice. We talk."

"You cannot talk to him anymore," Eve said. "You cannot walk home alone anymore. Do you understand me?"

"Yes. You're mean," Noni said. "You just don't want me to have friends!"

Eve took her daughter by both shoulders. She resisted the urge to shake her. "I will be picking you up every day after practice," she said. "You are not to go to the park. Do you understand?"

"Yes. Yes!" Noni shouted. "At least he listened!"

After that, Eve was hypervigilant. She told Jonah about the man in the park. She told the parents of Noni's friends. She called the homework hotline every afternoon. Noni slumped in the car after soccer, arms folded, looking out the window onto the dark yards.

Meanwhile, Marcus continued to flounder. He flunked two more math tests, and then Eve found a bottle of gin in his closet and poured it out. He tried to shrug it off. She watched it all happening, with the horrifying sensation of someone watching something precious wash down a drain. The waters were swirling, it was over their heads, and there was nothing she could do to stop it.

One night at dinner, none of them said a single word. Noni's face was bright red. Eve remembered what Jonah had said: "As long as he keeps talking, you're all right."

That night, after Noni went to bed, crying, she was so angry at the world—Eve took out a pack of cards and dealt them out between her and Marcus. "Gin rummy," she announced.

"I don't want to play," he said. There were blue

circles under his eyes. He wasn't getting enough sleep. God knew what it was he looked at on his computer these days. He played the same four or five songs over and over. Heavy metal, they sounded like nothing she had ever heard.

She dealt out the cards but didn't turn hers over. "I know you keep beating yourself up over the accident, for not being there," she said. "I know you're furious. But you did save a life that night, remember."

Marcus kept his head down. He was poking at an angry-looking cuticle on his thumb. "I'm not sure my life was so worth saving," he mumbled.

"I'm not talking about your life," she said. "I'm talking about Astrid's."

His head came up.

"If you hadn't gotten her so angry, she would have gone for that ride. Chances are she'd have sat in the front seat with those two boys."

Marcus was looking straight at her, with that greenish blue-gray gaze of his. It was like being held in the beam of headlights. Eve steeled herself and met the gaze head on.

"Astrid," he said.

"Imagine how she must be feeling," she said. "Living in that house. Thousands of miles from her home. I don't suppose you've talked to her about it," she added cleverly.

"We haven't talked much," he admitted. "Just at school."

"She probably needs someone to talk to."

"Yeah," he said. "She probably does."

Eve picked up her hand of cards and looked at it. "I thought you were a religious person," she said. "Doesn't that comfort you?"

"God does not bring comfort," he said. His words came out through the cards he held up in front of his face. "The *idea* of God brings comfort." He picked up the first card from the pile, rejected it and laid it faceup.

She picked up his card. "What about the sky?" she pressed on. "Or trees? Or anything you care about. If you believe in a higher power, surely all those things are His creations. So, in that sense, God comforts you."

"I just don't like Him very much right now," Marcus said. "I'm kind of pissed off at Him."

"But, still. According to you, He made the whole world."

"Yes," Marcus said. He threw down another card.

"The universe, in fact."

"Yes."

"Remember the Memphis planetarium we visited near Grandma's house? Every pinprick of light we were looking at, every dot of light, was a whole galaxy. Remember how amazed you were when they told us that?" She picked up another card.

"I do," Marcus said.

"I expect there is some kind of rhyme or reason to the things that happen. Maybe we're not big enough or smart enough to figure it out." She leaned one arm on the table and bent toward him. "And," she said, "you are making your little sister very unhappy, and that has to stop."

"Okay," he said, laying down a playing card.

"I mean it," she said. "Now."

He put both hands up. "Okay! I will."

"Good," she said, taking his card from the pile, then slapping another one face down. "Gin rummy."

A little while later she heard Marcus talking on his cell phone in his room. She was sure he was on with Astrid. His voice rose and fell a long time. She was not eavesdropping, but there was something she was listening for, and finally it came; a sound she had not heard in weeks.

It was Marcus, laughing.

Chapter 24
The Butterfly Closet

Chuck returned with the milder weather. He brought spring with him, warm winds and balmier nights, and his brand-new motorcycle, which he towed behind his Ford Focus, along with a doll that was too babyish, for Noni, and a lucky horseshoe with Marcus's name pricked out along its iron rim.

"Cool," Marcus said. He was spending time again with Danny Schwartz. It was Danny who had first stopped by the house after the accident, on his way to school.

"I'm here for Marcus," he said in his usual deadpan voice. Behind him, parked at the curb, was his father's dark gray Buick.

"I don't let Marcus drive with friends," Eve said. Marcus was still upstairs, luckily, brushing his teeth, or his hair, or whatever it was that took him an hour in the morning.

"Oh, right," Danny said. "Because those two kids got killed." He turned away. "Okay, 'bye."

Ten minutes later he was back. "I'm here for Marcus," he said again. Uncharacteristically, he looked Eve in the eye. "We'll walk . . . We'll walk."

Chuck returned as a stranger, his face looking unfamiliar, sharp and thin, like a fox. He moved into a farmhouse out of town, renting with an option to buy. "It's a hike," he said, "but I've got a great vehicle."

The acres and the trailer had fallen through. So had Donna. "She turned out flaky," he said. "That's how you want your pie crusts, not your women."

Eve winced. If Chuck still made her heart race

sometimes, just the sight of him standing by the front door, well, she'd get over it. *Desinas ineptire—et quod vides perisse perditum ducas.* Cease this folly—and what you see is lost, set down as lost. She remembered it from high school Latin.

When he first came to the house, Noni spent five minutes stiffly propped up in the living room with her father, then took off like a shot for her friend Anna's house. She did not return Chuck's many phone calls. She made other plans on the weekends.

Finally, Eve stepped in. "You're not being nice," she said to Noni.

"He doesn't live here, he lives on a stupid farm."

"They have cows and horses," Eve said. "Pretty soon they'll have calves, and foals."

"I don't care," Noni said. "—Baby horses, really?"

"Thank God," Valerie said. She stood in front of Eve's closet door, hands pressed together like a believer outside a cathedral. Mia was there, too, pencil and drawing paper ready. It was Valerie's job to orchestrate the overhaul of the clothing. "We'll take nothing for granted," she said. "As Rilke said, 'You must make your life new.' "

Mia's task was to envision a whole new use of the second floor. She made it her end-of-the-

307

year project. The teacher already loved her. Mia's work had been immaculate. She threw herself into each assignment wholeheartedly, a thoroughbred leaping a fence. Eve had watched each painstaking drawing emerge, proofread the written reports, and helped Mia plan her academic schedule for the following fall, with an eye on earning her degree. Mia would now be taking two classes instead of one. Then she helped one of Mia's friends.

"You should do this for your living," Mia said. "You are my real academic advisor."

Eve was flattered; she could almost imagine it, someday. She loved this kind of work, helping someone succeed. But Mia acted as if her life depended on doing this final project right, as if Mia weren't the one doing her the favor. She drew picture after picture, discarding each one.

"Okay," Valerie said, rubbing her hands together. "The first step is, we take everything *out*."

"Oh, no," Eve said. "I can't put anyone through that."

"Are you kldding?" Valerie said. "I'm like a pig in mud. I love this stuff."

"Come back tomorrow," Eve said. "I'll have it cleared out by then."

"Ignore her," Valerie told Mia.

"Better yet," Eve said, "I should just sell the house and move, and leave this for the next owner."

"You must be brave," Mia said. It was hard to tell if she was kidding or serious, but in any event she simply stepped into the closet in her stocking feet and lifted out a cluster of five blouses, still on hangers. Valerie followed her, grabbing an armful. You couldn't see her face beneath the mound of skirts, dresses, and slacks. Eve waded in behind.

There were clothes she hadn't worn in years, things she had forgotten about and greeted like old friends, and outfits—like a fringed weirdly dyed denim jacket with matching bell-bottoms—she would never wear again. "Ooh, perfect for the costume closet," Valerie purred, stroking the jacket, bleached and studded with silver stars on the pockets. "It's so sixties." There were boxes of old shoes with pointy toes and small sharp heels, shoes so ridiculous Mia had to sit down, she was laughing too hard.

"Maybe we should save some of these for Noni," Eve said, which set Mia off again till tears came to her eyes. She held up a pair of pink polka dot pumps with big bright pink bows.

"Well, you never know," Eve argued, though she realized Noni would have to undergo some kind of personality transplant before she'd want those pink pumps.

"Pick two pairs to set aside for Noni," Valerie commanded.

In the end, Eve chose midnight blue silk flats

and handmade Italian leather pumps on which she'd once spent half a week's pay.

"Classics," Valerie said regretfully, cradling them like puppies. "I was hoping you'd let these slide by."

They removed all of Chuck's things, organized them, piled them into cardboard boxes and bags, and set them in a corner of the garage. Eve hadn't realized how much room he'd been taking up. The closet looked empty on that side, it looked bereft. Then they began sweeping and vacuuming, and Mia mapped out the new space on paper while she and Valerie continued to wrangle over the clothes—Eve hanging onto things, Valerie systematically convincing her to let go.

"Keep only the things you love," Val finally said. "Really, why should you ever wear anything else?"

That made too much sense to argue. Out went the ugly but expensive clothing she felt too guilty to discard. Out with the cheap, flimsy, fashionable items she hated right after she'd bought them. There were blouses with price tags still hanging from them, mostly things on sale, bargains she'd never needed in the first place. She sacrificed heavy long wool kilts, fashioned by giant safety pins; silky wrap dresses that flew open in the first gust of wind. She moved Ivan's remaining things over to Marcus's closet, and kept his coat, a sweater, and one shirt. She unearthed papers and tax files from years earlier. She opened one box of woolens so old a cloud of moths rose from them, fluttering to the top of the closet as if they weighed less than the air around them.

"We will line the new closet with cedar," Mia said. "Drawers, shelves, everything."

"And remember to put three or four whole cloves in the pockets of all your wool coats," Valerie advised. "It really works."

Eve tried to pick out the things she cared most about. It wasn't much, when she was being honest, but what was left she truly loved—a rose-colored silk blouse, soft as the petals of a real rose; a bell-shaped teal blue wool skirt; a long gray cardigan with pockets; wide-legged black pants; her favorite jeans; a few old flowered blouses from Liberty of London in pale green and cornflower blue; a few summer dresses; a cobalt-blue sweater; a pink Lilly Pulitzer T-shirt she thought she'd lost years ago; the brown corduroy pants she'd worn on her date with Jonah; a black velvet dress. There were five pairs of shoes; one pair of red sneakers; sandals; and what Valerie called "a kick-ass pair of boots."

Eve had forgotten that the closet had wooden stairs inside; they must have once led to the attic. There was a small window facing these stairs. They would install new track lighting. She could have a place to sit down, if she liked, and look out the window, Mia explained. She would redesign better room for the hangers, and they could move her bureaus in here, opening new space in the bedroom. Still and all, when they were done emptying and sorting, it looked pathetic. The closet had more empty hangers than full.

"What happened to all my clothing?" she asked.

"You're molting," Valerie said. "Trust me, you'll fill it back up again. Try not to buy anything you don't absolutely love. See if you can imagine still loving it in ten years. Buy clothing that grows along with you, like a great book, or music, or a painting. Meanwhile, what do you want to do with all this?" She gestured at the sea of clothing around them.

"Get rid of the worn-out stuff," Eve said. "We'll give the rest to charity."

"How about a garage sale?" Mia suggested. "I could help. Sook-yun will help, too."

"No," Eve said firmly. "No garage sales."

The first time Chuck stayed for dinner, they ate off new dishes, ones Eve had picked out alone. She could not or would not remember which foods Chuck liked, which he hated. She passed him the Worcestershire sauce, forgetting he was allergic to it. He looked hurt.

It took diplomatic Marcus to make things seem normal again. Marcus and Chuck played chess in the living room. They were well matched. Chuck was almost childishly grateful to Marcus. They talked about movies and video games. They talked about baseball.

Chuck had his own large office now at Diute Ford, in the back, near where tires were displayed on the wall like big black rubber bracelets. The dealership gave him a generous raise. He bought Eve a new set of all-weather tires with stainless steel rims. He had to special-order them for her ancient Citroen. The car had developed what Eve thought of as a permanent cough. It sputtered and choked, and sometimes she had to run it for ten or fifteen minutes before it would shift into gear.

Its exhaust smoke was turning navy blue. She lay awake worrying about it. What was that term Jonah had used? A broken down hoop-dee. That was what she'd be driving. That's where her savings would go.

Except, as it turned out, Noni needed braces, and so much for her savings. The family dentist didn't like the gap between her front teeth, which Eve always thought of as cute. He sent them to an orthodontist, who said the gap was just the tip of the iceberg. Noni's bite was crooked, she was grinding her front molars while her back ones were almost untouched. She needed braces right away. Noni wept. She wouldn't wear one of those things that looked like a neck brace. She beat her fists on the padded arms of the orthodontist's chair, her small sharp face turning red.

As if by magic, the orthodontist produced a nearly invisible retainer. He gave her a coloring book and a sheet of stickers, and Noni hugged them gratefully to her flat chest, though she had outgrown such things long ago. She told Eve on the car ride home the orthodontist was "serious eye candy," which surprised Eve, since he looked perfectly ordinary to her, with large, prominent blue eyes of an unnatural shade she suspected came from contact lenses.

"Maybe you could marry him," Noni said.

"He's married," Eve said.

"He told you that?" Noni said disapprovingly. "How rude."

"He was wearing a wedding band," Eve said.

"You notice stuff like that, huh?"

The nearly-invisible braces, all the office visits, the X rays and fittings, were going to cost almost six thousand dollars. When she told Chuck, she could hear the sharp intake of his breath over the phone, then he let it out in a whistle.

"Trust me, I feel the same way," Eve said.

The Citroen had gotten so bad she finally brought it to the Turin brothers, her local mechanics. Years ago they ran a Chevron station, which had changed so many times through so many gas companies that Eve gave up trying to keep track. The four brothers still ran the place. Mr. Turin, Senior, the original owner, had long since retired—a bad heart, too many customers like Eve—and the four sons were all starting to look like him. They looked like each other, too.

"Excuse me," she said now, standing at the edge of the open garage. "Excuse me!" till one of the sons finally looked up and waved a wrench. He had been a sweet boy, pumping gas when he was barely fourteen. Now he was a man, sturdy, thick-necked, working on his own paunch. J.D. was the thin, handsome one, the serious mechanic. If you had a real problem, you talked with J.D. But he wasn't anywhere to be seen.

"Something's wrong with my Citroen!" She was always yelling over the noise of some machine. The place had been quieter when Mr. Turin ran things. "It's letting out blue smoke! Maybe something's wrong with a hose." That was her hope. Nothing serious. Nothing too expensive.

"Can you leave it?" he roared at her.

"I guess," she said. Her fear must have shown. He turned off whatever machine he'd been using and strode toward her. "Don't worry," he said. "Come back in the morning. We'll have it figured out."

"Thank you," Eve said.

She walked home. The April wind cut at her

face. She had no husband. She had no car. Her pocketbook hung heavily from her arm.

Marcus and Noni wanted pizza for supper. Eve said, "You want to walk to Pizza Hut?"

"Walk?" Noni said, staring. As if she didn't spend half her life running up and down a soccer field.

"Our car's at Turin's," Eve explained.

"Walk?" Marcus echoed. "Walk to Pizza Hut. That is so scrubby. Walk!"

Noni's little mouth tightened. "Have it delivered," she said.

Marcus was raving. "I knew it! All because Chuck left. We're scrubs now, aren't we? We're poor!"

"We aren't poor," Eve protested. "And stop using that word scrubs."

"I told you to get the car fixed," Marcus said. "I begged you!"

This was completely untrue, but Eve decided to let it go. "I am getting it fixed," she said. "We can live without a car for one night."

Noni was already on the phone, ordering the pizza. "Half with mushrooms, half with olives, right?" she said. "Mom, do we have any coupons?"

"Coupons!" Marcus cried. "Coupons. We're scr—we're poor!"

The next morning, Saturday, Eve felt a sinking in the pit of her stomach when she showed up at Turin's and was directed to J.D. It was like being sent to an open-heart surgeon when you'd hoped all you had was indigestion.

"Yep, it's bad," J.D. said. As usual, he spoke to the tool in his hand. He was handsome in a long, lean, suffering way that could make your legs weak. He was always tinkering around, inventing things, building things. His brothers were married, with children. J.D. was still single.

"How long will it take to fix?" Eve asked. Most of the cars around their lot looked like they had died there and been left out to rot.

"No use throwing good money after bad," J.D. said. "Sometimes a car gets to a point where it's going to be one thing after another, and it's just not worth fixing it anymore." He really could have been a surgeon, the way he spoke. All he needed was a turquoise cap and a pair of latex gloves. "Why don't you get yourself something easy to fix? An American car."

So this was the problem. Patriotic pride. Laziness. He didn't want to go through the trouble of fixing the Citroen. She should have gone to a foreign car dealer in the first place.

"It was a beautiful car," J.D. said gently, addressing the hammer in his left hand. "But it's done. Time to move on."

"Can't we just—patch it together?" she said. She hoped she didn't sound like she was begging. The bills were piling up—little things that

Chuck had always paid for, the cost of Noni's new soccer uniform, college applications, movies and gas and homeowner's insurance. She tried to imagine adding a car payment to all the rest. Where would she get a few thousand dollars for the down payment?

She remembered all the times she saw women stalled at a green light, or sitting in the CVS parking lot, smoke pouring from the engine. At the side of the road with the kids. How many times had she just driven by? Acts of kindness, she knew, could come back to haunt you—but acts of unkindness were sure to do so.

"Sixteen hundred dollars," J.D. was saying. "That's just the heating and cooling. Your main axle is starting to drag. You need a new muffler. The rear brakes are shot—"

"Enough," she said. She had never thought of herself as poor or rich. She had always worked, even as a teenager; she'd worked in a clothing store part-time during high school. She kept her own separate checking account when she married Ivan, and again with Chuck. But she'd always had some man's help. She had paid the mortgage, Chuck paid the utilities. He paid for cable, she covered the taxes. What if he stopped paying for anything? Men did that. Even with separation agreements. He might start a new family. She should have trained herself better for poverty. She should have been saving for a rainy day, steeling herself and the kids.

"You look terrible," J.D. said, which made her feel worse. "You've lost a lot of weight, haven't you? Sit down a minute." He dragged her over to a sagging, oil-spotted chair in the corner. The upholstery was scratchy. She probably should have been buying this kind of cheap furniture all along.

J.D. put some coins into a machine, punched a button and handed her a Coke. "Here," he said. "Can I give you a ride somewheres?"

"My mother's place," she said. "I told her I'd stop by. She lives off the Vestal Parkway," she added. "It's a ways."

"No problem," he told the hammer. He laid it down on the counter. He put a Yankees cap on his head, grabbed some keys off a pegboard on the wall.

J.D. drove carefully, the way he spoke. She arranged herself on her side of the front seat. It was hard being around a handsome man. Every day it seemed to be getting harder. She felt vulnerable to silly crushes, as if she were twelve years old again. It would have been easier if J.D. were ugly, or at least bad-mannered.

"You might get a couple hundred for parts," he told her. "Maybe more, on a Citroen. I can check around for you," he offered.

"Thanks," she said. The car was now torn apart in her mind—a fender here, a transmission there, the pretty hood with its red and blue engraved French ornament lying in a junkyard.

"You going to buy something new or used?"

"Oh God," she said. "Very used."

"Nowadays you find things on the Internet. I've seen some good deals. Of course, you have to get to where the car is," he added.

"Which is where?"

"Oh, all over. Colorado . . . Illinois."

"Here," she said, pointing at the entrance to Emerald Gardens. He drove so smoothly she didn't notice that he had put the car in park. If he had opened her door, it would have been like a date. As it was, she still held the cold, sweating can of Coke from the vending machine, feeling it would be ungracious to leave it behind.

Mrs. Dunrea was in a complaining mood. She complained about the noise next door. "It sounds like someone is constantly rearranging the furniture. You didn't pick a very good apartment." She moved on to the excessive heat in the building, the slowness of the aides, the salty food, the residents. "They sit there like a bunch of dummies. Some of these women have never been to New York City."

"That doesn't make them inferior human beings," Eve said.

"I didn't say that," her mother snapped. "What on earth is the matter with you?" she said. "Are you sick?"

"My car died," Eve said, and ridiculously, she began to cry.

"What are you crying for? It's just a car," her mother said, but her sharp face looked distressed, and her arms reached toward her daughter. "I always told you, don't cry over things. Things can be replaced."

"How?" Eve howled. "With what?"

"What are you talking about?" her mother said. "Take my car. I never use it."

Eve pawed at her face with a tissue. "No—"

"Why not? I'm glad to be rid of it!"

"It's your car," Eve said. "I can't just take it."

"I'm half blind and crippled," her mother said. "I can't see out of my right eye at all. Do you think I should be driving?"

"No," Eve said. "But you could sell it."

"It's costing me money to keep it. Insurance." She put the emphasis on the first syllable, *in*-surance. "As a matter of fact, why don't you buy a nice new car? A Toyota. I like their commercials."

"You can't throw money away on me," Eve said. "I won't let you." The used tissue was wadded up in her hand. The half-drunk can of Coke was sitting on a pile of her mother's magazines. Her mother patted her on the back, brisk, light little pats.

"I have more money than I know what to do with. Daddy left me a rich woman. Come on, now," she said. "Crying over a car. Really."

"It was Ivan's car," Eve said, fresh tears coming. She pulled more tissues out of her mother's box of Kleenex. There was a pink crocheted cover over it. Something from the Emerald Gardens gift shop. Made by one of the elderly residents.

"I know whose car it was," her mother said, tapping her on the back a few more times, then stroking her hair back from her forehead. "Cars die."

"People die," Eve said.

"Yes, but we are talking about a car," Mrs. Dunrea said. "And I would like to buy you a new one. If you are willing, I could give my old car to Marcus when he goes to college."

"Why are you being so nice?" Eve cried.

"I'm not being nice," Mrs. Dunrea said. "I'm being your mother."

Chapter 25
Hell Hath No Fury

The first thing Eve did with the new car was take her mother and Clem out to dinner and a movie.

"Make sure you get one with a roomy trunk," Mrs. Dunrea had told her. "No more wrestling with my walker. Get a big model. Don't be stingy with yourself. You take after your father that way."

Her new car was silver. It looked like an extremely elegant can of soup, with halogen headlights, a burgundy leather interior. It was last year's model, out of the showroom floor, five thousand miles on the speedometer. That dropped the price by a few thousand dollars. Lev, of all people, had come along to Jack Sherman Toyota to help her pick the car. He had been driving Toyotas for years, purchasing them from the same salesman, a man with a youthful face and a long Greek name.

"I'll get a coupon from the Little Venice out of this," Lev had told her early on. "We can go out and celebrate." He looked more at ease on the car lot, strolling up and down the aisles of cars, than he ever had at the university. He poked around, looking under car hoods, joking with the salesmen and mechanics. He bargained for her. It turned out his father had owned gas stations and repair shops in South Philadelphia.

"Didn't you ever think of going into the business?" Eve asked as they drove the new car away. It felt enormous, like something you might drive in an amusement park. She hadn't realized how rough the Citroen ran till she got behind the wheel of this new one. It was like driving a sofa.

"I wanted to get as far away as possible," Lev

said. "I wanted to be a jazz guitarist." He waggled his hand at her. "Broken wrist. No such luck." He looked at her. "You know, this car really suits you," he said. "It even sort of goes with your hair."

"My hair?" Her hand went up to touch it.

"Yeah. You have those—what-do-you-call-its? Red headlights."

"Highlights," she corrected him gently. She didn't want to end the moment, but he was already frowning, fiddling with the car radio, trying to get the university jazz station, his head cocked. The car's interior had that intoxicating new car smell. Maybe it had gone to his head.

"Hey—do you mind if I take Tracy to Little Venice?" he asked, waving the coupon at her. Eve felt a flush of something—annoyance, mostly.

"Of course not," she said.

"She's really been feeling down these days."

"It's fine." Now she felt guilty. Tracy was thin and haggard again, her hair lank and unwashed. She emitted almost an animal smell, and she hung onto her chow chow as if it was a stuffed animal and she was a small, sick child. She should have been inviting Tracy out more often, Eve thought.

"I try to stop by most days after work," he said.

"You're a good person, Lev," she said.

"Me? No. That's not why I told you," he said

curtly. Whatever feeling of comradery had briefly sprung up between them at the car dealership was severed, snapped like a twig. Lev was like that, moody as a cat.

Eve put on a skirt and blouse to take her mother and Clem out. Now she could find her clothing without having to wrestle to push all the rest of it out of the way first. There were drawers that pulled out, and soft lighting. Mia had helped her organize it by color. Eve sometimes thought she could live in that closet. Once in a while she sat inside on the little stairs, looking out the window, surrounded by blue, green, and rose colored cloth.

She chose carefully for this date. She dressed up more for her own mother than for anyone else on earth. She put on foundation, blush, mascara, the works. Noni sat on the edge of the bathtub, appraising her.

"Grandma's the one going on a date," she said. "Not you."

"Don't remind me," Eve said. "I'll never date again."

"I bet you do," Noni said. "I bet you do this month."

"Ha! You're supposed to be the realist." Downstairs, she put on her bright red wool coat with the black velvet collar—it had been a gift from Ivan, it was that old—and kissed her daughter on the head.

Marcus was lying on the sofa, reading Karl Marx. Only his white socks were visible. They were gray at the heels. "You need to do a laundry," she said. "And I think you have more mail." Even in April he was still getting invitations to apply to colleges. NYU sent him no fewer than sixteen separate mailings. They had started keeping count of them, as a joke.

"Have a nice time with the old folks," Marcus said. "Don't let them run you into the ground."

Charlotte and Clem hung onto each other's arms while they tried to move forward with their walkers, which resulted in the walkers tangling up with each other.

Then they argued about who would sit in the front seat.

"Ladies first, of course," Clem said.

"You've got the longer legs," Mrs. Dunrea said.

"I wouldn't dream of usurping your place."

"For heaven's sakes, Clem," Mrs. Dunrea said. "You'll be squashed in the back."

"I will not," he insisted, and he tried to crawl into the back at the same time Mrs. Dunrea pushed her way into the backseat from the other side. Eve ended up having to help both of them swing their legs inside.

"I'll be your driver for the evening," Eve said, alone in the front seat. "Where to?"

"You didn't make reservations?" Mrs. Dunrea's voice crackled with disapproval.

"It's a Thursday night in Binghamton," Eve said, "I don't think we'll have any trouble getting a table."

"A lot of people go out on Thursdays," Mrs. Dunrea said. "All the intelligent people. People who want to avoid the weekend crush."

"Not at five-thirty."

"Thirsty's?" Clem asked. "Isn't that a bar?"

"I wouldn't know," Mrs. Dunrea said. "You were born in this town, not me. He's very deaf," she added to Eve.

"Well I heard that," he said. "Where are we going?"

"I don't know," Eve said. "Where would you like to go?"

"Denny's is fine with me," Clem said.

"Denny's is horrible," Charlotte said. "We're going someplace nice. The treat's on me," she added a little more graciously.

"No," Eve said. "The treat is most definitely on me. How do you like the car, by the way?"

"Very pleasant car," Clem said. "Roomy."

"Your knees are touching your chin," Mrs. Dunrea said to him. "You should have sat up front like I told you."

"Where shall it be?" Eve asked.

"I don't care," her mother said.

"Neither do I," said Clem.

Eve put the car in gear. "Fine. How about Friday's?"

"Too noisy," Mrs. Dunrea said.

"I can't hear in places that are noisy," Clem said.

"You can't hear anyway," Mrs. Dunrea said. "You probably need a hearing aid."

"I heard that," Clem said.

"How about Touch of Thai?" Eve said.

"Is that Thai food?" her mother asked.

"Spicy food and I do not agree," Clem said.

"It's bad for my acid reflux," Mrs. Dunrea said.

"How about Chinese?"

"We had better Chinese food in Tennessee, if you can believe it."

"My dear, if you say it, I can believe it," Clem said.

"I guess Friday's is all right," her mother said. "Is the engine making a funny sound? I told you to get a brand new car. I don't know why you don't listen . . ."

"It's not making a funny noise," Eve said. "That's its normal noise." She pulled out of Emerald Gardens and headed onto the Vestal Parkway.

"Does it sound normal to you?" she asked Clem.

"Does what?"

"Applebee's!" Her mother suddenly poked Eve in the back of the neck. "Up ahead. I like their salads!"

"Is Applebee's all right?" Eve asked Clem, putting on her turn signal. "Mother, please don't poke me like that."

"I can if I want to," Mrs. Dunrea said. "Poke. Poke."

Her mother was acting childish, but then, it was really like taking two preschoolers out to dinner, as it turned out. Two ancient children who drank. Mrs. Dunrea ordered a gin rickey, Clem a Manhattan. Within minutes they were both drunk, or at least tipsy; Clem nearly fell sideways out of the booth.

They both ordered emphatically. "Absolutely no garlic on anything," Clem said. "Do I have your word on that?"

The waitress looked amused. "I wouldn't lie to you," she said. "You sure you don't want a drink, honey?" she asked Eve.

"Do you use butter or margarine?" her mother asked. "Because I am on a low-fat diet."

"That would be margarine, then," the waitress said, winking at Eve. Did that mean she was lying? Did she think because they were old they were stupid?

"I am on a low fat, low *sugar* diet," Clem said. "Do you have artificial sweetener?"

"Right on the table, doll," she said, tapping the plastic tray that held packets of white, pink, and blue sweeteners.

The woman could not have been more than

thirty, but she seemed ages older than all three of them. When Clem's water came, he sent it back for a slice of lemon. Then they both wanted straws. They blew the papers off, and Clem's flew to the next booth and struck a man on the back of his neck. The man's beefy hand went up to his neck but he did not turn around.

"We'll get thrown out of Applebee's!" Charlotte cried gaily. Eve had never seen her mother act so young and foolish.

Mrs. Dunrea ordered a second gin rickey.

"Are you sure?" Eve asked.

"What do you mean?" Mrs. Dunrea said. "I am not a child."

"What'll it be?" the waitress asked.

"Never mind," her mother said. "I suppose you're right. Drinking makes me sick to my stomach."

"Me, too," Clem said. "In fact I feel a bit queasy."

"You do?" The women turned to look at him. Clem had closed his eyes and was resting his great white head back against the dark red leatherette cushion of the booth.

His eyes snapped open again suddenly, like a doll's. "I'm fine," he said. "Let us eat."

Mrs. Dunrea complained that her Asian chicken salad didn't have enough crispy noodles on it. Clem thought he detected garlic in his Swiss steak.

"Who orders Swiss steak, anyway?" Mrs. Dunrea said, "I've never ordered it in my life."

"It is delicious, when prepared without garlic."

"I swear there's not a speck of garlic on it," the waitress said. She now looked closer to fifty than thirty. "But if you want me to bring it back to the kitchen, I will."

"No use wasting food," Clem said. "I suppose these mashed potatoes are from a mix?"

"Afraid so," the waitress said. "Would you rather have french fries?"

"No fried food!" Clem and Mrs. Dunrea cried together.

"Okay, then," the waitress said. "I'll get you those extra crispy noodles."

"Extra?" Mrs. Dunrea said. "Does that mean you're going to charge for them?" She looked ferocious.

"Not at all," the waitress said. "You're sure you don't want a drink?" she asked Eve again.

Eve shook her head.

"You know," Clem said after the waitress had gone, looking at Eve, "you remind me of one of my best friends. A lovely woman."

"You already said that," Mrs. Dunrea said. "Who do *I* remind you of?"

"You are sui generis," Clem said. "Unique unto yourself."

"Oh, now," Mrs. Dunrea said. When the bowl of crispy noodles came, they dipped them in mustard, then they tried ketchup. Then Clem tried A-1 sauce, which he said was truly delicious, though the noodles got soggy and began falling apart. Clem tried crumbling them onto his Swiss steak. Eve was afraid they'd be throwing them around next.

"I haven't eaten this well in weeks!" he declared. "Months."

"That's because the food at Emerald Gardens is so lousy," Mrs. Dunrea said. "I don't see how you can eat it."

"My dear," said Clem. "What choice do I have?"

"True," Mrs. Dunrea agreed. "We're old. We have to make do." She shot an accusing look at Eve.

Eve signaled for the check to the waitress, who came as if she'd been fired out of a cannon. Eve supposed she'd noticed the tabletop littered with the remains of crispy noodles. Eve left an extra large tip, but even so, the floor under their table was covered with noodles, straw wrappers, crumpled napkins, and food crumbs. Next time, she thought, she'd take them to Chuck E. Cheese.

Choosing a movie proved another challenge. Clem wanted to see a comedy. Charlotte wanted to see a famous one about a man whose child died.

"It sounds sad," Clem said.

"Life is sad," Mrs. Dunrea answered.

"Yes," Clem said. "That is why art should be uplifting."

"I hear this movie is very beautiful," Mrs. Dunrea said. "And sad. It's up for five Academy Awards."

Eve thought she had left more than enough time to get to the movie theater, but once again Clem and her mother surprised her. Both needed to use the restroom first. Eve went in with her mother. Mrs. Dunrea washed her hands and then reapplied her lipstick, a reddish pink. Their eyes met in the ladies' room mirror.

"Clem likes this color," her mother said. "Not that I listen to what Clem says," she added. "He likes everything. Swiss steak!"

The waitress hurried to meet them at the door. Clem had left his hat in the booth. He fitted the hat down, adjusting it at a rakish angle. "Thank you, my dear," he said. Then he turned to Eve. "And thank you," he added. "I'm not sure what I did to deserve this, but thank you anyway."

"You've been a good friend to my mom," Eve said. As she spoke, tears came, absurdly, into her eyes.

Her mother was already creeping ahead of them, moving with infinite slowness and determination toward the door. "Come on, we'll miss the movie!" she ordered.

• • •

The movie *was* sad. It reminded Eve of the two boys who had died, and she had to close her eyes through the scenes with the bereaved father. While she had her eyes closed she felt her mother tapping on her hand. "What?" she whispered. "Stop him!" her mother whispered back, and pointed.

Clem was trying to crawl through the metal bar in front of him, to make his escape from the movie. He had already gotten one long leg through and was trying to jam the other one. They had chosen seats in front of the elevated section, with low gray metal bars in front. Now Clem appeared to be stuck. A group of teenagers behind them were snickering.

Eve caught Clem's arm. "You need to sit down," she whispered.

"I have to get out of here." He shook his head and tried swinging the free leg over the bars. More laughter from behind. It looked as if Clem were riding the bars like some aging cowboy.

"Clem, please," her mother said.

"Come back," Eve said. They were trying to do this in whispers.

An angry woman in the movie threw a cup at the main actor, smashing it against a wall. She sobbed and punched the famous actor. Clem looked up and redoubled his efforts. Finally, Eve stood up, and pulled him into his seat.

"We'll go, I promise," she said. "This way." She pointed to the aisle and the steps.

"We'll come back for you," she whispered to her mother.

Her mother just shook her head, sitting perfectly straight. Her shoulders were jerking and small sobs escaped her. Eve had never seen her mother cry at the movies. She could count on one hand the number of times she had seen her mother cry at all. Mrs. Dunrea shook her head again, but when Eve offered her a tissue from her purse, she realized Charlotte was laughing.

She and Clem went into another theater and watched an animated movie for children about animals escaping from a zoo. Clem enjoyed it. He had a loud, infectious laugh. The movie was short, so they had twenty minutes left till her mother's movie was over.

"We could go back and watch the very end," Eve suggested in the lobby.

Clem shook his head emphatically. "Oh, no," he said. "I'm not going in there again."

Eve bought him some M&M peanuts, which he ate slowly and contentedly, while she sipped at a lemonade. He kept offering her the candy, and she kept saying, "No, thank you." Then she would offer him a lemonade and he would say, "No, thank you," or, "I'd be up all night." Finally, Eve left him and went to help her mother out of her theater. "I'll be right back," she told Clem.

"That's fine," he said. "I'll stay and guard your place."

Her mother said, "You two missed a very fine movie." Grumpily.

"It wasn't *my* idea," Eve said. Actually, she had enjoyed the children's movie more than the famous sad one. But she didn't have to admit that.

"I don't know what is the matter with that man," her mother said. "Honestly, he must be more nutty than I realized. He's a lot to handle. Now I know why he never married."

When they came back to the lobby, Eve had to scan the tables three or four times before she could believe her eyes. Clem was nowhere in sight. "Maybe he's in the men's room," she said.

"Maybe not," her mother said. "What if he's wandering along the highway? He could be killed!"

Eve ran for the manager, who checked the men's room for her. He came out a few minutes later alone, shaking his head. "Nobody answered when I called. I waited around to see, but there were no elderly gentlemen in there."

"Oh Lord," Eve said. She parked her mother at a table by the windows. "Keep watching. Maybe he just stepped out." She ran between the parked cars, calling Clem's name. It was a balmy night. This time of year it could well have been snowing. Her eyes scanned the far, dark shoulder of the highway. At least his white hair might be visible. She was heading back in just as Clem rounded the corner, hands in his pockets.

"Where were you?" she cried. She didn't know whether to hug him or shake him.

"I just went around the building," Clem said. He pointed at the sidewalk that circled the theater. "To stretch my legs."

Mrs. Dunrea lectured him furiously half the ride home, and gave him the cold, silent treatment the other half.

"I certainly am sorry," Clem said over and over. "I am heartily sorry."

"That's all right," Eve answered soothingly, till her mother cut in with, "It is certainly *not* all right. Very thoughtless. And here we were, taking you out for a nice evening. So we thought."

"It was a nice evening," Clem said. "I had a wonderful time."

All of this made Eve terribly sad. She had always imagined that old people were gentler, that they knew how to get along. She could hardly wait to get back to Emerald Gardens.

The white-haired woman at the front desk—a friend once called these workers "early admissions" cases—came out to hold open the door. "Such a beautiful night," the woman exclaimed. "Did you have a good time?"

"I did," Clem said.

Her mother said, "I'm exhausted. Get me to my

room." Eve kissed her mother on the cheek and shook Clem's hand. Her mother was already on her way.

Clem lowered his great, leonine head. "She'll never forgive me," he said.

"She will," Eve said, but knew her mother didn't have a forgiving nature. She cut friends over the smallest slights. Eve remembered grieving as if these friends had died, vanishing suddenly and completely from their lives. People just became more like themselves as they grew older. It must be like the grooves on an old LP. Over time the paths cut deeper and were that much harder to erase.

When she let herself inside the house, Noni and Marcus were sitting on the sofa side by side, as if they hadn't moved all night. Noni's face looked as rigid as her grandmother's. Her lips were in a thin line. In front of them, on the coffee table, lay an open manila envelope. Marcus had a strange smile on his face, a touch crooked.

"I got in," he said. "I got into Albany, first choice, on a full presidential scholarship."

Her heart swerving up and sinking, Eve said, "That's wonderful, honey! Congratulations!"

As if she'd been waiting all night, Noni burst into tears.

"Noni baloney," Marcus said tenderly, putting his arms around his sister.

"You're going away!" she wailed.

338

"I'll come home every vacation," Marcus said. "You'll be sick of the sight of me."

"I'll never," Noni sobbed, "be sick—of the—sight—of you!"

Every word could have come from Eve's own aching heart. It felt like there was an ocean in there, washing back and forth, waiting to spill over. But there could not be two weeping and wailing women in the house.

"It's wonderful news!" Eve said. "And Albany isn't so far away."

After Marcus had finally gone to bed—Noni went in early, all tuckered out from her crying jag—Eve sat out on the front porch, paying some bills. A cup of tea sat cooling on the wrought-iron table beside her, a garage sale item that had not sold. The April night air was as soft as June. It might have been global warming, as Samson Fleaback, the drawing teacher, declared gloomily, but Eve preferred to be hopeful. Living in Binghamton, you had to get lucky with the weather once in a while. She was carefully not thinking about Marcus going away next year. She remembered Scarlett O'Hara's "I'll think about it tomorrow!" and the little good it ever did her.

The porch light shone on the metal table; it was early enough in spring so no moths flew near the light; no one was out on the streets. All was calm and quiet. She heard whistling far off, which turned and headed up her street, a string of clear, jaunty notes. She peered down the street in disbelief. It was Lev Schooner, of all people. He noticed her, too, a few houses away, then stopped whistling and looked embarrassed.

"Oh, hey," he said.

"Hey," she said.

"I forgot you live right nearby."

"I live right here, in fact."

"I meant near Tracy," he said.

They were both silent a moment. "Nice night," she finally said.

Lev put his arms out as if to catch the wind. "Beautiful!" he said. "Amazing!" He spoke like a happy lover. Eve supposed he probably was one, out this late.

"Wouldn't it be nice if it stayed this way?" she said.

"It would be a miracle," he said. "Can I sit?"

She pushed the bills together in one pile, anchoring them down with her mug of tea. "Sure. Come up the steps."

Instead he vaulted lightly over the railing.

"I could never do that in a million years," she said.

"Believe it or not," he said, "I used to do pole vaulting. Back in high school."

"Believe it or not," she said, "I didn't. How's Tracy?" she asked.

His expression changed. "She's—coming along,"

he said. "All those medications." He shook his head. "I don't think she knows if she's in or out half the time. She was asleep when I left."

This was too intimate a detail to digest. Eve said, "Marcus got into SUNY Albany. That was his first choice."

"Did he?"

She looked out over the street. "He got a presidential scholarship, too. Honors College, the works."

"Good for him," Lev said. "You'll miss him, I bet."

"Don't get me started."

"I won't," he said, looking away, embarrassed. "So, did you hear about the Philosophy Department? They're talking about staging a revolt."

He stayed for a cup of tea, and went on talking even after Eve began to feel sleepy. He was one of those people who came awake after midnight, she realized. His voice became lighter and quicker. He talked about working at his father's gas station in high school, accidentally filling up a car with diesel fuel before he realized his mistake.

"My father found out anyway," he added. "When the carburator and the fuel lines gummed up. I was busted," he said, laughing.

When she offered him a refill on his tea, though, it stopped him cold. He looked at his watch, shook his wrist. "Wow, I've got to go," he said. "Tracy will wonder what happened. Ginger will be furious. She has a dog door, but even so . . ."

He offered to help bring everything inside, but Eve waved him off. "Go," she said. "Hurry. Hell hath no fury—"

"Right," he said, and as quickly as he had leapt onto the porch, he leapt off it—showing off? she wondered—and headed up the street. Just as he turned the corner back toward Tracy's house, his whistle, sweet, high, came trailing back behind. She felt a distinct pang, a deep regret almost like bitterness. She was sorry to see him go.

Chapter 26

Jonah's Dream

Lev had stopped by a few more evenings, to keep Eve company on her porch. He'd hop up, drink his one cup of tea, which stretched from a half hour to an hour, two hours, more—and then leave again, as abruptly as he'd come. She felt foolish, sitting out on the porch each night, waiting for him to drop by, yet she couldn't help herself. It was like having a wild animal come to your door—you didn't want to startle it away.

Being in love had made Lev happier. Eve could not quite put her finger on it. He and Tracy must have been seeing each other constantly, and one night Eve asked him why he didn't just stay over.

Lev looked guilty at the very idea. "Ginger would never forgive me if I spent the whole night away."

It was after two when he'd finally left. She dragged herself and the dogs to Rec Park next morning. Jonah was there, wearing a short-sleeve orange T-shirt, no jacket. He was mowing the grass but cut off the machine when he spotted Eve.

"Had a late night?" he asked, smiling.

"Does it show? Not the kind you mean," she said. "Just a friend coming to talk."

"Must be a very good friend," he said. "Me and Lorena," Jonah said, "we been going together three months now. Thinking it's almost time for me to settle down."

"Wouldn't that be nice!" Eve said.

He laughed. "You are all alike," he said. "I'm going down to South Carolina to see my mama before I pop the question. Driving down next week. Have some time in the car, get some thinking done. My mama's met Lorena, too, did I tell you?"

"No," she said.

"Came up in February. Her and my big sister. Had to look Lorena over. They think she a very nice woman," he said. "They were quite impressed. Lorena is not a flashy woman. She's a churchgoing woman. She is solid. She's respectable. I'm going down to Carolina as soon as I can get away from the park."

He told her, then, about the large number of homeless men who'd been congregating at Rec Park during the recent string of warm days and nights. "First thing every morning, I find them on the benches. That's why I left Brooklyn. I seen needles laying around on the grass where they been."

He crossed his arms. "Keep your kids away after dark. One man's been troubling me since the winter. Tried to borrow some money off me. Always wearing army fatigues, but I don't believe he's no vet. Plus now he's got him a couple of young friends. Cops caught them sleeping here the one time. I don't know if they hide when they see the cars drive up or if they just gotten lucky. It's not against the law for them to be here by day—I watch them watching these school kids coming through. I don't like what I am seeing."

"Most homeless people are harmless," Eve said. "Some of them are sick." But she thought of the stranger who'd talked to Noni.

"These men ain't sick. Sick of working," he said.

"Maybe you're being too harsh," she said.

"Maybe you ain't being harsh enough," he said. "Keep your kids out of the way."

"I will," she promised. "I am."

•••

"If we could take out this wall," Mia said, pointing to the narrow hallway that darkened the whole upstairs. She wore a long green skirt with wavy blue lines and a matching blue linen shirt. She was at the gun lap of the semester, but still dissatisfied with this final project.

Eve closed her eyes. She was not good at this. She touched the wall, trying to imagine it gone. "Let's get rid of the fourth bedroom," she said.

Mia's eyes widened. "You would sacrifice a bedroom?"

"It's tiny anyway. We don't really need it. We hardly ever use it."

"Make the upstairs bathroom so larger," Mia said eagerly, reaching for her drawing materials. "You could have more open space up here. I love this idea." She rapped on the wall of the hallway, then the bedroom. Both rang hollow. "No supporting wall. Easy."

"How easy?" Eve said. "Easy like I could do it myself?" She pictured herself swinging a hammer, breaking through walls. The idea appealed to her.

"Sook-yun worked construction in Korea, for his father. His father builds—" She put her hand above her head. "—high houses."

"Skyscrapers?"

Mia took out her pencil and paper and wrote down the word *skyscraper.* "Sook-yun can do," she said, sweeping her arm around the upstairs. "In a day, maybe two. With friends. Very sheeply."

"Cheaply," Eve corrected her automatically. "And I can help. I want to help."

Mia stuck her head inside the bathroom, studied it, turned back. "Maybe you will need a plumber," she said.

"I have a plumber."

But Mia was already busy sketching away. "This is so excellent," she said. "Will make all the difference." Her lips parted, her hair fell in front of half her face. She pushed it back. She had sat down right in the middle of the dark carpeted hallway, resting the pad on her knees, her skirt spreading around her like a green pond.

Jonah was not a man to pay attention to bad dreams. Normally he didn't even remember his dreams, and he doubted the veracity of the detail that other people recounted. "If I was that damn busy asleep," he'd say, "I'd be too tired to wake up."

Yet he woke from his nightmare shouting out loud, his own voice waking him. A car veered off the road, its driver's side door swinging open, was he the passenger? There was a white flash. He felt himself falling through empty space and woke with his arms and legs flailing, sending the quilt flying off the bed.

His bedroom clock's red Roman numerals

glowed in the dark. It was 4:00 A.M. Try as he might, Jonah could not get back to sleep. He stared at his suitcase standing in a corner of the room, by the door, and imagined getting in his car and driving down to South Carolina. He told himself to quit his foolishness. Moments later the phone rang.

"Don't come down, son," his mother said. "I had a dream about it. I'm sorry to call so early, but I was afraid I might miss you if I waited."

"Had the same dream," he said, before he could catch himself.

"I don't want you to—What's that?" she interrupted herself. "You had a dream, too?"

"Maybe," he said, "I'll just put off the trip this time around. Unless you think I could get a plane ticket?"

"I don't want you climbing into nothing that moves," she said. "Just stick close to home today. You can lie around in bed like you're always saying you want to."

"When did I say that?" he asked, teasing her, trying to draw her mind away from the dreams, the coincidence of having them together.

They talked a while longer, and neither said anything further about it till the very end. When they were about to hang up, his mother said, "I'm glad God give us a sign."

"Amen," he said. He felt lucky, blessed; he had been given a warning and so had his mother; as if God wanted to make doubly sure he got the message. Lying back, he decided: if he wasn't going down to visit his mother, he would not waste the day. He and Lorena would go to church services that night. He could say thank-you for not being run off the road on his way down to Carolina. It just wasn't his time yet.

Jonah drove to the park early. The sky was still stained pink from the sunrise. He felt like he ought to be doing something useful. He'd clean up some of his tools in the little shed behind the pool area. They'd be needing them soon if the warm weather days kept coming so early.

Usually he got to the park in time to see the middle-schoolers straggling in to school, dragging their book bags on the ground behind them, pushing each other and cursing. Today he saw the little kids heading off to elementary school. They looked brighter and happier than their older brothers and sisters. He waved to Noni, who waved back, hesitated as if she thought to come talk, then shrugged, smiled, pivoted and ran off after her friends. He watched them all gather at the back door of the school and swarm inside. Soon only one child was left in the park.

This little girl had her hair corn-rowed, with dozens of tiny white hair bows all over her head. She was dawdling, picking up sticks in the park and trying to stuff them into her backpack. They kept dropping out again. She'd bend to gather them, and shove them back inside, one by one, like trying to jam too many straws into a small drinking glass.

He was watching her from behind the mower. Sun was getting higher. She was playing just a few feet away, on the edge of the parking lot. Jonah heard a car screeching to a stop. He figured it was the little girl's mother, that the girl had probably forgotten her homework or her lunch.

But there were four men in the car, one in green army fatigues. The doors of the car flew open all at once. Like it had sprouted wings and was about to fly. Something metallic caught the glint of sunlight in the man's hand.

Jonah didn't have time to think. He threw himself at the girl, and pushed her down. There was a flash of white, a blinding pain, his own startled mind saying, *Good God Almighty that hurts,* and that was the very last thing he knew.

Chapter 27
Remembrance

The bagpipers lined up in the park, the way they always did for funerals, weddings, and memorial services. They were big burly men, with a few determined-looking women and one high school boy, his white-blond hair streaked with blue. He

349

covered it in the same dark blue peaked cap that all the pipers wore, which gave him a conservative look. Gareth Jenkins, former vice president of IBM as well as district assemblyman, led the pipers. He raised the pipe wand to his lips and blew a note, and the other pipers answered in a deep wave of sound. The pipers played "O Danny Boy." They marched in place, their white boots churning up and down, and midway through the song they formed two lines that parted like water.

And if you come, when all the flowers are dying
And I am dead, as dead I well may be
You'll come and find the place where I am lying
And kneel and say an "Ave" there for me.

Jonah threaded his way slowly through the opening they made, his right arm bulky in a white cast. It took a while to walk those thirty or forty feet, but he was beaming, his high cheekbones perfectly round. A young woman walked on his left side, an elderly woman in bright blue at his right. This had to be Jonah's mother—they did not look alike; in fact, she was an inch taller than her son. But only a mother could have looked so exalted, so rigidly upright, as if afraid to mar by one turn of her head the seriousness of this moment.

Jonah wore his Parks Department uniform with CITY OF BINGHAMTON blazoned across his back in large green letters. He had on a pair of black leather dress shoes, brilliantly polished. Eve had a sudden flash of intuition: one day he would be mayor of the city. But now he moved toward Mayor Garguillo to shake his hand, then the state senator's, and Tookie Jones, head of the Parks Department, with his bright red hair, and two or three other local officials.

It was a bright April afternoon, and the local elementary school half a block away had walked double-file to the park for the ceremony. The children's high chirping voices filled the air. The little girl with the corn-rowed hair stood at the front. At least fifty city workers were on hand; white cars with the green City of Binghamton seal on the side doors lined the lot by the softball field. Several park regulars had turned up for the event—joggers and dog-walkers; the elderly tennis players; the retarded boy still dragging his toy dog; the young mother with the jogging stroller, her baby looking more like a toddler staring alertly around. A few older kids had skipped school to be there, or were just hanging around and came closer, drawn by the crowd and the pipers. The ice cream man respectfully refrained from ringing his chimes for the moment. The pipers finished their song in a burst of harmonics from which the park echoed several seconds afterward.

The mayor stepped up to a microphone set on a

portable stand. Lorena and Jonah's mother fell back. The crowd quieted. The pipers stood locked in place, their posture rigid, eyes looking straight ahead. The crowd pushed around the carousel.

Mayor Garguillo thanked everyone for coming. He was wearing a double-breasted suit and a wide striped tie. His dark hair was slicked back. In photographs and campaign posters, even on the news, the mayor had a short, squat, comical look, but in person, Eve was always surprised by how handsome he was, with his black eyes and long lashes. He praised the elementary school principal and the children for their good behavior and "good listening skills. Thank you, boys and girls." He thanked the state senator for making time to be there. He went on about what a safe and clean city Binghamton was, how violent crime had dropped over the past three years. "I'm working to get my hometown back on top," he said—the line he'd made famous during his mayoral campaign. "Incidents like these are, thankfully, rare. No one should be afraid to come into the Binghamton parks. We've got more police presence, we've hired four extra officers to make sure that the law will be enforced. Trust me, the law *will* be enforced."

He turned at last to Jonah. "We thank this man," he said. "Today could have been a day of tragedy. Thanks to Jonah Cement it is a day of celebration, and I hereby declare that from this day forward, April thirteenth is declared to be Jonah Cement Day in Binghamton, New York!"

The crowd applauded, the children cheered. The retarded boy put his fingers to his lips and whistled.

One of the men handed the mayor a framed citation, which he presented to Jonah, pausing long enough in the handshake to let the photographers step up with their flash cameras going off. Jonah looked pleased and a bit overwhelmed. He bent his head, Eve thought at first in prayer, but then the mayor placed a medal around his neck, on a red, white, and blue striped ribbon. The medal was bronze, to match its twin, set in the pavement of the park.

Then the mayor stepped back and let the senator speak. The senator called Jonah "Judas" by mistake, mopping his brow in the warm spring sun. He looked tired, thinner; it had been a rough year—several fellow senators on his State Budgetary Committee had been indicted for fraud. He, too, paused to let the photographers step in with their flash cameras. When the senator was done, he shook Jonah's hand, and the assembled bagpipers lifted their bagpipes to their lips, but Jonah said, "I would like to say something."

The senator and mayor looked alarmed. Garguillo leaped forward and spoke into the mike. "And now our guest of honor would like to say a few words," he said. "Just a few."

"Thank you!" Jonah said. He stood too close to the mike, which exploded into feedback whistling squeals, and people clapped their hands over their ears. "Thank you," he said more quietly. "The city has been very good to me. I hear people say it ain't got nothing going on, but Binghamton has got heart. I am glad if I did something good for this town, because I love this place that has taken me in, and given me a good life. I thank God every day for that. That's it." He turned to the mayor with a helpless gesture. Then he turned back to the mike. "Thank you all."

The children cheered again, and the retarded boy whistled vigorously, even after the crowd began to break up and the children had been led off in two long, uneven lines, and the photographers had unscrewed their cameras from their stands. He whistled two or three more times into the air. Then he set off through the park, dragging the toy dog behind him on a thin red leash.

Eve stood on line to shake Jonah's hand. He chatted with each well-wisher, kissing the women and shaking the men's hands. It was Eve's lunch hour. She waited at the very end of the line, but it was that lull before the storm of final exams and critiques, and she didn't need to rush back to the university. Jonah introduced her to his mother, who sat on a bench nearby drinking lemonade from the ice cream man's truck, and to Lorena, who never budged from Jonah's side. For the first time since Eve had known him, Jonah was looking peaked. She said as much.

Lorena patted the arm in the cast, very softly. Her skin was scarred from what must have been a bout of adolescent acne, and she was thirty or forty pounds overweight. But she had a serene smile, and was clearly in charge. "We're leaving in ten minutes," she said, "I hope you don't mind my saying. Jonah got a bullet wound healing in his shoulder. He broke his arm when he fell. This man still needs his rest." She folded one hand gently, protectively, over Jonah's.

"They made that plaque in my honor," Jonah said to Eve. "I tole them I don't need anything like that, but the mayor insisted. My boss in Parks insisted."

"I agree," said Lorena. "Why shouldn't they honor you?"

They must have both told the story fifty or sixty times by now, but Jonah seemed glad to tell it again. "They had to special order the plaque in Albany. It has the seal of the Binghamton Parks Department by my name. I told them, if you want to do this thing, do it right, before everybody goes away for the summer. Not to mention I might have another ceremony in mind soon." He looked pointedly at Lorena.

Eve said, "Jonah, thank you. You were so brave, doing what you did."

"Was instinct," Jonah said. "I did what I did instinctively."

"That's the bravest way of all," Lorena put in.

Jonah leaned forward and spoke sotto voce. "I got lots of nice suits to wear, but this is my official uniform, and they are rewarding me in my official capacity. Plus the other city workers is jealous enough as it is. Man accused me of diving into that bullet on purpose. I said, 'I understand you have some trouble believing the *truth*. Maybe we need to set the record *straight*.' I told him, 'You have yourself a very nice day.' Lorena's training me to be polite."

"Working on it," Lorena said in an amused voice.

"I told you about them men, didn't I?" Jonah said to Eve. "Now the supervisor wants to promote me. City was ready to give me a job out of the park, but I told them, this is my park, I like what I do. But I wouldn't say no to a raise . . . So," he said in his normal voice again, "maybe soon I'll have more good news."

"The best news is you're still here," Eve said.

"Amen to that," said Lorena and Jonah together, and from the park bench Jonah's mother added, "The Lord be praised."

Mia and Eve collected Toys for Tots all month, in time for Easter. The people who ran it called it

Spring Bring, to make it seem more sectarian. They hit up their neighbors and friends, and Mia held a Spring Bring party at her apartment. The Americans brought one package, or two, wrapped in Easter bunny paper or pastels. The Koreans brought bags full of gifts, even the graduate students, who, Eve knew, lived on a pittance.

They loaded up Eve's Toyota and drove the gifts to the drop-off center in the Binghamton Plaza, a strip mall of soaped over storefronts. Once, there had been a movie theater there, and a pool parlor next to it, full of vaguely dangerous-looking teenagers, with a big picture window up front. There had been a Grand Union supermarket, a chain that no longer existed in the triple cities. There had been a barbershop; only its red and white striped pole remained. The drop-off spot for the toys, once the Ames, was now an immense, gray-looking space.

Bags of toys ran down the middle of the room, black plastic garbage bags stacked so they created a low wall. On the one side of this wall, Eve and Mia were directed toward the police captain who ran the operation, alongside Beds for Kids. He'd been doing this for so many years that Eve recognized him from TV and photos in the paper. He sat behind a small gray desk. On the other side of the bags came a steady trickle of people lined up to sign up for the toys. The line of people was as long as the warehouse.

They clutched paperwork, often a husband and wife side by side, usually speaking in another language. Nobody looked at the toys, which had spilled out of the bags or were stacked in towers—dolls encased in square plastic boxes, wooden blocks, picture books. They kept their eyes on the desk up front, as if afraid to be caught wanting something.

Eve was stunned by the sheer size of the operation—the vastness of the room, the number of bags, the number of toys inside the bags. Hundreds and hundreds. Could they all possibly go to people in Broome County? she wondered.

The police captain shook his head, in amazement or disgust. "Do you know how many of these people have nothing?" he asked. "They don't have a towel for their kids when they come out of the bath. Soap—shampoo, toothbrushes. Beds. Things we take for granted. Never mind teddy bears and dolls. We got more demand than supply. Every year the list gets longer. Yeah, we'll really give all these toys to the citizens of Broome County," he said. "Just look around you."

He probably didn't mean it literally, but she did look around. The cop who now emerged from the pile of toys and books to help them was the same bulldog-faced officer who had come to break the news of Ivan's death. She had not seen him close up for almost fifteen years. But it was the same face, the same sad mouth and slumped shoulders. She felt she had to say something, but had no idea what. Her mouth went dry. Her heart was pounding the way it used to at school, wanting to speak and not daring to raise her hand.

Mia was looking at Eve with concern.

"You are okay?" she asked. "Your back is hurting?"

Eve shook her head. They all walked out into the parking lot. She unlocked the Toyota and the bulldog-faced cop reached to take their bags from Mia, who looked tiny compared to them. Mia shook her head. "I can carry," she said. "I am very strong person."

"How about I take one and you carry the other?" the policeman suggested. His soft voice went through Eve like an arrow. It was hesitant, his way of speaking. She had been storing the sound all these years in some locked chamber of her heart. Mia lifted her bag of toys and marched back to the store, her back straight. The cop took one of the bags Eve had been holding. She could not look directly at him. He walked beside her into the large warehouse. It was as cold as a winter day in there. "I'm Officer Conlon," he said. "I remember you."

She felt a thrill as keen as if he had said he loved her.

She put the car keys in Marcus's hand. "Drive," she said.

She had been able to coax him back into the car from time to time, on the promise that once he got his license, he could borrow it occasionally for dates with Astrid.

"Where are we going?" he asked.

"You'll see," she said, settling back into her seat. She smoothed her dress down over her knees. She'd gotten dressed up for this occasion —high heels, makeup, the works.

She directed him right and left, then left again, through traffic, till at last they arrived at their destination.

"Oh, Mom," he said. "Oh, no."

"Come on," she said, more cheerfully than she felt. She climbed out of the Toyota and asked where to line up for their scheduled driving test.

"That's a brand new car, isn't it?" said the man who pointed her the right way. "You're a brave lady." He was a big, burly guy in his late fifties, early sixties, dressed in a bright red shirt, the color of a Santa Claus suit.

"Oh, well," she said, more airily than she felt, flapping her hand.

"Either you have a lot of faith, or a lot of money," he said.

"It's definitely not money," she answered.

He smiled, glancing at her flowered dress. "That's nice," he added, "dressing up for spring."

They had gotten there early. She'd made sure of that. And Marcus was wearing clean clothes.

She'd made sure of that, too. They waited for half an hour. And it turned out the man in the red shirt was Marcus's driving instructor. Now he was holding a clipboard. He said to Eve, "We meet again."

She laughed. "Yes."

"So this is the young man you have such faith in.—All right," he said to Marcus. "Let's see what you can do."

Before they drove off, she saw her son buckle his seat belt and adjust the rearview mirror. He did it like he'd been driving all his life. When she climbed back in the car twenty minutes later, Marcus waved his new permit at her. "I aced it, Mom!" He clutched the precious piece of paper and would not let go of it, even while driving.

They all went out to Red Lobster that night to celebrate. Mrs. Dunrea said, "Congratulations, Marcus." She sighed down at her buttered roll. "Now I have one more thing to worry about."

Spring came early and deranged, a bright brief flurry of lilacs and blossoming trees in full bloom by late April. There were more consecutive days of blue skies and sunlight than Eve could remember. People wore brighter colors; the high school kids wore fewer and fewer clothes to school, low-cut tank tops and high-cut shorts. Noni pleaded in vain to be allowed to wear them, too.

The cherry trees blew pink petals over both sides of Leroy Street. Eve got in the habit of sitting out on her front porch, evenings, setting out on the wrought-iron table candles, which fluttered festively, creating enough light to read or work by. More evenings than not, Lev stopped by on his way home from Tracy's. He stayed at least an hour, sometimes more. Eve began to expect him. He came on schedule.

One warm day she and Tracy finally had lunch together. It had been too long, Eve thought. They sat in Tracy's favorite café, half luncheonette, half bakery. Tracy always brought some cookies home in a paper bag.

"How's Lev?" Tracy asked, stirring her cappuccino. "I haven't seen him in a few weeks."

"You what?" Eve said. Swinging her hand forward in surprise, she upset her own water glass. Water spilled silver across the table. It streamed in a narrow line toward Tracy's plate. "Sorry," she said, mopping it up with her napkin and then Tracy's, then dabbing with the bottom of her own shirt. "Sorry!"

"I guess he's been busy," Tracy said. "We still talk on the phone a lot."

"What do you mean? Aren't you going out?" Eve asked.

"Going out where?" Tracy said. She looked at Eve. "Oh! You mean—We don't go out like that. We're friends."

"That's impossible," Eve said.

"I don't care if it's possible," Tracy said, irritated. "We're friends. That's it."

"But—" Eve shook her head as if to clear it. "I just don't understand. When did this all happen?"

"Nothing happened," Tracy said. "I haven't even seen him in weeks."

"Then what's he doing in our neighborhood?" Eve demanded.

Tracy looked at her in surprise. "Our neighborhood?"

Eve had to explain it several times. She described how Lev would round the corner night after night, always from the direction of Tracy's house. Tracy leaned back and looked down at her hands. Her fingernails were long and white at the tips, as if she'd had a French manicure, but actually, she'd once confided to Eve, that was just the way they looked naturally. They were artist's hands, nervous and elegant.

Tracy drummed her fingers on the table, a merry little tattoo of sound. "Beats me. You figure it out," she said.

Eve served dinner that night hardly knowing what she put on the table: cheese and bean tacos, corn bread—nothing she had to think about. She kept glancing out the window, the spring daylight darkening into dusk, wishing her kids were little again and she could pop them into bed at eight. Then she felt guilty for wishing to get rid of them. Noni asked to play Monopoly, the world's longest game. So they played, the three of them—the two dogs came to watch, too. They curled up on either side of her legs, Toaster leaning so heavily against Eve that her foot fell asleep. She thought the game would never end, and then when it did, she suddenly felt frightened.

Marcus had Debate Club practice before school the next morning, so he headed to bed early. She would get no help from him. He had lately joined the student government, as student senator-at-large, since he'd been offered a summer internship for their local congressman, a liberal Democrat famous for his fiery oratory.

Eve stayed downstairs alone and read, though she kept looking up from her book and could not remember from page to page a thing she had been reading. Then it was late, nearly midnight; surely Lev would not come tonight. Her heart was pounding wildly—ridiculous, she thought, for no reason at all. She should just go to bed, turn off all the house lights. But she stepped outside. The night air was warm. The street was black and empty. It stayed that way for a long time, nothing moving, except once a stray cat, and then Lev loped up the street, his legs almost invisible in black jeans taking wide, quick strides. He was whistling again. But he stopped at what must have been Eve's expression.

"What are you doing?" she said. She walked to the top of the porch steps.

"What do you mean," he asked, but his voice wavered. "Is it a bad night?"

"Not especially," she said. She wouldn't give him more than that.

"Do you want me to go away?"

She didn't trust herself to speak. She shook her head.

"Well, then." He came lightly up the first two stairs till he was inches away, his head one step's length lower than hers. He was wearing one of his Hawaiian shirts again: spring had come.

He took her hand and stepped up onto the porch. They were almost exactly the same height. He spun her around, which was disconcerting enough, and then, without preamble, dipped her backward. She laughed, out of surprise. While she was still laughing, he brought her back upright and kissed her with unexpected decisiveness.

She moved into his kiss as if there were something more under it, unsaid, something pulsing inside it. He put his hands on her shoulders, then the back of her neck, pushed his fingers through her hair. His body was small and confident. Everything about him surprised her. She came up out of the kiss like someone underwater. She staggered back a step. His face no longer looked familiar. He was smiling at her, a stranger.

"What was that?" she said.

"That was a kiss." He stepped forward as if to try again.

On the porch, the candles had burned down, and only the glow from the porch lamp cast a half-light on Lev's face. She could not read his unfathomable eyes. He stood tense as a cat, ready to spring off the porch and run off if she said a wrong word. She felt herself hanging in the balance, a pendulum that was swinging weightlessly for an instant but must soon move either one way or the other. A cloud touched the moon overhead. She had known him so long; it was her self who had been a mystery. She lifted her hands and took his.

"I know," she said. "Let's try it again."

Chapter 28
The Wedding

On the morning of the Van Gogh opening, a gray September day, people lined up around the Fine Arts building three and four deep to wait. Some had arrived the night before and camped out by the door of the museum. Olivia Zarembo, in a gesture of solidarity, had brought her eldest daughter and their own sleeping bag. It was featured on the television news and took up the front page of the *Press*, pushing to one side all other news, as if Van Gogh himself had marched into Binghamton. The only other event that had ever caused such a stampede in town was the opening of the large new Wegman's market, where people had driven fifty miles and slept in their cars to wait for the supermarket to unlock its doors. Van Gogh and Wegman's. The sublime and the ridiculous, that was Binghamton in a nutshell.

Noni eyed Lev as if he were a slightly dangerous animal coming around the house. She was polite but kept her distance till she met Lev's dog, the famous Ginger. It was love at first sight. Ginger let out a series of sharp, piercing yelps and sank down on her back, paws waving in the air.

Noni rubbed the dog's belly, which elicited more ear-splitting yelps.

"Calm down!" Lev ordered, but Noni was in heaven.

"See, Mom, we need a bigger dog, like Ginger. We need a third dog."

They drove to the Van Gogh show together—Noni in the back with Ginger, the girl and dog nearly intertwined. They had to persuade Noni that Ginger could not be permitted into the museum itself. "We can pretend she's my guide dog," Noni begged. "Okay, Mom? Ginger would be a great guide dog."

The exhibit consisted of twenty-four drawings and a handful of paintings, in two small rooms. It was designed to feel as if you had stepped into someone's house. The walls were painted a golden parchment color, roughly the same shade as the paper Van Gogh used for his drawings. The pieces were mostly in lithographic crayon and graphite, white paint as thick as Elmer's glue, portraits scratched in pen—there were a few watercolors, and two oil paintings had been loaned as well, for which the charcoal studies hung beside them: *A Farmhouse in Provence*, and *Olive Trees*.

The largest crowds gathered around the two oil paintings, in vibrant yellows and blues. After a week there was still a crowd in the museum; you couldn't move from drawing to drawing without bumping into someone or waiting in a huddle to move sideways again.

They took one of Olivia's guided tours. Olivia's voice was raspy, ragged from all the speaking she'd been doing, but she had never looked more blissful. More and more visitors attached themselves to the tour as she threaded her way around the rooms, pointing out details.

"Van Gogh did these pencil studies in the Dutch Reformed Old People's Home in the early eighties," she explained. "This man in *Worn Out* leans his face heavily in his hand—as if this were the last place he had to rest his head." She walked unhurriedly to the next drawing. She let people take their time, waited for the stragglers. "In *Old Man with a Top Hat* please observe the differences between the hat, the wool overcoat, and the dilapidated shoes. This is very telling, no? The feet. This is what roots us in the real world. Even for us, our shoes give us away."

True. Eve was wearing sleek black high heels. Her feet were aching after twenty minutes in the museum. Noni was comfortable in her sneakers. Lev, as always, wore hiking boots.

"After Van Gogh's work, we may look at light as a new phenomenon, not to be taken for granted. We notice gestures and expressions on people we pass. It occurs to us that the falling rain might be composed of hundreds of slanting lines. We wonder about the lives of people who have labored with their hands. We see faces differently. This is the highest calling of art—to make us look more deeply."

When Olivia thanked the group at the end of the tour, they burst into applause, startling the other visitors in the museum, who moved off and settled again close by, like birds.

It was a perfect day for a wedding, everybody agreed, and despite the complete, bumbling chaos of the moment, it was true. The September day was windy and bright. The sumacs' reds had come and gone, and the early birches burned sulfur yellow, as brilliant as forsythia. A few bright angled leaves had already fallen. Others flickered on the trees, as if still making up their minds.

Guests milled around out on the grass; not all of the folding chairs had arrived, and the striped green tent had been installed only minutes earlier. Young men and women in formal black jackets set out bottles of champagne in buckets under the shade of the tent. Musicians carried instruments in one direction and some in the opposite direction, and one man was hauling a bass viol across the grass as if pulling a lawn mower. Eve saw two guests bump heads in their effort to navigate around each other, something she had certainly never seen in a wedding on TV or in the movies. Wedding guests were supposed to look sedate and composed, dabbing at their eyes. These looked like people waiting to get on a bus, except, of course, they were too dressed up.

Jonah was dapper in a chalk-striped suit and electric blue shirt the shade of the cloudless sky. He held Lorena's hand, he was a solid figure in an ocean of frantic movement. His arm was out of its cast. Lorena wore a flowered dress that matched his shirt and the kind of broad-brimmed hat worn in church, though the wedding ceremony was being held out of doors, the weather permitting.

Even the guests were put to work. Jonah left Lorena and began carrying extra folding metal chairs, hooking two over each arm. He set up the seats and went back for more. He kept doing this till the young man who'd been bringing them out of the church threw up his arms in despair—they had run out of chairs. The musicians clumped together at one side. Some were still struggling to set up their music stands. The chairs began to settle into rows.

Jonah winked at Marcus, sweating inside a dark blue sport coat. Marcus was too nervous to wink back. He had come from Albany for the occasion. He was best man, and had the wedding ring inside a box in his breast pocket. His fingers kept returning to the pocket.

Noni looked slim and tall, in pale pink; she was the flower girl—if you could call it that, said her Grandma Dunrea dryly. The formal wedding party was small. There were no bridesmaids, no groom's men. It was Noni's job to sprinkle flower petals along the walkway, to clear a path for the bride and groom. She looked as delicate as a pink peony, but she'd cleave a path if she had to knock down several old ladies to do it. "It's what I do as center," she noted, so proud of playing offense on the traveling soccer team that she found some way to work it into every conversation. A few of her teammates and their parents mixed in among the other guests.

Noni waved at them, light glinting off her not entirely invisible braces. She bounced on her heels.

Eve stood quite still, surprisingly nervous, her fingers tightly laced with Lev's. Sweat trickled down her side. You were not supposed to sweat at weddings, she thought, you were allowed only to cry. Even that, discreetly. It was the first time they had stood in public like this, on display as a couple. Lev was wearing the dark blue suit he'd worn to the Thanksgiving dinner almost a year earlier, his one good suit, though he was wearing a tuxedo shirt with two rows of white pleats down the front and a pair of tortoiseshell cuff links from Eve in honor of the day's significance.

She had combed through in her closet and, it seemed, in every store in the tri-cities area look-ing for the right thing to wear. Three weeks before the wedding she still had no dress.

She must have reached some instant's equilib-rium, she thought, for every single thing she owned fit her—clothing she'd worn when she was still on the plump side, and clothing she'd bought when she was skin and bones. But for today, of course, she needed something remark-able. White was out of the question for this wedding; so was black.

As a last resort Eve dragged her mother to the Oakdale mall and asked her to decide. "You're old enough to be dressing yourself," Charlotte

Dunrea grumbled, but was glad to have her opinion solicited. The clothing looked identical from store to store. Only the age of the salespeople varied. Anything even slightly formal looked like a prom dress. At the opposite extreme were racks and racks of career clothing. In desperation they went to a store that specialized in bridal attire, but Charlotte wheeled around as soon as they stepped inside. "Barbie doll outfits," she said. She hobbled away, pushing the walker.

They drove at the end of the day to a small consignment store in town. This was Eve's idea. It was quiet and empty in the shop; compared to the mall, it felt like an oasis. One other customer, a heavyset woman, pushed through a rack of sweaters and kept up a steady stream of conversation with the owner.

Charlotte collapsed into a flowered armchair. "I'm too old for this," she said. Then she pointed across the room, without getting out of her chair. "Try that," she said. She gestured at a row of vintage clothing hanging on a free-standing rack. She was pointing to a long green dress, iridescent beads sewn down the front in a pattern like leaves, delicately intertwined. Eve carried it to the dressing room, feeling like she was holding something alive. It fit snugly around her hips, then flared to the floor in a fall of shimmering green silk "It's elegant," Charlotte said.

"And I'm too tired to look at anything else."

The dress was ridiculously expensive, but Eve bought it anyway. Once home, she could hardly believe her good fortune and foolishness. She hung it on the outside of her closet door so she could look at it each night before she went to bed, like a lovesick girl. The gown was entirely hand-beaded; trumpet beads cascaded the length of the dress, making it shimmer even in the dark. It was amazing that she had never worn anything this beautiful in her life. What had she been waiting for?

Now, a man holding a French horn came up and whispered that while the soprano was ready for her aria at the ceremony's end, her accompanists were nowhere in sight, and no one had brought the keyboard out of the church. Eve disengaged her hand from Lev's and hurried inside the church, nearly colliding with a tall thin man carrying the keyboard out. He was wearing glasses, and he pushed them back up his nose as if Eve had knocked them askew.

"Are they miked?" the man asked.

"Who?"

"The bride and groom."

"They don't want to be miked!" Eve said.

"But no one will be able to hear a thing."

"They don't care," Eve said. "Has the damned accompanist shown up yet?"

"I am the damned accompanist," the man said.

Eve didn't have time to apologize. She followed the man back out to the wedding, which was beginning to pour itself into a shape, still liquid, but starting to resemble an actual formal gathering. Most of the guests had found seats. Marcus was helping to escort others to empty chairs, while some sat in wheelchairs that only needed to be rolled up to their proper places.

Charlotte and Clem stood in a small pool of calm, facing one another. It happened that the sun fell directly on them, so Clem was squinting at his future bride, and Charlotte's hair was lit like a sheet of tissue paper.

She stood upright, but wavering, a candle flame, one hand on her walker. Her head was shaking a little, from nerves, though Eve doubted anyone else would have noticed.

Charlotte had agreed to a church wedding for Clem's sake; he'd served as organist here. The Universalist Church was a large, soaring edifice, its interior like the ark of a ship, with a bowed wooden ceiling and stained-glass windows in deep blues and violent crimsons. Charlotte balked at holding the ceremony inside—her first marriage had been in a city hall, she said, and she hadn't had to perjure herself in order to be wed.

"No talk about Jesus, either," she said. "That's where I hold the line."

Clem remained sweetly oblivious. "I care not

a whit," was his answer. "What I want is the bride." But he had arranged for the church and minister; he called his old musician friends, including Lily, the granddaughter of his deceased best friend. An up-and-coming violinist, Lily looked too young to be in college, much less a silver medalist, but she carried a Stradivarius in one hand. She had bought an extra plane ticket for the violin, she explained, rather breathlessly, after she came running across the church lawn, a red ribbon bouncing up and down in her long black hair. Lily took her place between the keyboard player and the soprano, close enough so Eve could hear her whispering a greeting on either side. Clem's arrangements did not extend to petty details—hence the last minute rush for tent and chairs. Eve had provided the food and drink under the tent and back at Emerald Gardens afterward.

"Half of them won't know what it's for anyway," Charlotte said. But she insisted they provide a wedding cake and ice cream at Emerald Gardens. "And real champagne," she added. "It won't kill them—most of them, anyway."

"Are they going to move into the same room at Emerald Gardens?" Noni asked. "Are they going on a *honeymoon?*"

The answer to both questions was no. They might attempt a short trip later to New York City, if they felt up to it after the fuss of the wedding.

"New York isn't the same without the Plaza," Charlotte grieved, put out, but Clem said placidly, "The Waldorf-Astoria is nearly as good." They were still maintaining their own rooms, though they now occupied the same wing. "I like my own bathroom," Charlotte said. "Besides, Clemente snores."

Marcus remembered his Grandfather Dunrea —better than Noni, she was only three or four when he passed away—but both of Eve's children thought of Grandmother Dunrea in the singular —never the plural. She had always been so self-sufficient, so absolute, her marriage to anyone seemed as improbable as trying to marry off the wind or rain. Yet here she was, looking at Clem with a piercing gaze. Clem met her look and smiled quizzically back, tilting his head. A famous jazz saxophonist in his early eighties, who still played with Dave Brubeck, had flown from Chicago for the wedding. Lev drove the man to and from the airport. He confided to Eve that having coffee with the musician in the airport lounge was one of the highlights of his life.

Lev saw nothing foolish or whimsical in any of this. So it was up to Eve to ask her mother why on earth she was getting married.

"Well, people do," was Charlotte's first response.

Then she said, "Why does anyone get married? Why do middle-aged men leave their wives, or women abandon their families and run off to Tahiti? Why does anyone bother to become friends with anyone, or adopt a child, or own a pet, for that matter? We're all going to die sooner or later, if that's what you're thinking," Charlotte said. "That's life. Nothing we do can change that. We're all going to someday say good-bye. We're all going to have to cry, little girl," she said, putting one hand out to touch Eve's hair. The touch did not quite happen, but hovered, and then settled back down, like a butterfly, still quivering. "We might as well be happy while we can."

Charlotte looked happy now. Absorbed, interested, as Eve remembered her playing bridge or gardening, her hands in the earth, years ago.

The minister was tiptoeing around talk of God, speaking about being part of a community and a higher power, generalizations that might have made Charlotte wince on any other occasion, but at this moment she actually appeared to be thinking about it; she had turned that clear, gimlet-eyed gaze on the minister and was giving him her full attention.

The words sailed over Eve's head. They winged past her ears, but nothing settled. The breeze swirled the long green dress around her legs and feet. And then, too, it was such a motley crowd she was looking at—workers from Emerald Gardens; aides, housecleaners, women she had only seen working in or near the kitchen, always in uniforms. She barely recognized them wearing their own dress clothes. The facility's director was there, and the round-faced sweet-tempered woman from Admissions, with her husband at her side—an enormous man, it turned out, a former football player with wild blond hair whitening at the sides. He stood so close to his wife that they were always touching. Half a dozen of the residents had made the trip—those who were mobile or willing to travel in the medivan.

"There are people," Charlotte had said, half disapprovingly, half with the pitying, superior tone that was her trademark attitude, "who never leave these walls at all. Some grew up on farms and have never even been to the city of Binghamton, much less New York. One of them told me, 'If you've seen one museum, you've seen them all.' They probably feel the same way about weddings."

Jack Veneer was there, along with his assistant, Valerie, who had apparently given up smoking for good. Jack's wife had passed away at last early that spring. Eve had attended the memorial service, a rowdy affair, more theater than funeral, with performances and bawdy stories about Edith's wilder days. The actors were drunk by the end of the evening; even Jack, the ever upright and reliable, had tears falling down his handsome face as if running off a tall stone statue. He went weaving back and forth across the room, sobbing on people's shoulders. He looked lost without Edith, like a one-armed man.

Now and again tall skinny Valerie patted his sleeve, and Eve realized, startled, that the two had probably been in love for years. She simply hadn't noticed.

Cummings and his wife stood toward the back. The art faculty had signed a large card on which Frederick scribbled one of his pencil drawings, along with a gift certificate for an inn near Ithaca, overlooking Lake Cayuga. The gift included the night's stay, dinner, Sunday brunch, and champagne. It was an extravagant present.

"You should use it," Charlotte told Eve when she opened the envelope. "You and Lev," she added a little awkwardly. "I can look after Noni for one night. Clem and I are too old for this kind of bed-and-breakfast thing."

"Clem would love it," Eve said. "You both would. I'll drop you off and pick you up again the next day."

"It's too long a trip," Charlotte said. "We'd have to pack all our medications." But her resistance was weakening.

Eve was close enough to touch her mother. The violinist, soprano, and the man with the keyboard hovered nearby, ready for their part in the program. The soprano would sing "Anch'il

Mar Par Che Sommerga," from Vivaldi's *Bajazet*, as soon as the ceremony concluded, though as Charlotte said with a grimace, "I hate opera."

Soon, Eve knew, she would have her one line to say. Charlotte and Clem leaned toward each other—they must be tired of standing by now. Clem was looking a little gray, and she thought, What if he dropped dead on the spot?

Beyond them were all the assembled guests. Women wore hats. Men looked grave. They could have been at a funeral. Chuck stood at the back, looking handsome and young and ill at ease in a gray suit. He had brought a date, a young cashier from the Service Department. Mia and her family were seated sedately, like visiting royalty from another country—which in some sense they were. A few Emerald Gardens residents were growing restless. One bent old woman piped up every few minutes, asking, "When is my mother coming to get me?"—her voice growing louder and more urgent. As if in response, the minister raised his voice and spoke faster. The aide tried to hush the little old woman, but finally wheeled her away to a far end of the green lawn. "When is my mother coming to pick me up?" the woman begged.

Musicians were still arriving, even now, one man wielding a tuba in his arms, the brass glinting in the sunshine. He zigzagged over to the other musicians and mopped his brow.

It reminded Eve of the Van Gogh show, that other strange and crowded affair. That was nearly a record for her life in Binghamton—two major events in one week.

"Oh Mom, you're not going to go all gaga, are you?" Noni whispered.

This wedding party had the same aspect of colorful birds gathered together. The breeze was riffling through the turning leaves. People did not simply sit still, fixed in place. They gazed around, turning their heads. Some looked at the sky.

Children and old people fidgeted. It must have been difficult to hear the minister sitting in the back rows, and many of the old people were hard of hearing. A few of the Emerald Gardens residents had brought umbrellas to the wedding—whether to protect themselves against rain or sunshine, it was hard to say.

One flowered umbrella, with lilac handle and a broken spoke, escaped its owner's hands. It blew across the church lawn, skating slowly in one direction, then the other, turning gentle cartwheels across the grass, like a giant flower. The umbrella looked as if it might take flight. Eve fought the urge to run after it. The minister's voice grew louder, or perhaps the finality of the words gave them a stronger timbre. He asked if Clem took this woman to have and to hold, in sickness and in health till death did them part.

Lily, the young Chinese-American violinist—her feet in sneakers and bright red socks—was tapping her foot as if already hearing the music she was about to play.

Marcus lurched forward and produced the ring with a look of relief. For the first time all morning he smiled. Now the minister asked who would give the bride away, and Eve stepped forward, her heart beating in her throat—she had never been comfortable speaking in public—and she grasped her mother's hand at exactly the moment when she was supposed to let go.

Her mother looked at her expectantly. In that instant's flicker, Charlotte's agate-colored eyes looked unusually bright. Eve squeezed her mother's bony hand and released it. "I will," Eve said, and her mother said, "I do," and then the keyboard, violin, and soprano all burst into song.

Discussion Questions

1 Why do you think this book is called *Home Repair*? Who and what is broken in this novel, and how does it get repaired?

2 Eve initially responds to her situation by going on "The Heartbreak Diet" and dressing out of her hamper. Does this ring true to you? How have you, or the people or other literary characters you've known, reacted to heartbreak?

3 They say that a tragedy ends with a death, and a comedy ends with a marriage. Since Home Repair has some of each, do you think this is more of a tragic or a comic novel?

4 In some ways, *Home Repair* is about change. What are some of the notable changes in this novel?

5 There are many minor characters all through the novel: Mia; Jonah; Clem; Devin; Maxine Schwartz, etc. How do you feel they strengthen or distract from the novel?

6 The last chapter of the book has a surprise

element. What did you think was going to happen? What did you want to happen?

7   What is the role of family in *Home Repair*? What is the role of friendship?

8   Marcus goes through some tough experiences in this novel. Are they believable, and do you think teenagers really have to face challenges like this?

9   What is the role of Rec Park in this book? Does it represent anything beyond itself?

10 There is a big, messy Thanksgiving dinner in the middle of this book. Why do you think the author chose Thanksgiving for this scene? What is the meaning of this scene for the rest of the book?

11 Marcus challenges the senator to a debate. Should young people be more or less involved in politics? How can they be involved effectively?

12 Who would you say is the most heroic character in this novel, and why?

13 Charlotte says to her daughter, "We're all going to someday say goodbye, little girl.

We're all going to have to cry." Do you believe this is true? If you had to say one thing to someone about loss, what would it be?

14 In the chapter called "On the Diet" Eve realizes "she simply didn't have any time or space to weep in. She'd have to give it up and move on." In what other ways is she constrained? What are some of the ways people make space for themselves in this novel? How does the idea of an open space come to play in the book?

15 What is the meaning and purpose of Van Gogh in this book? Olivia says that "Art can save lives. . . . Van Gogh's failures teach us never to give up hope." What do you think the role of art should be?

16 Did you love this book enough to send the author five hundred dollars? If so, here is her address.

Inspiration for Home Repair

About five years ago my husband and I were having a garage sale. At one point he sort of disappeared for about ten minutes and it suddenly occurred to me, wouldn't it be funny if somebody's husband actually walked out on the family in the middle of a yard sale? I didn't so much mean ha-ha funny as strange—how strange to have such a life-shattering event occur in such an ordinary and unexpected way.

For me, a lot of fiction begins with that sort of aimless daydreaming. What if the roof collapsed and my best friend and I were stuck together for three days? What if an astronaut went into outer space and refused to come back? What if someone broke into our house in the middle of the night, how could we escape? I once went into such a vivid daydream about that worry that I actually started climbing out the window toward my son's bedroom. Most of those thoughts never go beyond a few minutes of aimless imagining. But now and again an idea takes hold.

There was something about that middle-aged woman left behind at the garage sale that captivated me. What would happen to all the things they had laid out to sell? What if she had children, too? And what if her strong-minded mother happened to be visiting when the husband took off?

Home Repair was the first novel I ever wrote for adults. I wrote it over the course of about two years, but I didn't try to write it chronologically, from beginning to end. I just wrote whatever scene came most clearly to mind—whatever I wanted to write. Sometimes pieces of scenes, snippets of dialogue. Often this happened while I was out walking the dogs. Then I would hurry back to my study and try to write it down before I forgot. Eventually the scenes began to fall into place, and the plot took shape, with one event hurrying along the next. But because I didn't try to write in a straight line, it was some of the easiest writing I've ever done.

I love these characters. They seem as real to me as some of my own real life relatives and friends, and now and then I forget that I don't actually know these people—that I myself don't live in a house with an enormous, crowded, walk-in closet. (I wish I did!)

It's also my hymn of affection for Binghamton, the small, low-key, peaceful, slightly run-down upstate New York city where I've lived for the past thirty years. Writing about it has made it feel that much dearer. I think writing is all about love, anyway. And I discovered that writing novels is like eating potato chips. All I wanted to do when I finished this book was to start the next.

Is Home Repair *a sad novel or a comic one?*

Yes to both. Laughter and tears are such close companions, sometimes you hardly know where one ends and the other begins. The novelist Fred Busch said that what Americans really want is a tragedy with a happy ending. I think that is what I attempted to do in *Home Repair.*

So what are some of your favorite books?

Well—there are so many. I started reading at the age of two. I can't remember a time when I wasn't reading voraciously. But I would have to say that the books of J. D. Salinger influenced me enormously. And then I love all the novelists of big fat books whose secondary characters are as great as their heroes and heroines—writers like Charles Dickens, Jane Austen, Dostoevski. I'm fairly addicted to nineteenth century fiction. Among the more modern writers, I seem to be drawn to women writers—like Virginia Woolf and Jean Rhys, Allegra Goodman, Anne Tyler, and J. K. Rowling.

I need to add that my best creative writing teacher ever was also my first husband, the novelist John Gardner. (Author of *Nickel Mountain, Grendel,* etc.) I never write a word without having his listening ear somewhere in the back of my mind. If you haven't read anything by John Gardner you should run out, immediately, and get one of his books.

Home Repair takes place in Binghamton, where you live. Eve has two children, and so do you. How much of this novel is autobiographical?

Almost none of it—and in other ways, almost all of it. My husband David is certainly nothing like Chuck. He likes to say that he's been chasing after me since I was seventeen and he was eighteen— he is a true romantic, and really, the ideal mate. My life is nothing like Eve's. But I think even the most fantastic kind of science fiction is grounded in moments of reality. We all have to root ourselves in the real world, no matter how otherworldly the creation that flowers from that root. I took real-life places, like Recreation Park, and peopled it with real and imaginary characters. My mom resembles Charlotte, probably my favorite character in the book. A novel becomes a sort of sack into which you throw absolutely everything you know, everyone you've ever loved, everything you are thinking or worrying about at that moment. Then you whirl them all together, in the safety of that imaginary world and see what happens next.

Often I think I write just so I can make things come out better than they do in real life. I take real-life enemies and turn them into friends, for instance. I try to come to terms with sad events, with deaths and departures. And also to celebrate the ten thousand things of the so-called floating world.

You have published books of poetry and books for children and teenage readers. Do you decide ahead of time what kind of audience you are writing for?

I don't decide ahead of time. Some stories want to take shape as poems. Others find their way as children's stories. All writing has certain common elements. I used to think there were enormous distinctions between one type of book and another—but I don't anymore. I will say that poetry has some place in everything I write. I love metaphors and beautiful language. And I always make room for children in everything I write—I can't imagine living without children even in an imaginary world. They are absolutely essential. But I can honestly say I never think about audience. I do think about readers.

Who is your ideal reader for this novel?

My ideal reader for *Home Repair* is anyone who has ever been left alone in the middle of his or her life. But it's also for the woman sitting in the hospital waiting room, trying to distract herself. It's for the insomniac—the man awake reading at three thirty in the morning. That's why I write, to comfort those people and to keep them company. I have no doubt about that, and have never had any doubt about that.

About the Author

Liz Rosenberg's work has appeared in *The New Yorker*, *The New York Times*, *The Atlantic Monthly*, *Harper's*, *Paris Review*, and elsewhere. She has published award-winning books for young readers, prize-winning books of poems, and two documentaries have been made about her work: *Six Artists Who Happen To Be Women* and *How a Book Is Made*. She is a professor of English and Creative Writing at Binghamton University where she lives with her husband, daughter, dogs, and her son when he's home form college. *Home Repair* is her first adult fiction novel.

Center Point Publishing
600 Brooks Road • PO Box 1
Thorndike ME 04986-0001 USA

(207) 568-3717

US & Canada:
1 800 929-9108
www.centerpointlargeprint.com